Family BLOSSOM

SKYLINE MANSION BOOK FOUR

NOLA LI BARR

Edited by Corina Douglas
Cover design by The Red Leaf Book Design / www.redleafbookdesign.com

ISBN 978-1-956919-08-0 (ebook)
ISBN 978-1-956919-09-7 (paperback)

www.nolalibarr.com

The Lin Family

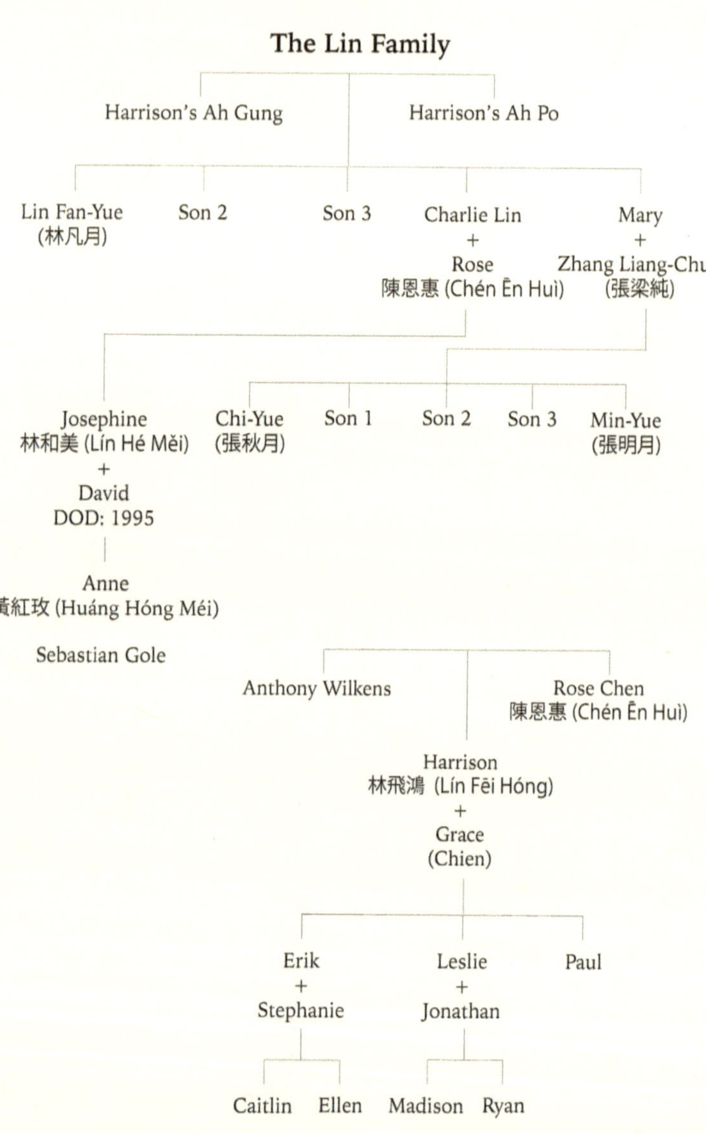

The Wilkens Family

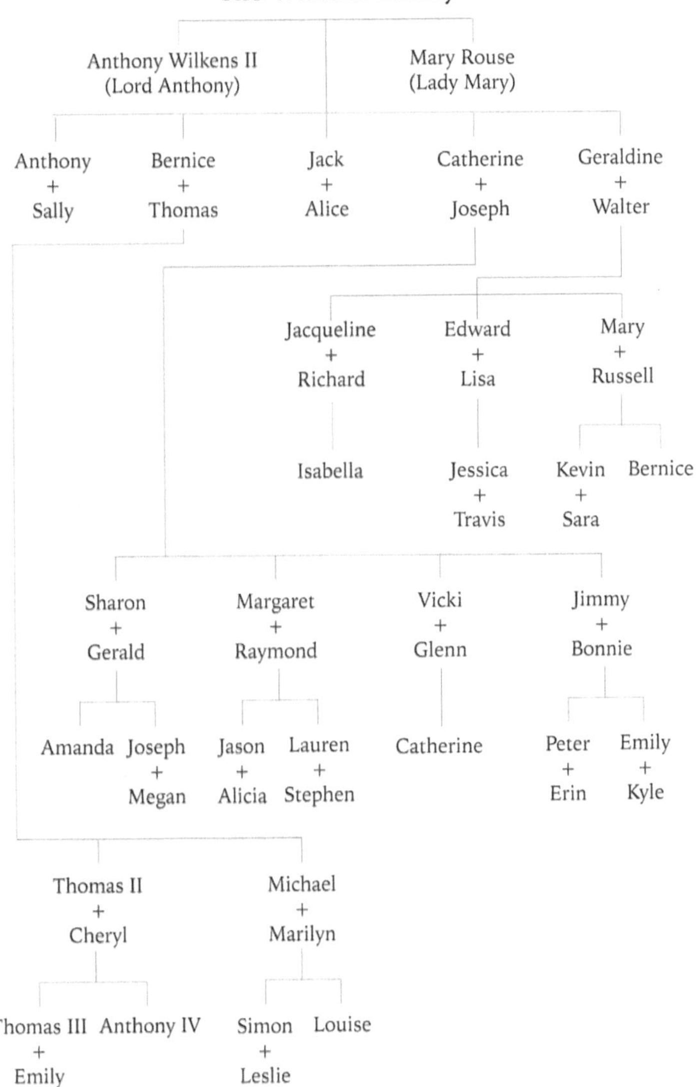

The Donaldson Family

Bruce | Joan

Cecilia
+
gardener

Sebastian Gole

The Crowell Family

Patriarch | Matriarch

The Gole Family

Frank Gole | Molly

Sebastian

The Cambell Family

Cassie | Roger Cambell

Brody | Ryan | Kelly

ABOUT THIS BOOK

Anne is the happiest she's ever been, and her wedding is just around the corner. This is meant to be the biggest moment of her life—a chance to celebrate the love she has found with not only Sebastian but also her new-found family.

But Anne is the wealthiest woman in town and her upcoming nuptials provide an opportunity for her enemies to undo her newfound happiness. As the big day draws closer, the complications keep mounting, and Anne is torn four different ways: planning the wedding of her dreams, bridging the gap within her family, fighting off slanderous attacks, and supporting her husband-to-be when his own long-kept family secrets are exposed.

Being true to herself could very well mean losing the family she's only just found.

CHAPTER 1

"SO, WE HAVE FLOWERS, DRAPED CLOTH, A BEACH, and a sunset in the background." Victoria turned to show me a page out of the magazine she was holding. "This is the dream destination wedding! What do you think?"

I shifted on my bed, knocking a pile of magazines on the floor as I leaned in for a look. I scrunched up my nose at the images. "Um, flowers, yes, but I was thinking that we'd stay in Portland and have the wedding in the garden out back. You know, with some twinkly lights for outdoor lighting. Nice and simple."

"What fun is that?" Victoria exclaimed, staring at me as if I'd grown horns.

"But it's all that's needed."

Her eyebrows shot to her forehead. "You have all the money you could ever imagine to throw a big wedding and *that's* all you want? Wait—don't answer that! I already know what you're going to say. I'm just saying it might be fun to throw a big party that's for you and not others for a change."

Victoria was throwing out ideas at me while we flipped through the pages of *Wedding Boutique*, ogling beautiful pictures of dream weddings. We'd been best friends since high school, and, as Victoria knew wedding planning was the last thing I wanted to do, she'd planned a sleepover party around it. We'd had fun doing our nails and watching romantic movies, but now she was making me look at wedding magazines.

I loved the weddings that looked simple; nothing too over the top. But the only thing I had learned from the bundles of magazines Victoria had bought for us was the more I looked, the more confused I was. I had absolutely no idea what I wanted or where to start finding out. Dreaming about my wedding was not something I did growing up. But now, here in front of me, were images of happy couples with beautiful color-coordinated decorations. *Ugh! I could never pull this off.*

Victoria's phone buzzed, and she shoved a new magazine into my hands before turning to pick it up. I looked down at the cover to see this one focused on winter weddings. My musing was cut short when Victoria announced, "Oh, it's Paul. He just texted me to say he's leaving campus and wants to see me." She looked at me with pleading eyes. "Do you mind?"

I laughed at the absurdity of the question. "Of course, I don't mind."

Relief hit her features. "I'll help you with more ideas tomorrow, okay?"

"Sounds good. Go. Have a fun night with Paul."

Her face split into a smile. "You're the best, Anne." She jumped off the bed and gave me a hug before grabbing her purse and running out of the house.

I hadn't seen Victoria this happy in a long time, and it made me happy to think that if Paul proposed, she would also become my cousin. I looked back down at the magazines and realized all my excitement had left with Victoria. Pushing the pile aside, I called Sebastian.

"Hi, my love," he said after only one ring.

"Hi! I keep looking at this glittery ring wondering if this is all a fairy tale."

"Nope, it's all real." There was a muffled sound, as if he'd placed his hand over the phone, and then I heard him call out to his secretary for a file.

"You sound busy," I said as he came back on.

"I'm just buried in paperwork."

"With the thing that you were telling me about yesterday?"

"Yes, I'm working on 'the thing' as you call it, among other projects," he said, laughing.

"Hey! I don't need to remember all that lawyer jargon."

"It's just you with words." He continued chuckling, and I heard papers rustling in the background.

"Did Jack make a final decision?" I asked.

"He did. He's going to take a more active role on the board, hence why I'm buried. It's something he's never done before, because Anthony was always around. But now that he knows the extent of how much Geraldine had her hands in company matters, he wants to see if there's any other fishy things going on. So, he's hired me to be the head lawyer of the Wilkens fortune."

I frowned. "Wouldn't I have to be in agreement with that? I own the largest stake in the company."

"Would you disagree?" he asked, sounding a bit worried.

"No! Of course not!" I said, laughing. "I just wanted to play with you a bit."

"Very funny. Ha ha."

"I trust you with all my heart," I said while flinging myself back on the bed. A deep sigh escaped me, and Sebastian chuckled.

"I love you too, Anne. Why don't we go out and have a nice dinner tonight, just the two of us?"

"That sounds fantastic!"

"It's a date. I'll see you at home about six o'clock."

We hung up, and with new vigor, I picked up the magazine closest to me and vowed to have some sort of color scheme picked out by the time I got to the last page.

Sebastian sat across from me, still dressed in his work suit, looking disheveled and handsome all at the same time. "Have you thought more about Grace's proposal?"

"What proposal?" I asked, lifting a large forkful of spaghetti and the largest meatball I had ever seen to my mouth.

He raised a brow. "You know exactly what I'm talking about."

"You mean to go live with them for a couple weeks, get to know my extended family, and let them show me around San Francisco? Or to become bosom friends with my new cousin, Leslie, who Grace thinks I can tame?"

"All of the above."

I wrinkled my nose. "I was being sarcastic."

"I know, but I think you should do it. It'd be a change of scenery. Victoria could meet you there, and maybe the three of you could go wedding dress shopping together."

"Why would I pay sales tax in California when I don't have to pay any here?"

He looked at me in amusement. "Money is not an issue anymore, remember?"

"Right. Doesn't mean I need to spend willy-nilly, though."

Sebastian put his fork down. "Anne, you need a trip. We never did get back on that topic of intervention. You've been at home mostly by yourself for months now. You're someone who likes to travel, meet new people, eat a variety of food, and explore. Going to hang out with Grace and Leslie will be good for you. Plus, they're family, and knowing you, you want to get to know them better."

I sighed. "You do know me well. All right, I'll do it. I'll give Grace a call tomorrow morning."

"Fantastic! Now, on to more important matters."

"Uh oh, I don't like the sound of this."

Sebastian started laughing, and it was with great impatience that I waited for him to catch his breath. The whole time my brain was spinning as I wondered what Geraldine had come up with this time.

Sebastian twined the last of his spaghetti onto his fork. "I would like to know if you've picked out the wedding colors?"

That was his big and important question? "As a matter of fact, I have. I would like our wedding colors to be purple and light pink with a dash of green."

"Okay, I can go with that." Having finished his meal, Sebastian leaned forward and took my hand. His thumb rubbed across the top of my knuckles. "I want you to have the wedding of your dreams."

"That's the problem, Sebastian, I've never dreamed of my wedding. It just wasn't something I ever thought about."

"Well, think of it as a blank slate. You can let your imagination go wild. Just remember you're able to afford it."

I grimaced. "It's exhilarating having all this money, isn't it? I could go crazy. But is there anything you want for our wedding?"

He grinned. "A full bar, that I do want. And what do you think about getting a live band?"

"That sounds like fun! I never thought of that."

"See, you're excited too," Sebastian said, smiling at me.

"I am. I'm quite excited now. But I just had a thought— what if we did the wedding three weeks from now?"

Water almost spewed from Sebastian's lips, and I quickly handed him a napkin before he asked, "Why so quick?"

"Well, everyone we know is here, and I just remembered I saw a deal on a trip to Bora Bora. Do you want to go there for our honeymoon?"

Sebastian had to take the napkin and cover his mouth for a second. He was laughing so hard his whole body was shaking.

"Why is that funny?" I asked with a scowl.

"It's just so you. You want to do a quick wedding because you found a deal, not because you're pregnant or you want a certain venue and that was the only available date for years they had left."

"Well, I don't want to miss out on going to Bora Bora." I was a bit miffed he was laughing at me about this.

"Anne—"

"I know I have all the money in the world, and I shouldn't get hung up on deals anymore, but it's ingrained in me. I can't help it."

"I'm sorry for laughing, but you've got to see it's a bit funny."

I willed my breath to even out, and yes, if I thought about what I said it was a bit funny. I felt myself smiling. "Yes, yes, I suppose it is. But if you want to go to Bora Bora, I'm still going to book this deal. What do you think?"

"Yes, I'd love to go to Bora Bora."

"Great!" I exclaimed, and I made a mental note to look into it tonight. I couldn't wait to marry Sebastian and spend the rest of my life with him!

Sebastian was in bed next to me, snoring. I gave him a light shove to see if he'd roll over, and, when he did, I breathed a sigh of relief. With the quiet peace resettled, I went back to thinking about Grace and Leslie. I would love to be able to hang out with my family a bit more, and it did sound like a lot of fun to involve them in my wedding, especially since we were now looking at having it in three weeks. Given the short timeframe, any help would be welcome.

The more I thought about it, the more excited I got. To have my aunt and cousin by my side as I tried on wedding dresses, picked out flowers, and designed my invitations brought a thrill of anticipation. I couldn't wait. It was decided —I would call them first thing in the morning.

CHAPTER 2

LESLIE

"Mom!" Madison called from the other side of the house.

I rolled my eyes to the ceiling. "I swear, if Madison calls me one more time I'm going to scream," I said, both hoping and not hoping that Jonathan would hear me.

He sat at the dining table, eating breakfast and looking very smart in his new designer suit and blue silk tie. Ever since we got back from visiting Anne, he'd been wanting a smarter suit. Said he had to spend money to look the part of a board member of a startup. I thought it was a ridiculous notion, because just last year he was telling me we had to be frugal, and here he was buying a thousand-dollar suit! Although, I did have to say he looked pretty good in it.

Jonathan sighed behind me. "You need to lay off her, Leslie. She's just six."

"Weren't you the one that said we need to let her know her boundaries, and I was the one who wasn't doing that?"

"I did, but you also have to give her space to let out her energy every once in a while."

I turned from doing the dishes to look at Jonathan again.

He was busy drinking his coffee and reading his phone. I doubt he even really knew what he just said. Let Madison scream? Like he could stand it if he knew he was staying home instead of going to work! I turned back around and started scrubbing the dishes harder than they needed to be.

There was a rustle behind me, and then Jonathan stood. "Well, I'm off," he said, coming over and giving me a peck on my cheek.

I didn't say anything, but I heard him sigh as he walked to the door. When I heard the car start up and drive off, I threw the dish towel on the counter and went to sit at the kitchen table, placing my head in my hands as I willed my tears back. I might think bad thoughts about Madison and Ryan sometimes, but I still loved my kids and didn't want them to see me like this. They should know happy parents.

"Mom?"

I looked up to see Madison had walked into the kitchen, her teddy clutched to her chest. She only did that when she got scared. I wiped my face with the back of my hands and stood up to wash the dishes again. Forcing my voice to sound neutral, I asked, "Yes, Madison?"

"Mom, I tried to call you, but you never came."

"I was talking to Daddy. He just left for work. I would have come up as soon as I was done here. But as you're here now, tell me what you need."

"I'm here because you never came."

I was about to open my mouth to argue when I realized this was exactly what my therapist told me not to do. She was six, I needed to remember that. There was no point in arguing with a six-year-old, I would always lose. No . . . that's not the words she used. She told me I was her mother. I needed to guide her and not keep telling her what to do. *Ugh.*

After almost losing Madison at Anne's place, I didn't dare

not tell Madison what to do. What if she ran off again and got lost or stuck somewhere that was even worse than under the mansion? There was that boy that fell down a well. What if she fell down a well? Okay, bit extreme; no one near us had wells—we lived in San Jose. With my back to Madison, I put my head back in my hands and rubbed my eyes until my face felt warm.

"Mom?"

Oh my goodness! I whirled to face my daughter. "Madison!"

"You forgot I was here again, didn't you?"

My stomach plummeted. "I . . ."

"It's okay. I sometimes forget you're here too."

I didn't know how I felt about that. I eyed her, my mind racing to recall normal tasks and what kids and parents usually enjoyed doing together. "Madison, do you want to go to the park today?"

"Yes!" she squealed.

I released a sigh of relief. "And what was it that you wanted to ask me about?"

"Nothing. I just had a nightmare last night, but I'm good now. I want to go to the park!"

"Me too!" Ryan said, running into the room, and I noticed he was still in his nightgown.

"Okay, let's get dressed, have some breakfast, and then let Mommy finish up some chores first." Sometimes, I wished Jonathan was home with the kids or that they could go to daycare and I could go back to work. Wrangling these two was a lot harder than going back to work, but it wasn't an option as I didn't trust my kids with strangers.

"Phone," Ryan said, waddling toward me with my phone in his hand. I was always misplacing that thing. As my hand closed around it, I found it was vibrating, and I looked down to see that Anne was calling.

Holding the phone up to my ear, I said, "Hi, Anne" while

shooing the kids back to their room and motioning that they should get dressed. "It's so nice to hear from you."

"Did I catch you at a bad time?" Anne asked.

"No, not at all." Because every time was a bad time. I would never talk to anyone if I had to wait for a good time. "We're just getting dressed and heading to the park."

"Oh, well, I'll be quick then."

"There's really no hurry. We're not on a set schedule."

Anne paused for a moment, and I wondered if I'd been too quick to placate, but then she said, "Well, I was wondering if I could come down to see you this weekend? I know it's last minute, but if you're free, I thought it'd be nice for us to hang out, and maybe you could help me pick out a wedding dress?"

"Oh, I'd love that! But I don't know, Anne . . . ." Thoughts of who would watch over the kids ran through my mind. "I'm pretty busy. Let me think about it."

"Oh, okay, just me know. I'll probably stay at a hotel in San Francisco."

"That's nonsense. You can stay here; there's no need to book a hotel." *Oh my goodness, the kids are being too quiet! What are they doing in their room?*

"That's awful nice of you. I thought—"

"I'm sorry, Anne. I have to go check on the kids. I'll think about it, okay? I can't promise anything, though. I'm so swamped with the little ones these days."

"Can Jonathan help?"

Can Jonathan help? He didn't even feed the kids their breakfast in the morning or get them dressed. He can't be depended on to help! "He does when he can, but he's at work most of the time."

"I get it—"

"Sorry, Anne, I have to go. I'll let you know what I decide."

I hung up before I said anything else that might hurt my new cousin. It was odd that she had just popped up out of the blue. She and her mom were nice people, but we didn't really know each other. Why did I just say that I would let her stay in my house with my kids? We didn't have a mansion like she did, where everyone could be spaced out with lots of room to stretch their legs. Our guest room was also the game room, and right now, it was piled high with toys everywhere. There were game boards, Lego, plastic kitchen appliances, and food, as well as who knew what else was hidden underneath all that stuff for who knew how long.

I walked into the kids' room to see Madison teaching Ryan how to play Candy Land. He wasn't really paying attention, but Madison was playing for both of them. I stood by the door just watching them, awed that the screaming child from this morning could also be so silent and sweet. But my presence alerted them, and next thing I knew, they were both jumping up and down, Madison yelling she wanted to go to the park, and Ryan just excited because Madison was excited.

After another hour, we were finally on the road. I told myself we were not in a hurry, that the park was open all day long, and it was still early in the day. There was plenty of time. Deep breaths, my therapist had said. Deep breaths and to keep telling myself that I wasn't in a hurry.

I had texted my childhood friend, Amanda, before we left to let her know we were headed to the park and I wondered if she and her kids wanted to join us. So far, there'd been no response back, and I steeled myself that I would be at the park by myself with the kids for the next hour or so.

"We're at the park! We're at the park!" Madison was clapping her hands and singing, she was so excited. I tried really hard not to ask her to be so loud.

But then Ryan decided to join in. "Ahhhh!"

I couldn't stand it. "You two need to pipe down!"

"I don't want to pipe down!" Madison cried. "I'm so excited to be at the park!"

I quickly parked and got out of the car. Shutting the door, I walked to the back of the minivan where I took some deep breaths.

"Hey, Leslie!" a familiar voice cried out, startling me. "Sorry, didn't mean to scare you."

I turned, relief rushing through me that it was Amanda. "Amanda, it's so good to see you." It really was. Amanda's daughter, Sadie, and son, Aiden, were the same age as Madison and Ryan. It was a big relief to know they not only had playmates to play with on the playground, but that I also had an adult I could talk to.

Amanda was my best friend from middle school. She knew everything about me and my family. Our parents were all from Taiwan, and, growing up, we'd got together for Lunar New Year, Christmas, and, well, any chance we could get. Our parents became fast friends, and it didn't take long before Amanda and I followed suit. These days, we got our families together for Lunar New Year and Christmas, but other than that it was just Amanda and me with the kids at the playground, except she looked so much more content with her life than I felt.

"Ready to go?" she asked, glancing into my minivan.

I caught sight of Madison and Ryan waving frantically. I forced a smile. "Sure! Give me a second and I'll get them out."

I let the kids out of the car, and they immediately migrated to Sadie and Aiden.

I reached for Madison and Ryan's hands so we could cross the car park and enter the playground. Amanda followed suit with Sadie and Aiden. As soon as our feet touched the grass, the kids ran off toward the swings, Amanda and I slowly following.

"You look like crap," Amanda said.

Clearly, I wasn't fooling her. I'd put my hair up in a messy bun before leaving the house. Amanda, of course, looked like she had all the time in the world this morning to freshen up and look human. I gave a wry laugh. "I feel it, too, especially since we came back from meeting my new cousin."

"Oh! How did that go?"

"It went okay. Madison was Madison and got herself lost. I freaked out, and my brothers made fun of me. Same old, same old. Look at her now—she's probably already forgotten the incident while I'm still turned inside out knowing I almost lost her in that gigantic house Anne has."

Amanda looked intrigued. "Is it very large?"

"It's a legit mansion with a ballroom and secret tunnels."

"Wow!" Amanda's eyes were so big I thought they might pop out of her eye sockets. "I'm glad Madison is okay."

"Yeah, us too."

"How's Jonathan been?" Amanda asked as we got to the kids, who were now clamoring for us to push them on the swings.

"Jonathan has started acting like he has a lot of money now and wants to show it off, though where he thinks this money is coming from is beyond me. He just told me that we had to budget cut last year."

Amanda sent me a small smile. "He's probably just on one of his kicks. Give him another week, and he'll revert back to his old self again."

"I hope so. But that's not all, I feel like I'm losing him."

Amanda gasped, one of her hands lifting to cover her mouth. "Is there another girl?"

"No! Nothing like that." That was one thing I knew about Jonathan—he was loyal and would never cheat on me. "He's just working so much we hardly see him anymore."

"Have you talked to him about it?" Amanda asked, going back to give Aiden another push.

"No, of course not. He would just tell me I'm crazy and a worry wart."

"You are a worry wart."

"Thanks, Amanda!"

She laughed. She actually laughed. "You are, though. And you know it too."

I sat there in silence for a bit, telling myself to calm down. It wasn't the first time Amanda had told me this. And I did know it. Goodness, we'd spent enough on my therapist for me to know it forwards and backwards. I worried way too much. But wasn't that what a mother did? Worried about the kids, worried about the house—basically worried about everyone but themselves?

"Leslie, can I suggest something?"

"Sure." Anything would be better than living in my head.

"I heard from Maxine the other day that her husband is letting her take a two-day sleep away at the Four Seasons. She's going to get to do whatever she wants for two whole days!"

"People get to do that?" I had never heard of anyone doing that before, and my face must have shown it, because Amanda started laughing.

"Yes, Leslie, people do that. I suggested the idea to James the other night, and he immediately agreed to it. Said it'd be good for me to reset. He's going to watch the kids this weekend for me."

"Wow, that's amazing." Jonathan would never go for that. He'd say I was taking time out of his work hours. The deal was I would take care of the kids while he brought in the money. "No takesie backsies," as Madison would say.

"Ask Jonathan," Amanda pushed. "You might be surprised by what he says."

I lifted a brow. "Ha."

"Just try. You so need the break, Leslie."

I bit my lip as I gave Ryan a push. "It wouldn't work. He's too focused on his job. I sometimes wonder if he even knows we have a second child."

"That's harsh, don't you think?"

"Yeah . . . I suppose it is." I went silent for a while, the offer spinning in my mind. Then an idea hit me. *This could be the perfect plan!* I turned to Amanda again. "I might be able to ask him in a different way."

"Oh? What way would that be?"

"My cousin, Anne, called me before we got here. She said she wanted to come down to the Bay Area and go wedding dress shopping with me. Jonathan likes her and thinks highly of her."

"That's wonderful!" Amanda said, but I could see she was confused as to why I'd brought this up.

I clarified, "He might say yes to allowing me to stay in a hotel with Anne for a couple of days while she and I went around trying on wedding dresses. It means I could still leave him with the kids without really asking him outright for the days off."

Amanda's face lit up. "Do it!"

"Yeah?" I asked, now helping Madison and Ryan off the swings as Amanda did the same for Sadie and Aiden.

"Yes! I want to get a call tonight saying you've asked him. You deserve this, Leslie. You so do. Every mom out there deserves this. It's a thankless job, and as much as you love your kids, you need to take care of yourself too. They need a mom who's there for them because she's happy."

As the kids ran off, I looked into Amanda's eyes, taking note of the worry and sincerity in them. "Okay, I'll do it. I'll ask him tonight."

That night, I made Jonathan's favorite food of beef noodle soup. It was my mama's recipe, and he'd loved it the first time he had it. It had been served for dinner the night I'd brought him home to meet my parents. Jonathan was fourth generation Taiwanese American, and, therefore, some of the traditional meals had disappeared from his family meals. He loved it all—beef noodle soup, fresh spring rolls, beef with white radish that had been cooked in a thick sauce for hours, sticky rice, and much more. But cooking wasn't my favorite thing to do, so the traditional meals only happened every once in a while. I usually baked casseroles or chicken with a side of broccoli; simple food that didn't take a lot of prep work.

"Wow, that smells delicious!" Jonathan said, walking into the kitchen while loosening his tie.

"Daddy!" Madison cried, jumping into his arms as Ryan came waddling behind her. He held up his chubby arms as far as he could stretch them to get his dad's attention. I had to admit Jonathan was a good dad. He loved the kids, and he had an easy way with them.

After he'd greeted Madison and Ryan, I said, "I made beef noodle soup for tonight."

"Yum!" He moved forward and gave me a kiss on the cheek. It made me realize there wasn't enough of those little gestures of affection these days. I immediately reminded myself we were grown adults who had responsibilities; there wasn't much time for intimacy.

"Dinner's ready now, kids," I told Madison and Ryan, urging them to wash their hands and take a seat at the table.

I set out the food and watched my family devour the delicious meal. Jonathan and the kids were laughing, and everyone seemed to be enjoying themselves. It turned out to be a pretty fun evening, and I felt a surge of hope that it would influence Jonathan in saying yes to my request.

After the kids went down and the two of us were settled on the sofa with my feet in his lap, I tried to work out the right words to phrase my request as he massaged my toes. But my mind was a mess. I realized I just had to bite the bullet and do it.

"Jonathan?"

"Mmm?" His eyes were closed, and he looked like he was going to fall asleep right there on the couch.

"I was wondering if I could . . ." I trailed off, my sweaty hands tangling together in my lap.

"You could what?" he mumbled.

"Ah, let me start over. Anne called this morning."

"Anne?" His eyes popped open.

If I didn't know Jonathan was only interested in Anne because he was infatuated with her money, then I would have been jealous at the sudden interest. "Yeah, she asked if she could come down and hang out with me. She also wants me to go wedding dress shopping with her."

His hands stilled on my feet. "You should invite her to stay here."

"I did." I could tell my voice had gone a bit quiet, and Jonathan noticed.

He sighed. "But you think our place is too small, and she's not used to this kind of living, right?"

"No! You know she only just inherited the place. It's not like she grew up living in that house or having all that money."

"Then what is it, Leslie? I'm tired. I'm going to head up to bed if you don't start talking."

If he was going to be like this, then fine, I was just going to spit it out. "I'd like to book a hotel room and have Anne and I stay there. I'd like to really bond with her without the kids around." *And have some time away from my life.*

"Well, sure, I could take the kids this weekend, and you and Anne could go wedding dress shopping and do your girl things." He yawned and stretched, and I knew he really was ready to go to bed—but he was actually agreeing!

"Really?" I couldn't help saying.

"Why are you so surprised?" He turned to look at me with a raised brow. "I'm not holding you here on house arrest."

"No, of course not!" *But it'd be nice to have you help around the house a bit more. Though, he does bring in the money. Ah, doesn't matter! He agreed!*

"Okay, I'll call Anne then." And then it hit me what he'd just agreed to. "Oh, sweetie!" I crawled over and gave him a big kiss, which I could see surprised him. I felt his arms wrap around me. Next thing I knew, I was on my back, and he was giving me light kisses all over my face and neck.

"We don't have any time to ourselves anymore. Maybe if the kids don't overpower me this weekend, we could try this again, but this time with a babysitter?" he suggested in a husky voice.

I froze and looked at him, all thoughts of affection vanishing. "You know how I feel about that, Jonathan. No babysitters. They're still too young. I don't want strangers looking after our kids."

"What about your parents, then?" he said, leaning toward me in an effort to continue the intimacy, but it was already lost on me. The thought of a stranger with my kids scared me, and my parents . . .

"My mom isn't capable of watching both of them. They'd wear her out in thirty minutes. And my dad. Well, he's not so good with kids. It will be better when they're much older and more self-reliant." I pushed at him and moved to get off the couch.

"Leslie . . ." He grabbed my waist.

"I'm tired too. Why don't we head up?" I gave him a peck on his cheek. "Thank you, Jonathan. I really need this, and it's very generous of you to offer to take care of the kids this weekend."

"Of course, Leslie." He had a quizzical look on his face, but I ignored it as I took his hand. We walked up to our room together, and I was asleep before my head hit the pillow.

CHAPTER 3

ANNE

"Did you call Leslie?" Victoria asked between mouthfuls of pasta.

"I did. She said she had to think about it. She didn't sound too excited about me coming down to visit, though. I think you and I should just plan the whole thing here in Portland."

Victoria shook her head. "No, I want to go to San Francisco, and you're going to come with me. There's no reason we have to buy everything in Portland, although that bridal shop Lauren got her dress from is pretty posh."

I nodded in agreement. "I know, I was really hoping Leslie would say yes. I was looking forward to getting to know my family a bit better." I hadn't realized how disappointed I'd feel when Leslie hadn't agreed to jump on board with my plans. But then again, we had only recently met each other.

"You still will, Anne. I think we should still go to San Fran, and while we're there, we can touch base and see if Leslie would like to join us. She might be more comfortable with the idea once we're there. Oh! Maybe we could do a girls' night out? A spa, dinner, movie, dessert—you name it! It would be fun."

I gave Victoria a knowing look. "I know what you're doing."

"What?" she asked, feigning innocence.

"You're trying to get me excited about traveling again."

"Of course, I am! Where's the adventurous Anne I used to look up to?"

"What? You don't look up to me anymore?" I said in mock horror.

Victoria rolled her eyes. "That's not the point. I hate seeing you sitting at home all the time, brooding."

"I do not brood!"

"Oh yes you do! And"—Victoria held up a hand to shush me as she continued—"I haven't gone on a trip with you in a while. Let's do this for old times' sakes. What do you say? Want to go this weekend?"

I had to admit I was excited about the prospect of traveling again. "All right, let's do it. We can book ourselves into one of the nicest hotels in San Francisco."

"Yeah!" Victoria whooped.

I went to grab my phone to start looking at hotels when I saw Leslie's name pop up with an incoming call. I picked up before it could ring. "Hi, Leslie. Victoria and I—"

"I'd love for you to come!" Leslie said before I could finish my thought.

Huh? Well, this was a nice turn of events. "That's fantastic," I said. "I'm at lunch with Victoria, and we just agreed to head down and book a hotel for the weekend."

"Oh! That sounds fabulous. I know I offered our house as a place to stay, but can I join you guys in the hotel? Jonathan is going to give me the weekend off, and I'd love to join. If that's okay, of course?"

I felt a smile break out on my face and didn't hesitate to

say, "Of course, it is! We were thinking about having a girls' night out."

"Oh, I can't wait!" she said.

This was a very different Leslie than the one I had called this morning. When she hung up, Victoria was looking at me with a quizzical expression. "What was that all about?"

"Leslie is going to join us at the hotel."

"That's fantastic!"

I nodded eagerly, still struggling to believe how it had all worked out. Then a thought popped in me as I stared at Victoria. "You know what I just realized? Leslie could be your sister-in-law. Then we'd all be related!"

"That's true," Victoria said, but her smile dropped a second later. "Don't jinx it, though. Paul and I are taking it slow."

"Well, don't take it too slow. We're not getting any younger."

"Not something you need to worry about," she said with a laugh. "I think it's only a matter of time, but Paul wants to finish his degree first and really needs to focus on his work right now."

"Maybe we could do a double wedding?" I said, meaning it as a joke and knowing there was no way Victoria would go for that.

"Oh, I don't know, Anne. I don't want to rush Paul."

My mouth fell open. "Victoria, I was just joking! And I would want you to have your own special day all to yourselves, anyways."

She gave me a brief smile. "I want that for you too, Anne. And speaking of your wedding, you should totally ask Leslie to be one of your bridesmaids."

"That's a fantastic idea. You're going to be my maid of honor, though, right?"

"Do you really have to ask?" Victoria laughed. "Let's go book that hotel."

After lunch, we returned home and booked a room at The Mark in San Francisco. A terrace room to be exact. It had a view of the city and was incredibly luxurious. I was going to bask in this wedding planning trip with my best friend and my new cousin. I was so excited.

The last time Victoria and I were in San Francisco, I had not received my inheritance, nor had I any idea who the Wilkens family was. I was traveling on a budget, couch surfing, finding hostels, and camping where needed. At that time, never in a million years would I have thought I'd be able to afford a hotel room at The Mark!

"Here's to your next adventure," Victoria said, returning to the library with two champagne glasses in hand. "We should celebrate this new journey that we're going on."

I laughed, placing the book I'd been reading on the table beside me. "You're too much! It's just a trip to try on dresses."

"You know you're excited. Come on, let's celebrate!"

"You're right, I should. Here's to San Francisco," I said, clinking Victoria's flute. She beamed at me, and I realized with that look that she had been worried about my self-imposed seclusion, as the worry lines on her face all but disappeared. I vowed to keep it that way by making sure we had a blast on our trip.

CHAPTER 4

THERE WERE HUNDREDS OF PEOPLE MILLING ABOUT the Oakland terminals.

I sighed. "I know it's only been a month or so since I've been flying commercial, but I had forgotten how crowded a big airport could be. I already want to return home to Portland."

"Stop being a whiner," Victoria replied as she paid for some snacks at the shop across from our terminal. "You're the one who didn't want to take your own plane."

"It felt too excessive. There are perfectly good planes already flying."

"But you're now thinking that it wouldn't have been quite a bad idea to take your own private plane." Victoria was looking at me with a raised eyebrow, and I couldn't blame her. I was totally thinking that now. I had my own plane, and it should be used.

I decided to change the subject. "I'm looking forward to some spa treatment. That massage you were talking about on the plane sounds divine."

Victoria laughed. "That's the spirit!" She turned, scanning the airport, then she pointed at a lady jumping up and down. "I think that's Leslie."

She was so far away and there were people blocking our view that I wasn't sure it was Leslie. But as she got closer, we heard our names coming from her direction. I couldn't help it, I ran to give her a hug. I'd always wanted to do that—be welcomed back at the airport by a relative, and Mom didn't count.

"I'm so glad you two are here." Leslie was beaming. She was holding our hands and looking between us as if she couldn't quite believe we were in front of her. She looked almost crazed, and Victoria and I exchanged a glance while we walked hand in hand to the baggage claim area.

"I think we should go have lunch first in the city. Do you two have any preferences?" Leslie asked, having let go of our hands so we could grab our luggage.

"I'm not picky," I said.

"Nor am I," Victoria said, reaching down to grab her bright red suitcase.

"In that case, how about Crab House? They have Dungeness crabs slathered in garlic—absolutely delicious. It's been a long time since I've eaten one." She looked at us with such pleading eyes that there was no way we could have said no, but good thing neither of us wanted to. Dungeness crab slathered in garlic was right up our alley.

The drive from Oakland Airport was bumper-to-bumper traffic. I'd forgotten about big cities and their lack of space. There were cars and people everywhere, and we were surrounded by concrete. The Bay Bridge was magnificent, though. It gave a three-hundred-and-sixty-degree view of the Bay. I could see ship liners parked in the water waiting for their turn to unload, and there were ferry boats going to and from San Francisco, carrying people to and from work or just for a day's sightseeing. The day was beautiful too, not a cloud in sight.

I had gotten so used to Portland weather that it was dazzling to be in an area where everything looked and felt so crisp and shiny. There was a nip in the air too. Leslie had warned us that it was summer in San Francisco, so that meant it was chillier than normal here than in Portland. I was glad I had brought my jacket, because with it on, the weather was perfect. We got dropped off on Embarcadero. There were seagulls flying overhead as well as walking around the pier in front of us.

"We can walk to Pier 39," Leslie said, hooking her arms through both of ours.

"You miss this, don't you?" Victoria asked me.

"Yes," I said at the same time as Leslie.

Leslie suddenly stopped, realizing Victoria had been referring to how I missed traveling. "Sorry. I haven't been by myself in a long time, and I've missed coming out," she said.

Victoria patted her shoulder. "Don't worry about it. You're here now, and we're going to have a fantastic weekend." She looked around. "Is Pier 39 close? I'm starving."

Leslie gave Victoria a relieved smile. "Not far at all."

And she was right. Not more than five minutes later we were at Pier 39, tourist central it seemed. There were wall-to-wall shops with a big walkway and lots of restaurants, but what caught my attention were the cookies, chocolates, and ice cream shops. I made a note to stop by after our meal.

Leslie led us into the middle of the Pier and up some steps. At the top was the entrance to Crab House. The restaurant was cute. It had a diner feel with narrow walkways between tables. We were seated right next to the window where we could see a big part of the city.

We each got our own Dungeness crab, because when could you get away with being gluttonous except on vacation? A side of garlic noodles and some vegetables were added to make us feel better. There was silence while we devoured every morsel of food in front of us.

Leslie was the first to break it. "So, what do you want to do next? I could take you down the Embarcadero where we can see the sights, or do you want dessert after this?"

Between bites of crab, I said, "We'd love to see the sights, but could we actually go to the hotel first to unpack and freshen up?"

"Oh! Of course, I'm sorry. I just haven't been out for so long. I'm pumped up with adrenaline."

"We can tell," Victoria said with a chuckle. "It's actually great because I'm hoping we'll have a fantastic trip this time and pack in as much as we can."

I looked at my cousin closely as I ate my next forkful of crab. She looked almost manic. "Leslie, are you doing okay?" I asked.

She nodded. "I'm okay, I just need to calm down. Having young kids means I never get to go out anymore, and I think this is the first time I'll be without the kids for more than a day. It probably doesn't help that I had about two cups of coffee this morning, either."

"Aren't Grace and Harrison and your brother's family around too, though?" I asked her.

"Erik has his own family, but his kids are older, so I don't want to burden him with our young ones. Mom and Dad, well, they help, but they can't babysit for more than a day. Oh! But here I am rambling on and on about my problems when we're supposed to be having a girls' weekend."

"But Leslie—"

She raised a hand. "No, I don't want to talk about it." She

changed the subject. "Before we leave, we should see the sea lions on the docks at the back of Pier 39."

I felt a worm of worry at her response, but then Victoria started laughing.

"Did I say something wrong?" Leslie's brows furrowed, and I could see worry starting to creep into her eyes again.

"No!" Victoria gasped. "I'm laughing because on our last road trip Anne made me stop at a tourist trap to see a cave filled with sea lions."

"Oh, that is funny," Leslie said, seemingly placated by the response.

I figured the three of us would be a bit awkward around one another until we got to know each other more, but I sure hoped it would happen quickly so Leslie didn't have to tiptoe around us for much longer.

We got to the hotel and both Victoria and I collapsed on the bed. If it wasn't for Leslie hovering over us, we would have stayed right there for the rest of the day.

The first and last day of any trip was always the hardest, and I had forgotten how draining it was to travel to your destination. But Leslie wasn't having it. She would sit for a few minutes, lost in her own thoughts, and then, as if realizing where she was, she'd ask us if we wanted to go to a Broadway show, eat at a certain restaurant, or go on a Napa tour. I had never seen anyone so jittery. I wondered, not for the first time, if it had been a good idea to bring Leslie into the bridesmaid fold. Maybe Victoria and I would have been better off with just the two of us . . . .

I chided myself at the thought. Leslie was my cousin! Until recently, I'd had no other family member besides Mom, but I'd always wished I had more. Now I had them—uncle, aunt, and cousins but this was a strange phenomenon for me, and I wasn't sure how to navigate it. I did know one thing—this was my chance to make a good impression. With that thought in mind, I turned to Victoria.

"We should probably see some sights before dinner."

"Oh, do you two want to see the Golden Gate Bridge?" Leslie asked, and I could see she wasn't going to let this opportunity pass on by like her other requests had, especially after I had voiced interest in getting moving again.

"That sounds great, Leslie," Victoria said, rolling off the bed.

We drove through Golden Gate Park, and I marveled at how similar it was to Central Park. It made me a bit nostalgic. I missed the big city life and being able to travel to my heart's content. *Though,* I quickly corrected myself, *it's not like I can't do that now*.

Originally, Leslie's mom, Grace, had invited us to stay with them, but I politely declined. She then asked if we would like to join them for dinner, but I was able to push it to the next day. I was feeling glad for that right now, because I was still feeling tired.

When we got to the Golden Gate Bridge, the structure was much larger than I had anticipated. There were people milling about all over the place, and it didn't help that the parking lot was tiny and cramped. Large tour buses were navigating the mass of cars, and I was glad Leslie was driving, because I cringed every time we came close to vehicles or pedestrians. So much for living in New York City for two years.

Once we'd parked, we walked across the bridge and were lucky enough to see some seals. I took lots of photos while Victoria and Leslie chatted.

"Did you know that prisoners tried to escape Alcatraz?" Leslie said.

"Is that the island over there?" Victoria asked, pointing to an island straight across the water. "It looks like a little town."

"It kind of was. The warden and all the people who worked there lived on the island, including the children. I believe they even had a school there."

"That's crazy," I said. "I can't imagine living on a secluded island with all those prisoners."

"What was that you said about them escaping?" Victoria asked.

"Well, they didn't really. The water is super cold, and there are sharks in here," Leslie said.

"Ugh. I wouldn't want to swim in that," Victoria said. "Nooo, thank you!"

"But I see swimmers now." I pointed to some heads bobbing in the bay.

Leslie shrugged. "Yeah, some people do. Some wear wet suits, but I swear, those who don't are impervious to the cold."

"I am definitely not one of them," Victoria said.

"Me neither, though more power to them," I added.

We stared out at the scenery for a bit longer until I felt Leslie tap me on the shoulder. "We better get going," she said.

"Really?" I wanted to stay a bit longer.

Leslie simply pointed over my shoulder, and I turned around to see the ocean on the other side of the bay. My mouth dropped open at the vista. "Oh, that's beautiful. I'm always in awe at how expansive the ocean is compared to everything else."

Leslie frowned. "Yes, but—"

"What Leslie is trying to tell us is that the fog is rolling in. I read about this," Victoria cut in.

I felt my eyebrows raise. Victoria gave me the stink eye, preventing me from saying what I was about to blurt out. Instead, I pointed to the fog and asked, "What's so bad about it? We get fog in Portland all the time."

"But it's more like mist there," Leslie said. "At least, that's what Paul says. This fog is more like a soft, cold, wet cloud. It's not bad, it's just not preferable when we can head somewhere warmer. A fun fact for you, though: it's nick-named Carl."

"There's a nickname for the fog?" I asked.

"Yeah, because it's such a big part of life here in the city."

"Carl. I love that," I mused.

In the time we had stood there discussing its presence, the fog had ventured closer at quite a speed. I could feel goosebumps forming on my skin. "It's time to go. I'm getting prickles all over me. Let's head to dinner." With that, Victoria hooked my arm and we headed back the way we came.

When we walked back over the bridge, Leslie said she had to make a phone call, which was just as well, because I was burning to ask Victoria about the fact that she'd read some-thing. As Leslie walked ahead, I immediately turned to Victoria.

"You read about the fog?" I asked, giving her another raised eyebrow.

"Yes, as a matter of fact I looked up some things to do while we're here, but Leslie is the perfect tour guide, so I decided not to bring it up."

I stared at her. "You never look up anything about the places we go."

"I do too!"

"Like what?"

"Like . . . that time we went to Kentucky. I found the BBQ place we ate at for lunch."

"Only after we found out the places I looked up were closed. Besides, we were starving, and the BBQ place was across the street from where we were standing." This time I couldn't help it, I started to laugh.

"Don't laugh at me," Victoria said, and she looked so serious I stopped laughing immediately.

"What is it? Did something happen?" I asked in a low voice.

"No. It's just that we're eating dinner with Paul's family tomorrow—who's your family too," Victoria quickly added, "and I want to make a good impression. So, I spent some time reading up on the area before we came. You know, so that I could have something to talk about—or not say the wrong things, for that matter."

I reached for her hand. "Oh, Victoria, just be yourself. They already love you."

She swallowed, suddenly looking unlike her usual confident self. "You know how in high school you told me that you stood out like a sore thumb because you were Taiwanese and most of our class was white?"

"Yes," I said, wondering where she was going with this.

"Well, that's how I feel about going to dinner with Paul's family, especially because he won't even be there."

"Oh . . . I hadn't thought of it that way." I really hadn't.

"Yeah, it's given me insight into how you felt at school."

My chest tightened at her comment and the memories that arose, but I forced a smile, trying to placate her. "Well, let's look at the bright side—I'll be there to keep you safe." I gave Victoria a smile. A smile that I didn't really feel inside. I had no idea Victoria had felt like this. Why hadn't she told me?

"Hey, slowpokes!" Leslie called, already at the end of the bridge. "I made reservations at another Dungeness crab place in the Outer Sunset area. It's not far from here."

I could have sworn Victoria said under her breath, "Another one?"

CHAPTER 5

THE NEXT MORNING WAS JUST AS BEAUTIFUL AS yesterday, sunny and warm. A fleeting thought of moving down here crossed my mind, but I already had a house—no, a mansion—in Portland to live in. And Mom was close by. The ten months of rain, though, I would not miss. I gave a big sigh and thought back to how Victoria kept telling me that I should get out of the house more. I'd just have to ensure that when I started traveling again, it was to more sunshine-filled locations.

"You ready to go?" Victoria asked, knocking me out of my thoughts. "I'm sure Leslie is already jumping up and down in the lobby with impatience."

"Yeah. And be nice," I said while pulling on my coat. "She's going through a rough time. She said so herself that this is the first time in a long while that she's been able to go out on her own."

"I know I'm being snarky, but she seems so desperate, and I kind of regret asking you to bring her along. I wish this weekend was just you and me."

My heart went out to Victoria. We had a special connection and were always there for each other. Me getting married was as much a big deal for her as it was for me. I turned to her and held her hands in mine. "I promise that we'll get some quality time together, just the two of us."

"Promise?"

"I promise."

"Okay." Victoria was instantly happier, and I was glad to see it. She was the livelier of the two of us, and I needed her to be happy today. "Let's not keep her waiting, then."

She turned on her heel and was off. If I'd known better, others would think this was Victoria's wedding. I hurried after her, feeling more than just a bit excited that I was about to try on wedding dresses.

"Anne!"

I whirled at the familiar voice, my jaw dropping open when I saw two women enter the shop. "Mom? Grace? What are you two doing here?" I didn't bother waiting for them to respond. I couldn't run fast enough into Mom's arms. We had left Portland so quickly and Mom was so busy with her art that I hadn't thought to ask if she wanted to come along on this trip.

"I decided to surprise you," Mom said when I pulled out of her arms. "Grace called me this morning asking what my favorite food was, and I had no idea what she was talking about."

"I assumed that your mom was joining you, seeing how you're trying on wedding dresses," Grace explained.

I blushed, realizing that any other girl would have thought of that and treated this trip as something big that her own mother would join in on, no matter what. Me, on the other hand, who had never thought about my wedding, just took it as something I had to do. I felt ashamed.

"Mom, I'm sorry. I should have asked you to come."

"Just don't forget to invite me to your wedding," she said with a wink.

"Of course not!"

Mom laughed. "I know, Anne. It's okay. Big to-dos have never been our thing, so I understand why you forgot, but I couldn't not be here for my daughter's special wedding dress shopping trip." She gave me another hug.

I beamed, feeling very loved. My family and best friend were here all together. I marveled at the fact that just four months ago I hadn't known they existed, but here we were together, shopping for my wedding dress.

Grace stepped forward. "I know we're seeing each other for dinner tonight, but you're my niece, and I was keen to come along with your mother. Leslie told me she was taking you here, and Ms. Lu is one of my closest friends."

"Ms. Lu?" I asked.

"She's the owner of this store," Grace explained. "She'll take good care of you. I've known her since we moved to America, and she designs some of the prettiest dresses I've ever seen."

A petite lady with auburn hair tied up in a bun came out of the back. "Hi, Ms. Lin."

"Emily!" Grace said. "Where is Ms. Lu?"

"She sends her deepest regrets. She was called away last minute. There was an emergency at a wedding downtown, but before she left, she picked out the dresses she wanted Anne to try."

"Oh, then let's get started!" Victoria said, passing out champagne to all of us.

Before I knew it, Emily's eyes were only on me. The last time I was the center of attention like this was when I was in

Anthony's office at the will reading with the Wilkens family. All twenty-five pairs of eyes were on me, and not in the best kind of way either. I remembered wanting to shrivel up and hide for the rest of my life, if only to dodge their scrutiny. But this was different. Under Emily, Grace, Mom, Leslie, and Victoria's attention, I felt like a princess.

I was ushered behind velvet curtains. For a moment, all I could do was stand and stare. The room was no bigger than a dressing room I'd use in Target. But instead of white walls with dirty fingerprints all over it, a wooden bench that had seen better days, and a grimy floor where I didn't dare go barefoot, this room felt like a tiny drawing room. It felt inviting, and all I wanted to do was take off my shoes, sit in the cushioned ornate chair to the left, and be pampered.

Mom called out asking if I was okay, and I realized everyone was waiting for me to come out in dress number one. It was a reminder that I better get started. The first dress was covered in lace from top to bottom. It was strapless and formed a straight line across the bodice and had sleeves that reached my elbows. It hugged me tightly around the chest and midsection before flowing like water down my legs, creating a pool of white foam that swished this way and that while I walked. With it on, I definitely felt like a princess.

"Oh, sweetheart!" Mom said as soon as I walked out of the dressing room. I swore I saw tears brimming in her eyes. Everyone else had big smiles on their faces. Grace was dabbing at her eyes, and the knowledge that she barely knew me but was moved by what she saw somehow made me even happier.

I turned to look at myself in the floor-to-ceiling gold gilded mirror and gasped. The dress was exquisite. I had never seen myself in anything this formal or beautiful before, and I could feel tears forming in the corners of my own eyes.

Mom came up behind me and gave me a hug. "You look lovely!"

"Absolutely stunning," Leslie agreed.

"Okay, on to the next one!" Victoria said, and I had to laugh. Of course, she would be heralding me forward to keep trying on the next one and the next one. If it was just me, I would have decided on this dress and been done with it. Not with Victoria, though.

I tried on dresses for a good two hours. All but one was long. The one that wasn't came just past my knees and looked more like a cocktail dress than a wedding dress. Victoria told me not to discard it because I might want to change into something I could move a little easier in at the reception. I hadn't even thought of that. But then Leslie piped up that a qipao would be better for the wedding, and I realized I hadn't thought of that either. But I did like the idea of wearing a traditional Taiwanese dress to the wedding. Maybe it was a good thing that Leslie had joined us after all. She was someone who had gone through a wedding before, and she had kids. Maybe she would be my sounding board when I was ready to have kids too. I liked the idea of calling up my cousin for advice.

Victoria lifted a hand and began ticking off her fingers as she said, "Okay, so we've narrowed it down to the lace dress, the boring silk dress—"

"Victoria, I really liked the silk—"

"Very boring," Leslie interrupted, and she and Victoria gave each other a knowing look.

"Oh, fine!"

Victoria continued, "As I was saying, there's also the mermaid dress—"

"I really liked the goofy one with flowers covering you from waist to toes," Leslie piped in.

"Which one? There were three of them," I said. *Or were*

there only two? There were too many dresses. Thank goodness Victoria and Leslie were here.

"There was the third one with the sweetheart cut and strapless bodice," Mom said, and I could see Grace nodding beside her.

"But I—"

"Yes, that one is gorgeous!" Leslie exclaimed. "Oh, Anne, you must get that one. It really stands out."

"Maybe we should look at some other stores," I said in rapid fire, trying to get my opinion in before someone else could cut me off. "I was thinking of wearing something simple."

"Nonsense! It's your wedding day and you should look like a princess," Leslie said.

"I agree," Mom chimed in.

I had seen Mom getting more and more excited as I tried on the dresses. It made me smile to see her so happy. Maybe I should just go with the dress they liked? "Okay, what about if I—"

"I vote for the lace dress," Victoria exclaimed.

"The one that looked rustic?" Leslie asked.

"Yes, that one was beautiful. It's also my favorite," Mom added.

I blew out a breath. "Okay, that's the dress, then."

Grace began walking to the front of the store.

"Wait, what is Grace doing?" I asked, a suspicion beginning to arise when I distinctly saw her take her wallet out. Without waiting for anyone to respond, I quickly walked up behind her. "Grace, what are you doing?"

She looked at me like it was obvious. "Buying your wedding dress, of course."

"You don't need to do that! It's far too much."

"I want to, Anne. Plus, Ms. Lu is giving us a family discount."

"But . . ." The words: *"I'm so rich and I can cover everything I need for the wedding"* rolled through my mind like a neon sign.

Grace placed a hand on my arm. "Hush. I'm buying you this dress. Think of it as your wedding present." With that, Grace turned back to Emily and handed over her credit card. I managed a quick glance at the invoice before Emily hid it from my sight. There were a lot of zeros.

"It's okay to let others buy you stuff for your wedding," Mom said.

I turned to see her standing behind me, her arms wide open. I immediately stepped into them.

Mom hugged me tight and said softly, "I know it's odd to have family members buy you stuff. I had the same problem when I met your dad. His family was so giving I thought it was unnatural. But people love to gift, and when they give from the heart, it's okay to receive that gift and appreciate it."

"But it cost—"

"It's not up to you to decide how much they want to spend," Mom cut in.

"I don't think it's right, though," I said, stepping back. "But I do understand there are customs that I'm not used to, so I'll take your word on this."

Leslie stepped in and put a hand on my arm. "Take your mom's advice, Anne. My mom loves to gift, and you'll be insulting her if you don't accept her offer."

"Okay, okay. I accept." How could I not?

Grace finished up at the counter and walked over to join us. "Now, how about we all go back to my house? I have some tea and zong zi."

"Ooooh! Are those the sticky rice rolls wrapped in bamboo leaves?" Victoria asked.

"Yes," Grace said, beaming.

I had to give it to Victoria, she had done her homework.

It had taken close to an hour to get to Harrison and Grace's house, even though we were only going from one side of the bridge to the other. Leslie said the commute time was normal when there was an accident, and we were lucky it hadn't taken longer. It made me rethink the idea of moving down here. Though, the tunnel on twenty-six wasn't all that better sometimes.

Grace pulled into the driveway, and all I could think was how wrong Nick had been—the neighborhood wasn't posh, yes, and the house had seen better days as roots had cracked the sidewalk and were tripping hazards, but it was beautiful. There was a peace to the area. The houses were all built on a hill and had a boxy feel to them, squished right up next to each other. Old trees lined the sidewalk. They looked as though they reached up to fifty feet in the air. Some houses had a front yard, and in those, I could see toys, a swing swaying from a tall limb, and makeshift gardens in every corner. It felt homey, and I loved it. It reminded me of how I'd grown up in a complex where every neighbor helped each other out. A sense of nostalgia washed over me as I exited the car and walked toward Harrison's home.

"Welcome!" Harrison said, opening the door for us to enter.

Before I could reply, Madison had her arms around me and was simultaneously jumping up and down while hugging me, exclaiming how much she had missed me and asking when she could visit again.

"Madison, that's enough!" Leslie said, appearing from behind me. She had taken a detour and put her luggage in Jonathan's car.

I started to tell her that it was okay, that I liked Madison's greeting; it made me feel loved. But Leslie was too quick for me as she said next, "Let your aunt go, Madison!"

I'm an Aunt. I smiled at the thought. I pinched myself to make sure I was really in my family's home.

Madison let go, and I felt a bit sad that I couldn't hug her anymore. She was definitely my favorite of all the children.

"Jonathan, you really need to catch her before she jumps on people like that. It's not okay," Leslie exclaimed as she now moved into the living room and extracted Ryan from a pile of wooden trains to give him a series of hugs and kisses.

Grace and Mom had disappeared into the house before we had taken off our shoes, but I could hear voices in what looked to be the kitchen, so I started that way, only to have Stephanie, my cousin Erik's wife, give me a quick hug and kiss on the cheek before running to Victoria and doing the same to her. I heard Stephanie tell Victoria how excited she was to have her here. I could tell they were going to become bosom buddies, and I felt a tinge of jealousy. Apparently, being the only girl that wasn't blood related to everyone had its downside, and she clearly saw Victoria as an ally in the same position.

"It's good to see you again, Anne," Erik announced, having just entered the room. One of his daughters followed behind him, her face buried in what looked to be Erik's phone.

"Caitlin, right?" I asked her.

Caitlin, Erik's oldest child, looked up and gave a slight nod and then went back to watching whatever she was watching as she walked into the living room. I turned to her father. "Erik, it's good to see you too."

He gave me a wry smile. "Sorry about that. I had to give Catlin my phone because the three of them were driving me crazy. Two is a better ratio."

Before I could respond, I heard arguing coming from one

of the rooms in the back. Erik groaned and excused himself, mumbling something about Caitlin and his other daughter, Ellen, driving him crazy.

"Anne, come over here!" a voice called.

I turned to see Mom beckoning me into the kitchen. I looked at Victoria to make sure she was okay. She gave me a smile, and I took that as a good sign. This morning before the wedding dress marathon, I had told Victoria I would be by her side the whole time this evening. Clearly, that wasn't going to be possible; there was too much going on, and people were everywhere.

"Anne," Mom called again.

"Anne, over here," Grace tacked on, beckoning me to the other side of the kitchen.

"I'm coming," I called back and hurried over.

"Grace has some extra supplies for making zong zi, and I thought it'd be fun for us to make some fresh. What do you think?" Mom asked.

She looked so excited, how was I to say no? Plus, I had always wanted to learn how to make zong zi. "Okay, but before we start, where is Harrison?"

"Oh, don't worry about him," said Grace. "I sent him out to buy some milk for the children, but he tends to end up in his store and paint or whatever he does in there before coming home."

"Oh, I heard his store got ransacked. Is it okay?"

"You heard about that?" Grace asked, giving me a quizzical look. "We're not sure who did it. The security camera is so old that it didn't capture a clean shot. The person was too blurry. Harrison has been very down about it."

"I'm sorry it happened. Maybe I can stop by while I'm here and help out?"

Grace beamed. "I think he'd like that. He'll probably show

you some of his paintings while he's at it. But no more about Harrison, let's make some zong zi!" Grace gestured to a tub of really long leaves sitting on the counter. "You see those bamboo leaves? They've been soaking long enough. Bring them over here."

I brought them over to Mom and Grace.

"Now, I've set up everything in a line," Grace continued, gesturing at the array of ingredients laid out. "There's the sticky rice, the pork, boiled egg yolks, mushrooms, and the peanuts. You want to take two of these leaves and cross them. Then cup the middle so it's sitting in your hand with a big opening to put all the food in. Put the rice in first in a nice thick layer, then add one piece of pork, an egg yolk, a couple slices of mushroom, and a sprinkle of peanuts. Then, top it off with more rice and fold the leaves in so that it's wrapped up like a triangle. Next, take some string and wrap it around the zong zi a few times so it holds the leaves together. And there you go." She held up a perfectly wrapped zong zi.

Mom and I just stared at Grace as if she had just performed magic. She made it look easy. Mom and I had attempted to make zong zi a long time ago, and let's just say we didn't know what we were doing, and it didn't look like that!

Leslie and Victoria came to join in, and over the course of the next hour, I was able to make five decent zong zis and was starting to get the hang of it. In the end, it wasn't as hard as it looked. You just needed to know how to hold the leaves and what direction to fold them in. Leslie was as proficient as her mom, and in the time it had taken me to make five, they each had at least twenty of them hanging off their strings ready to be steamed.

While the food was cooking, I pulled Victoria aside. "How are you holding up?" I asked her.

"Pretty good, actually. Leslie and Stephanie have been really nice. If anything, it seems they have other stuff to be concerned about rather than who's dating their brother."

"That's great to hear." I felt relieved for Victoria.

We mingled with the rest of the family in the living room and played board games with the kids, talking about life in Portland and the Bay Area. In the middle of all this Harrison came home.

"Baba!" Leslie cried. "Where have you been? We've been home for hours."

"Your mama sent me to get milk."

"Hours ago!" Erik said, and everyone laughed.

"I can't help it if I have the urge to paint."

"We know, we know," Leslie said. "But Anne, Ah Yi, and Victoria are here. They've been waiting to see you."

We hadn't really. We'd had fun interacting with everyone that I'd forgotten Harrison wasn't there, but Leslie seemed bent on making a point about my uncle being late.

Grace suddenly yelled from the kitchen, "Food is ready!"

There was an instant cacophony of sound as recliners were lowered and large and little feet moved simultaneously in the direction of the kitchen.

"That smells divine," Caitlin said.

"Where did you learn to use that word?" Erik said, laughing.

"From you and Mommy," she replied. To which everyone laughed.

"Victoria, you come and sit next to me," Grace said.

Victoria sent me a shocked look before turning to go and sit next to Grace. I decided to follow her but was pulled back by Leslie, who gestured at me to sit with her on the other side of the long table.

Grace waited till everyone was seated before saying, "I am so glad to have Josephine and Anne here today. If it wasn't for Anne's persistence in finding Harrison, we wouldn't all be together right now as a family. And Victoria, I'm so happy you are here with us as well, and I hope you'll be a formal part of this family soon too."

"Mom!" Leslie said, turning red on her mom's behalf.

"What? I'm not getting younger, and Paul and Victoria clearly like each other."

"But Mom—" Leslie began.

"It's okay. I'm glad to be here too," Victoria said, and I didn't miss the flush creeping up her neck.

"Great! Then, as our guest here tonight, you have first choice of the zong zi," Grace announced.

"Oh, um . . . I'll just take this one. Thank you." Victoria flushed even more at the lingering attention, but I could see she was also pleased. My worry meter was instantly tampered down.

"Now, eat, eat! And enjoy, everyone," Grace said, putting zong zi on our plates.

I was part way through my first bite and savoring the delicious taste when Leslie leaned over and whispered, "Would you be up for a Broadway show tonight? *Cats* is showing."

I swallowed my food, surprised at the request. "Tonight? It's a bit late to get tickets, no?"

"I bought them a while ago for Jonathan and me, but he's not a big Broadway fan, and when I asked if I could offer his ticket to you, he was more than happy to not go."

"Wow, okay. If you're sure, that'll be fantastic. I'm sure Victoria would be interested too."

Leslie frowned. "Oh, I did check, but I wasn't able to get a third ticket last-minute. They're already sold out." She glanced at Victoria as she asked, "Do you think she'll mind if she can't go?"

"Um . . ." An image of Victoria going off with Isabella and Lauren came to mind, and I shook my head. "No, she'll be fine. To tell you the truth, she was nervous about coming here tonight, but she seems okay now."

Leslie's brows rose. "Why? We don't bite."

"Oh, it's not that. It's because she felt the odd one out. She pointed out that I'm uncomfortable when I'm the only Taiwanese person in a group of people, and she told me she felt the same about coming here."

"Oh, I hadn't thought of that."

"That's what I said too."

"Now I want her to come with us, so she doesn't feel left out."

I thought on that for a moment, then said, "Why don't you and Jonathan still go? Goodness knows, you two probably need the time without the kids, right?"

"Well, yes . . . but he won't be too excited about it after I already told him he's off the hook."

I touched Leslie's arm. "I'm sure he'll love spending time with just you."

"Yeah."

Her response was odd, but before I could question it, I remembered I had something to ask her. "Oh! I almost forgot. I wanted to ask you if you would like to be one of my bridesmaids?"

A squeal came from Leslie that was so high-pitched that everyone stopped talking and eating to see what the commotion was.

"Anne just asked me to be one of her bridesmaids," Leslie explained in an excited rush. This elicited a lot of cheers from the adults and questions from the kids, but before we could say anything more, Harrison stood up and announced he'd like to do a toast. It was the most confident I had ever seen him.

"I wanted to say my own welcome to Anne, Josephine, and Victoria. This wouldn't be happening if not for Anne.

And, as Grace says, I'm a stubborn old man, and I tried so hard to keep my past silent, but I'm happy we are all together as a family now. To Anne." He raised his glass to me.

I blushed as everyone followed suit and raised their glasses to me as well. Madison was cheering at the top of her lungs, and I couldn't help laughing. It was then that another thought came to me—my wedding would be the perfect place for Harrison and his mom to finally meet. Without thinking, I blurted out, "Harrison, what do you think about inviting Mary to my wedding? We could have the whole family together again."

The room went silent. *Great, Anne, you sure know how to kill the mood. Should have kept my mouth shut.*

"Victoria, honey, please help me clear these dishes," I heard Grace say quietly.

I could feel my neck turning red, and even Leslie was being awfully quiet.

Thank goodness Harrison started speaking again. "Anne, why don't you come with me to my office? It'll be easier to talk there."

Now what had I done?

I nodded and got up from the table and followed Harrison to his office in an awkward silence. Once we were inside, he quietly closed the door. I almost wished he had slammed it, as the quietness was starting to get to me.

Looking at me, he said, "Anne, I think it's a great idea to invite Mary."

"Harrison—" I began at the same time. Then I paused. "Wait, what?"

"I said I think it'll be a great idea to invite Mary to your wedding."

I stared at him. "You really have no concerns?"

He gave me a wry smile. "Of course, I do. I'm terrified. I want to say 'no' to you, because I knew you would ask me this when you came tonight. Grace warned me about it, too, so I have been thinking about it today. It's why I took so long buying the milk earlier; I had to go to my shop where I could think. You've seen how it is here when the family comes over —there is no quiet time, and Grace would never allow me to hide here in my office while our family is here."

Relief surged through me. "I agree. I think having Mary come to my wedding will be really good for everyone. Would you like to be the one to invite her?"

"No," he said, laughing. "I am not that brave."

"Okay, I'll ask her as soon as I get back home, as I didn't bring her number with me."

"I don't think there is any hurry, no? You and Sebastian are not getting married immediately." I saw a twinkle appear in his eyes. "Unless there's something you haven't told us?"

"No, of course not!" I laughed. "Well, okay, yes there is. If everything works out, we've decided to have the wedding in a few weeks. I'd like to invite her soon so she has time to prepare. I really am excited to get you two together again."

Harrison's brows rose. "So, there *is* something you're not telling us if the wedding is so soon?"

I flushed, suddenly aware of what he was thinking, especially given Rose's past. "No, it's not that. I found a deal for a trip to Bora Bora, which I thought could be for our honeymoon. I wanted to take advantage of it."

Harrison relaxed slightly. "Ah, I see. Well, I cannot blame you there. You should invite Mary soon then, but maybe give it a couple days to allow the idea to sink in, yes?"

I was fine with that—relieved, actually, that he'd said yes. "Okay, no problem, Harrison. But do you mind if I let the others know?"

He seemed surprised at the question. "Of course not. Why would you ask?"

I gestured at the room. "Because you took us into your office."

"Oh, that's only because it's such a sensitive topic that I didn't want all the drama that came with it while we talked—and not from you, but from the rest of the family. But now that we've come to a decision, we can allow the drama to happen outside of this office." He smiled wryly.

"Okay, got it." I stood up and headed to the door.

"Anne?"

"Yes?" I said, one foot already out the door.

"There is no rush, okay? Just let this decision sit for a bit."

"Okay, Harrison. No problem."

I left the room thinking that was easier than I'd thought, but my uncle was still very much an enigma.

CHAPTER 6

"How many times has he called you now?" Victoria asked while lounging on a chaise in my sitting room.

It'd been three days since we got back from San Francisco, and Harrison had called at least twice a day to change his mind about asking Mary to the wedding. "This will have been the fifth time."

"And which way is he leaning now? I can't keep track anymore."

"He does not want me to invite Mary at the moment."

"The man is conflicted, isn't he?"

"You think? I thought it was way too easy when he agreed the first time. He can't make up his mind, and it's driving me crazy. I'm tempted to make the call without his agreement."

"You should. Why wait? You're going to eventually do it, no matter what he says."

"I know, but it would be nice if everyone was on board with the idea. I don't like the thought of calling Mary behind Harrison's back."

"Yes, because waiting for Harrison to make a decision was always the way to go." Victoria rolled her eyes.

"No need to be nasty."

"Sorry, I just want you to stop fretting about it. Mary has an invitation as far as you're concerned, and it is *your* wedding. Not Harrison's. And Sebastian has already given you his blessing."

"All right. I'll give her a call."

"You should do it now while your brain is still in agreement with the rest of you," Victoria urged.

"Yeah, yeah." She was right, though.

I pulled out my cell. I had almost dialed Mary's number multiple times already, only to be stopped by Harrison. Let's just say I had it memorized by now, and all I had to do was wait for someone to pick up. It rang and rang, and I was about to hang up when a young voice picked up.

"Hello?" It was almost a whisper, but it was clearly a little boy's voice.

"Um . . . hi, is Mary home?"

"Mary?"

The couple of seconds of silence seemed to drag on forever, but then I heard the boy yell for his grandmother, and I had to hold the phone away from my ears.

Ming-Yue's voice came on the line. "Who is this?"

"It's Anne—Hong-Mei. I'm He-Mei's daughter."

"Oh, Anne! So nice to hear from you. Mary and I have been wondering how you've been doing. Are you still searching for Harrison?"

"Ah, that's actually why I'm calling."

"Oh. You've found something? Another clue?"

"Well . . . no, not a clue. More like a person."

There was silence on the other end of the line, and then I heard her walking in the background. Was she going to get Mary? I could feel my hand starting to sweat as I held the phone. It really should be Harrison that was making this call, not me. Why was I the one who had to face Mary? He's the one who ran away. *But it is my wedding,* I reminded myself. I was inviting her to my wedding, so I should be the one to call. Ugh.

"This was a bad idea," I whispered to Victoria as the silence rolled on.

She just shrugged and waved for me to continue. Clearly, she had no idea how much this affected me right now.

A whisper came over the phone. "Anne?"

At first, I thought it was the little boy again, but my name was followed by heavy breathing. It couldn't be him, it had to be Mary. But she sounded strained, not the force of nature I had met only a couple of months ago. "Is that you, Mary?"

"Yes. I was wondering when you would call. I have wanted to talk to you." This was followed by heavy breathing again, as if the words themselves drew excess energy.

"Mary, what's wrong?" I felt my heart rate go up. I was thinking all sorts of horrible things that might have happened to her. Maybe me not finding Harrison hurt her more than I thought?

Mary's voice brought me back to the present. "Anne, listen to me. Ming-Yue just gave me some pain medication—"

"Why are you taking pain medication?" I cried out.

"Because I am old, and my body is not what it used to be. It's just a cold," she snapped, turning once again into the Mary I knew. "Now, listen to me, and stop changing the subject."

"Okay."

She released a sigh. "You need to stop looking for Harrison. Ming-Yue said you found someone, but I have found so many people over the years and none have led me to Harrison. Every path has only made my heart crack open that much more. Do not follow in my footsteps. Harrison is a grown man, and if he can hold a grudge for this long, then he deserves to be alone. You and your mom's visit made me see life in a different way. We have many in our family who love us, and that is enough. We should—"

"I met him," I cut in.

"I appreciate . . . What?" The heavy breathing had stopped, and panic started to overcome me as I wondered if Mary had stopped breathing altogether. But then she said in a very shallow voice, "What did you say?"

I released a deep breath and admitted, "I met him. He came to my house and gave me his journal to read, then he brought his entire family to Portland with him, and we had a family reunion."

There was silence, and then I heard Mary's voice from a distance, speaking to Ming-Yue. "Talk to Anne, I need a break. Tell her I will talk to her later." There were the sounds of bedsheets rustling and then a door clicking shut.

I swallowed, waiting for Ming-Yue to say something. I could almost sense the woman's confusion.

"What did you tell Mama?" she finally asked.

"That I've met Harrison." And then I repeated, "He came to the house and gave me his journal to read, then he brought his family to Portland to meet me and my mum, and we had a family reunion."

"I see . . . . That is big news."

What was going on? I thought they would be more excited than this. "I know this is a lot to swallow. I wish Harrison had called you himself or even flown over to see Mary in person, but he won't."

"It's been a long time. I can't blame him for being hesi-tant," Ming-Yue said. "Mary, however, might not think otherwise."

"You think she'll not want to see him because he's caused her so much hurt over the years?"

"Yes, I fear that," Ming-Yue confessed, and I could hear the heaviness in her voice.

I felt there was nothing more to say. I was well aware I'd dropped a bombshell. "Ming-Yue, please let me know if Mary would like to talk more. I can send her his address, and maybe they could write? I know Grace would have my back on this."

"There is no need. Mama will be in touch when she's ready. Do not worry. This has been on her mind since the day Harrison ran away. I know she'll want to follow up with you soon."

Relief hit me. "Okay, but if there's anything I can do . . ."

"I understand, Anne. Do not worry. I must say goodnight now. It is bedtime here."

"Oh yes, sorry. I'll talk to you later."

Victoria watched as I hung up and sat down with a thud. I hope I didn't kill Mary with this news.

As if reading my thoughts, Victoria came over and sat next to me. "You did the right thing," she said.

"Yeah? Then why do I feel wretched? Oh—drat!" I clapped a hand to my forehead.

"What is it?"

"I never invited her to the wedding!"

"Anne, just breathe. It'll be okay. You haven't even made the invitation to invite anyone to the wedding."

"Oh, right. Good point." I tried to catch my breath. I wanted this to work. Harrison and Mary were going to meet up if I had anything to do with it. "Let's see if she calls back then."

"She will," Victoria said without hesitation.

"Well, if Mary is ready to talk to me again, I'll offer to fly her out. She can obviously stay here."

"I think that will be a nice gesture," Victoria agreed. "And speaking of invitations, you need to make yours. Were you still going to go with Anders Printing?"

"I am. The ones she made for Lauren were beautiful. I have my heart set on a letterpress invitation now too."

"Great! And how is Lauren, by the way? Have you talked to her?"

"Yes, I—oh! I never responded to her text!" I opened my phone again and clicked on Lauren's name, bringing up a message from a few days ago. She had arrived home and was asking if she could call to chat. Apparently, she had a lot to share.

CHAPTER 7

"You've got to go to Lucia for flowers!"
Lauren excitedly exclaimed.

"I know." I couldn't help laughing. We got back home
from San Francisco yesterday, and I'd called Lauren first thing
this morning. She had been shouting her responses to me the
whole time. She seemed very excited, and it was contagious. I
couldn't help smiling and laughing along with her.

"Of course, you do. You're the one who saved the day!"

"I wouldn't say I—"

"Don't be modest, Anne. Own it!"

"Now you're sounding like Isabella," I pointed out.

"Well, it's true. And speaking of Isabella, have you heard
from her?"

"Lauren, you might not have picked up on the vibe at
your party, but Isabella and I—"

"I know, I know! You two are mortal enemies."

"That's a bit dramatic, but yes, we dislike each other a
lot."

"Well, if you hear from her, can you let me know?"

"Of course, but why are you asking? You keep in touch regularly."

"That's the thing, we usually do, but ever since I got back from my honeymoon I haven't been able to reach her. I've left her voice message after voice message and still nothing. Not even a text telling me that she'll talk to me later. I even went to her house and knocked on her door, but no one responded. I know, she probably was just out and about, but I have a feeling. You know how you know someone so well that you just know when something is wrong? I have that feeling, Anne. Something's wrong with Izzy, and I don't know what it is. It's making me very nervous. Promise me you'll let me know if you hear from her?"

I smiled. I'd forgotten how chatty Lauren could be. "Lauren, I already said I would. I'm sure everything is fine. Isabella has probably just gotten super busy with her work."

"No. That's not . . . Well, I guess so. She's more than just family, though, Anne. We'd do anything for each other. But I swear something's not right."

"Okay, as I said, I'll let you know if she contacts me, but you should probably call her actual friends, as there's a better chance of her calling them than me."

"I already have. I've called everyone—even Nick! That boy fawns over Isabella, even though she just uses him. I've told her time and again to let him go so he can find a nice girl for himself. He could have a family of his own instead of pining after her, but she just says he would never listen to her and changes the subject."

"You have to admit they are cute together." *I can't believe I just said that. Since when did I notice Isabella in a cute framework? And Nick was not someone I would associate cute with, either.* Lauren was rubbing off on me. That's what I was going with.

"They are, though, aren't they?" I heard her sigh. "Anne,

you know how I shared all that information about Isabella with you when we were in Hawaii?"

"Yeah." How could I forget? Lauren had had a bit too much to drink that night. She'd shared her story about her ex, Rudy; who, after breaking up with her, had caused a catastrophe for both their family businesses because they depended on each other. But Isabella had smoothed everything over in the end, thereby solidifying her and Lauren's friendship.

"She stopped talking to me for a couple months when she was sorting out my mess," Lauren continued. "I thought she despised me, but then I found out it was because she was taking care of my problem with Rudy, and she was staying away so I didn't get my hopes up. It was so sweet of her. I'm worried that there's something going on that she's trying to fix, and this time I want to help her."

"Maybe it's not for you to know," I suggested.

But that was too sensible an answer for Lauren. "No! We're sisters, Anne. We might as well have been from the same parents. If she's hurting, I hurt. I tell you, I just have this feeling. It's not good. Something's up, and as she won't tell me, she's avoiding me. You just wait and see."

"I'm sure she's fine." I needed to change the subject fast. Lauren was going to drag me down this spiral with her if I let her keep going. I was hoping what I said next would get her mind off Isabella. "There is something I want to ask you, Lauren."

"Of course. Here I am, talking away like usual." She laughed her beautiful musical laugh.

Without any lead up, I said, "Would you like to be one of my bridesmaids?"

"Ahhhh! Anne!" I heard running and then an "oomph." Had she just tripped? There was a mad scramble, then

Lauren squealed, "Stephen! Stephen! Anne just asked me to be her bridesmaid!"

I heard him telling her to calm down, and I couldn't help laughing. Good thing she was so excited she didn't notice.

The phone was transferred, and Stephen came on the line. "Anne?"

"Yes?"

"Are you sure about this?" He sounded a bit worried.

Before I could answer, I heard a smack, and the phone sounded like it was jostled around before Lauren came back on the line. I could hear Stephen laughing in the background and then saying loudly, "You know how she is, Anne!"

"Don't listen to him!" Lauren cried. "He's just jealous that I get to be in your wedding, and he'll just be a guest."

I could see her sticking her tongue out at him. Part of me felt a bit jealous that Sebastian and I didn't joke around like the two of them, but then again, I was definitely not like Lauren, so there was that.

"I assume Victoria is maid of honor?" Lauren now asked.

"Yes, and I also have Leslie, my cousin, in the bridal party, but she lives down in the Bay Area."

"Excellent! Okay, since I am now an official bridesmaid—and yes, I accept!—I'm going to coordinate a brunch for the three of us. I'll book it in for tomorrow—oh, can you make sure Victoria is free?"

"Yes, I'm sure she is. She and I were planning on going to lunch tomorrow anyway."

"Perfect! Okay, I'll book lunch and let you two know where it'll be. Talk to you soon. I'm so excited!"

She hung up, and I couldn't help but grin. Between Victoria, Lauren, and Leslie, I wouldn't have to lift a finger.

"You sure you're not mad that I asked Lauren to be a bridesmaid?" I asked Victoria as we walked toward the place Lauren had booked for lunch.

"Why would I be mad? I'm so happy you're making new friends!"

"Ha ha ha." I rolled my eyes at Victoria.

She didn't smile back. "You laugh, but it's a concern."

"Yes, I know, I know. Let's just go in now."

"Have you ever eaten here?" Victoria asked as we came to the door.

"No, but . . . wow!" I said as I looked at the venue.

"Yeah," Victoria said under her breath.

I should have known that when Lauren said "brunch," it wasn't just to the fast-food joint down the corner. A sense of guilt hit me as I remembered the first time we had treated Lauren to brunch—we'd taken her out for fish and chips. She'd seemed very out of place, and looking at this restaurant, I could see why.

Victoria and I were planning on going to The Pancake House today, but this was so much better. It felt like we had walked into an oasis. Everyone was very put together for living in Portland, whereas Victoria and I looked shabby in our jeans and t-shirts. If it wasn't for Lauren bouncing her way toward us that very second, I was positive we both would have bolted and called her later to say our car had broken down or some other story.

"I'm so glad you two are here!" Lauren exclaimed, giving us the tightest hug. Her smile made my nerves immediately settle. I could tell it had the same effect on Victoria, too, because her hand finally let go of mine.

I opened and closed my fingers a few times to get the blood circulating again as I said, "This is quite the place. I've never heard of it before."

"Oh, you wouldn't. It's exclusive to the rich. Stephen says

it's for the snooty. Honestly, some of the people are, but the food is absolutely out-of-this-world. Come on, I have a table ready for us."

Lauren hooked both of our arms and led us to the back terrace, where we had a grand view of Portland. Firefly lights hung above us, and I could imagine how magical it looked at night. As if reading my thoughts, Lauren looked up and sighed.

"It's really pretty here at night, but I just couldn't wait until dinner to catch up with you both. I wanted us to start planning immediately. I even talked to my wedding planner, and she said she would totally take you on—with your assent, of course. But I hope you'll work with her. She made my life so much easier."

"Lauren—"

"Have you picked a venue yet? Oh, sorry, I just love weddings, and since it's not mine anymore, I'm so excited to enjoy the process this time." She quickly added, "Not that you'll have a bad time of it."

"What do you mean?" Victoria asked.

"Oh, it's just that when it's your own, it's not really your wedding."

"But of course, it is," I said, a bit baffled where this was going.

At this time, a waiter came by to take our drink and appetizer orders, to which Victoria and I grabbed our menus, apologizing for not having read them already. But with one finger and a nod from Lauren, the waiter left, saying he'd give us another minute.

Lauren looked at us as she said, "He's waiting on us, not the other way around." She paused for a second longer and seemed to make a decision right then. "Yes, we are going to use my wedding planner. I'm going to call her right after this brunch and get our first meeting set up."

"Why don't we meet her first and then decide?" I felt embarrassed that I had apologized for not having my drink decision made before the waiter came by, but this sudden decision from Lauren about using her wedding planner had spiked my heart rate.

"Yes, that's a good point. You'll have to gel. That's a must, but I think you'll like her. You two will definitely get along. Oh, I'm so excited!" she squealed. "Now, let's see what we want to eat and drink before he comes back." She picked up her menu and started perusing it, not noticing the look Victoria and I shared before we picked up our own menus.

Behind the menus, Victoria whispered to me, "Are you sure about this?"

I knew exactly where that question was pointed. "Yes, I'm not going back on asking her."

Victoria just raised her brows but said nothing.

The waiter came and took our orders. When he left, Lauren took out a notebook that had a bunch of tabs down the side. The notebook looked like it was stuffed to the brim.

"This is my wedding book," Lauren explained, beaming as she handed it over to us. "It has every detail that was included in my wedding, right down to the type of lace that lined my veil. Feel free to flip through it and come up with answers to some of the questions on the first page. Eda will want to know these answers in order to help you plan. But first things first, what colors are you choosing for your wedding?" Lauren looked at me with expectant eyes, and I could tell Victoria was trying to hide a laugh. She knew I was very much out of my comfort zone.

"Um . . . I was thinking of purple and light pink with a dash of green."

"Ooooh, that sounds so pretty! It'll be like a farmhouse wedding. Oh, I think I might know of a barn we could rent. We can go for that rustic feel, you know, that feeling of grunginess. Give me back my notebook for a second; I'm writing this down. We can share all this with Eda when we meet her. Oh, she's going to be so excited. She has always wanted to do a farmhouse wedding, but her brides always wanted a beach or church wedding. This is going to be so much fun!"

Our appetizers came, and I found myself so distracted by the delicious food going into my mouth that I didn't have time to wonder at the decisions being made for me.

During the main course, Lauren continued to talk on and on about her wedding and what I should consider for mine if I wanted a rustic feel. "I think this a fantastic start," she was saying. "Make sure you call your mother to see if there's any Taiwanese traditions she'd like to add. It'll be such a pretty blend of rustic and Taiwanese culture. I can see it now."

"Actually, Leslie called yesterday saying she had thought of some traditions to add to my wedding, but I said I had to talk to Mom first."

"Oh! Your cousin who's also the other bridesmaid?"

"Yes. We were able to go wedding dress shopping with her the other day."

"You already went dress shopping?" Lauren's excited face fell.

I quickly jumped in. "Ah, yes, we did get a dress already, and it falls into that rustic look really well. It's lace all over and drops in a gorgeous pool around my feet. My aunt bought it for my wedding present."

"Oh, well." She collected herself. "That's fantastic. That's one thing we don't have to worry about then. But there will be plenty of other stuff you'll have to think about. You should put Leslie in touch with me and Victoria so we can all plan together. We'll want to organize a bridal shower next." Lauren winked at Victoria, and I sighed.

But I couldn't help thinking that was a close one. Lauren

had looked so disappointed that she'd missed out on the wedding dress shopping trip, but we hadn't planned much of anything past that, so there was still a lot to do.

Lauren continued throwing out ideas all through brunch, and I continued eating, hoping Victoria was able to remember more of what was being said than I would.

"I had no idea it would be so involved," I said to Victoria, my head resting on her shoulder. "Is it too much to ask that all I want is a quiet wedding behind the mansion with close family and friends? It's all that's really needed. Nothing fancy."

We had returned home and were on a mission trying to come up with answers to the questions the wedding planner would be asking. Victoria had pulled out the wedding magazines I'd slipped under my bed and neatly displayed them on the floor for us to peruse. By the time I'd flipped through the last magazine I had an idea of what I wanted—and a headache.

"That doesn't sound bad at all," Victoria replied. "At the end of the day, it's your wedding, Anne. So, if you want a small one, then let everyone know."

She made it sound so simple. "I know, but . . ."

Victoria turned to me. "You're also a bit excited about throwing a big party and having all the trimmings, right? Why not keep an open mind?"

"Yeah, you're right," I said, smiling at Victoria. She knew me well.

"Then let's do it. Let's go for the whole shebang. Every last detail. And then let the wedding planner put it all together."

That sounded good right now. "Yeah, I'll do that."

We both leaned back against the bed again, and I felt at peace with the decision made tonight. The silence between us was broken by the buzz of a phone.

"Oh, Lauren just texted," Victoria said, passing my phone over.

I looked down at the screen and, sure enough, Lauren's name was at the top with the words:

Eda will meet us tomorrow at ten. She's very excited to meet you and to be planning your wedding!

"Guess we're going with this wedding planner," I muttered to Victoria.

"Everything is a trial until you finalize it, Anne. Remember that. But first, you need to call your mother and ask if she has anything she wants to add."

"Right. Let me get a hold of Mom." Thank goodness for Victoria. I leaned back against my bed and dialed Mom's number.

Mom picked up on the third ring. "Hi, Anne, how's the wedding planning going?"

"It's going well. It's actually why I'm calling."

"Oh? Something I can help with?"

"Yeah, Victoria and I are meeting with Lauren's wedding planner tomorrow, and I was wondering if there were any Taiwanese traditions you'd like to add? Leslie had given some suggestions, but I didn't know if they were necessary."

"Oh, well, I'm probably not the best person to ask. I had a tiny wedding of just your dad and his parents. It was at the courthouse, and we brought some flowers. I dressed in a simple white dress, and your dad was in a suit. Nothing fancy. I think it's safe to say that you can do whatever you like. I don't know of any customs to add."

"Great! That will simplify things. Thanks, Mom. Lauren is excited about me meeting her wedding planner, but I'm thinking I don't need one. How hard can it be to plan a wedding? I planned the Christmas Gala not long ago. Even though it was very last minute. It went great."

Victoria piped in at this moment. "Remember, though, Anne, that the Christmas Gala had been running like clockwork every year; there weren't too many details to take care of that the staff didn't already know."

"True, but we're looking at a small wedding. Even Sebastian agreed to a small wedding."

Mom said something, and I had to ask her to repeat it. "Of course, you don't need to hire a wedding planner," she said. "But you can afford one, and she might help take some of the stress away."

"What stress? Planning the wedding will be fun."

"Parties from scratch always have some stress attached to them," Mom said. "But why don't you meet this woman first and then make a decision? Aside from that, are you and Victoria having fun organizing the wedding?"

I looked at Victoria, who was once again immersed in one of the magazines. She had a pen in hand, circling who knew what. "Yeah, Mom, we are. I never thought I'd say this, but we are having fun planning this wedding."

"That's fantastic to hear. It makes me happy that you invited Leslie to be one of your bridesmaids too. I think that means a lot to Grace and Harrison. Now that I think about it, it might be nice to add some of the Taiwanese traditions Leslie is thinking about. Wouldn't hurt, and it'd invite that side of your family into the mix."

"Yeah, that's not a bad idea. I'll think about that. I'm glad

I invited Leslie too. Hopefully, this will give us a chance to get to know each other better."

"You've done good, Anne, by bringing this family together."

"Thanks, Mom," I said, blushing. "Who knew a surprise inheritance would have so much reach?"

"Who knew, indeed. But it's been well worth it—you put me in touch with my brother. Just remember, sweetheart, that it's your wedding, and you can do whatever you want."

CHAPTER 8

We met Lauren at what looked like a boutique store but was really a studio of wedding planners. The whole place was polished and feminine, and I felt very out of place. But Lauren immediately skipped toward us and gave us a hug.

She pulled back, a big smile plastered over her face. "I'm so excited. You're going to love her, Anne!"

As if on cue, a very poised lady walked toward us. She was dressed in a pencil skirt and fitted button-down shirt, the sleeves rolled precisely to her elbow. Her gray hair was tied back in a tight bun, with not one loose strand visible. She had a warm smile, though, and her handshake was firm. I liked her and had the thought this wedding planner thing might actually work. There was also the fact I wouldn't have to lift a finger and would only need to say "yes" or "no" to questions. It was more than appealing.

"It's very nice to meet you, Anne. I'm Eda. I've been looking forward to meeting you ever since Lauren told me you got engaged."

"It's nice to meet you too, Eda," I said, returning her

smile. "This is my friend, Victoria. She's the maid of honor, and of course, you know Lauren. I have one more bridesmaid, Leslie. She's my cousin, but she lives near San Francisco, so she won't be able to make it up here often."

"That's not a problem. I can work with anyone in your wedding party, no matter where they are."

Lauren chimed in, "Eda is the best. You can't go wrong with her. She will take care of everything."

"You're too kind, Lauren. It helps that I love what I do. But why don't we head into my office so we can continue our discussion there? I have water and snacks available."

I looked at Victoria, and I could tell she knew what I was thinking. Eda was so poised it was more than a little scary. She stood straight, her smile and eyes warm and welcoming, but who could smile like that all the time? There wasn't a wrinkle on her clothes, and she . . . she reminded me of Isabella! I heard Victoria giggling next to me as we followed Eda and Lauren into the office.

"Be quiet," I said to Victoria.

"You're thinking of Isabella, aren't you?"

"How'd you know?"

"Because I had the same thought."

"We're so bad."

Victoria patted my arm. "Just keep telling yourself that she's not Isabella. Eda should be allowed to start on a clean slate."

I grimaced. "That's what I'm trying to do, but all I can see is Isabella planning my wedding."

We were interrupted by Eda ushering us into the dullest room I could imagine. There were four chairs all facing a small circular coffee table in the middle of the room. A big binder was positioned in the middle of the table.

"Have a seat," Eda invited, gesturing to the chairs. "Would you like anything to drink?"

"I'll take a mimosa," Lauren said.

"Oh, I'll take one too!" Victoria said.

I smiled. "I guess I'll have one too."

"Excellent, three mimosas coming up." She clicked a button, and a young girl appeared to take our order. She had the glittering eyes of someone who loved her job, and when she saw Lauren, her smile became wider.

Lauren noticed her at the same moment. "Maggie, it's so good to see you again!" Lauren went and gave the girl a big hug before turning to introduce her to us. "Maggie is Eda's number one helper. I couldn't have gotten through my wedding without her."

Maggie was blushing. "Whose wedding is it?" she asked, her eyes alighting on Victoria.

"It's mine," I said, holding out my hand in greeting. Maggie's eyes went big when she saw me. Not in a frightened way, but more of a surprised way than anything else.

"It's very nice to meet you," Maggie said, shaking my hand. After the introductions, she left to get our drinks.

"Isn't she the best?" Lauren announced. "She's very professional too. You wouldn't even know she's only sixteen."

Just then, Maggie poked her head back into the room. "Lauren?"

"Yes, Maggie?"

"Briel wanted to say hi to you while you were here. It's just that she's going to head out soon. Can you spare a moment?"

Lauren's face lit up. "Oh, I'd love to see her! Anne, will you be okay here without me for a bit?"

"Yes, I'll be fine." I couldn't help but laugh a little inside. I hadn't known Lauren that long, but she treated us like life-long friends. It felt good.

"Victoria, do you want to come with me? We can meet

some of the other staff that help Eda. We'll be working with them more closely than Anne." Without waiting for Victoria's reply, Lauren reached out and took both my hands in hers and looked me in the eye. "I'm so happy for you, Anne. I'm also very glad we found each other. Your wedding is going to be the best one ever. I can already tell."

With that, she took Victoria down the hallway, and Eda and I were left alone.

Eda gestured to two of the seats. "Why don't we have a seat?"

I sat and then didn't know what to say. What did one ask a wedding planner? What was there to plan that I needed a wedding planner? But Eda had no trouble starting the discussion. "I want you to know that we have not signed any contracts, so you are under no obligation to work with me or my staff if you don't want to—no matter what Lauren says," she added with a genuine smile.

I laughed. "She's just full of life."

"I know, and she was lovely to work with."

I instantly warmed to Eda. "Thank you for not putting pressure on me. I'm honestly not sure I need a wedding planner right now. Mainly because there's not much for us to plan except the flowers, a dress, and maybe some tablecloth colors."

"Absolutely. My job is to not put pressure on the bride or groom. This is your wedding. And I want to apologize for Maggie. Since you inherited the Wilkens fortune, you're very well-known here, and, without beating around the bush, we were hoping you would be interested in working with us."

I didn't know what to say to this. Me? Well-known? "I . . ."

Eda saved me from blubbering a clumsy reply by waving her hand and saying, "Anyway, let's talk about your wedding. Even if you don't hire me, I could give you a tip or two."

"Yes, lets. That would be great." I wasn't used to being the center of attention, but focusing on the wedding was a good change of direction after what she had just said about Maggie. "I have to warn you that, aside from the wedding colors, I would just like to keep it small and simple."

"That's a great start. Would you like to look at some photographs of weddings I've done first?"

"That would be great." I was actually excited. I wanted to see what Eda had made possible, even if I wasn't planning to hire her.

She picked up the binder from the table and opened it up. Inside, there were beautiful photographs of outdoor and indoor weddings. I saw weddings within castles, beach weddings with the sunset in the background, mountain-top weddings, gorgeous buffets, indoor water fountains, stunning flower arrangements as tall as me, and a whole heap of happy, smiling people dancing the night away. It stirred a desire inside me—a desire I didn't know I had, and I almost broke down. Who wouldn't want a beautiful princess-like wedding? And the best person to hire for the job was sitting right beside me.

Eda broke into my thoughts. "What do you want your wedding to feel like?"

I tore my gaze away from the photographs to look at her. "Feel like?"

"Yes, what do you envision? When your guests walk in, what is it that you want them to feel about the occasion?"

"Oh, I haven't really thought about that. I know I want it in the backyard with some Christmas lights . . ." My voice trailed off. Clearly, I had no idea what I wanted except 'something simple.'

Eda smiled, and there was no judgement to her expression. "Well, it's something to think about. Once you've got that sorted, you'll be able to create an overview of the day, and this will help you decide on the smaller details."

"Right." It did make sense, and this was a great place to start.

"Flowers usually help," Eda suggested.

"Yeah?"

She nodded. "The type of flower you pick can set the mood for everything else. It could be elegant, relaxed, homey. You'd be surprised at the emotions a flower can convey."

"I see . . ." Not really, but I wasn't going to admit that.

"Let's start there, then. Do you already have a florist in mind?"

"Oh yes, it's Lucia. She's a friend, and we were going to pay her a visit right after this meeting."

"Wonderful. You can choose your bouquet, and then if you're interested in our service, I can explain where we go from there."

"That sounds great." And it did. I already felt like things were under control.

"Okay, let me get you some info." Eda got up and went to a shelf that I hadn't noticed in the corner of the room. She picked out a white binder that had my name labeled on the front of it. "This is yours. I've included my pricing and payment plan in there too. Let me know if you have any questions. I am very excited to work with you if you decide to come on board."

"Thank you, Eda. I appreciate your time and advice and will definitely take a look at this when I get home. I suppose I should go grab Victoria and Lauren."

"Allow me." Eda went to press the button again, and Maggie appeared as if she had been waiting at the door this whole time. "Can you let Lauren and Victoria know Anne is ready to head over to Lucia's?" Eda asked her.

"Of course." Maggie flashed a warm smile my way, and just that small gesture made me feel more welcome.

Within a couple of minutes, we heard Victoria and Lauren's voices coming down the hallway. Eda and I met them partway, and we all walked to the front entrance together.

"Isn't Eda the best?" Lauren announced. Without waiting for my response, she asked over her shoulder, "When do we meet with you again, Eda?"

"I told her to go home and think about it," Eda said, putting a hand on Lauren's arm.

"You mean you haven't signed on yet?" Lauren asked me, eyes wide with surprise. "What is there to think about? Eda's the best."

"Some like to plan their own wedding," Eda said. And her voice was soothing. It was obvious she could calm anyone down, and I was very tempted to hire her right then and there.

"Interesting," Lauren said.

We left it at that, but it was clear Lauren was in a daze as we said our goodbyes and headed over to Lucia's.

At Lucia's, we crowded into her shop, and I breathed in the fragrance of fresh-cut flowers. That and Lucia's motherly hug always made me feel like everything was right in the world.

"Are we throwing a party?" Lucia asked after she'd greeted us all.

"We are!" Lauren exclaimed, and I couldn't help wondering how in the world did she keep this energy?

"I wanted to ask if you could do the flowers for my wedding?" I said to Lucia—before Lauren could.

"Oh, Anne! Yes, I'd love to! I was hoping you would ask,

but I didn't want to get my hopes up," she gushed, pulling me in for another big hug. Releasing me, she stepped back and looked at me with tears in her eyes. "This is the happiest day of my life. You and Sebastian; I couldn't be happier."

"Oh, Lucia." I gave her another hug before she pulled away and dried her eyes.

Lauren, absorbed in the choices in front of her, yelled out, "Anne! What about this beautiful pink orchid?"

"Yes, you love orchids, Anne," Victoria chimed in.

"I do, but can we use those in a wedding?"

"Absolutely," Lucia said. "Let me go grab my binder, and I can show you some examples."

While we waited for Lucia to come back, Lauren started explaining that orchids were perfect because they exhibited elegance and came in a variety of colors. I was getting excited just listening to her. Who knew picking flowers could be this fun?

"Here we are," Lucia said, reentering the room and carrying a binder chock-full of different wedding bouquets. "I've been collecting these images. I find it helps the brides get a visual of what they want."

"That's fantastic!" Lauren said. She grabbed the binder before Lucia could open it. "Let's take a look."

"Shouldn't Anne be the one looking?" Victoria asked with a raised brow.

"Oh yes, of course." Lauren looked abashed as she passed over the binder.

I opened it and browsed the contents, and it wasn't long before Lauren became animated again. "So, which one do you like?" she asked.

"Why don't I show you what I'm thinking of for orchids first?" Lucia cut in.

"Yes please, there's a lot in this binder, and I'd appreciate your advice," I said, handing the binder over to Lucia, who I could see was not happy that Lauren had taken the binder in the first place.

Lucia began to purposely flick through the pages. "There are some beautiful teardrop bouquets that I think will work really well. What colors were you thinking of?"

"I was thinking purple and light pink with a dash of green."

"Ah, let me show you some of these options." Lucia flipped to a page that showed bright blue calla lilies and blue hydrangeas. Next to it was a teardrop bouquet made up of purple and turquoise orchids, with big tiger lilies as the center piece. They were gorgeous.

"I think there's a bit too much blue for me, but I love the teardrop look," I gushed.

Victoria and Lauren were oooing and ahhing right next to me.

Lucia then showed us a picture of big white lilies cascading down from a traditional bouquet that included white peonies, pink roses, and freesias, all complimented with pops of light green, velvety-looking leaves and thistles. She then showed us a bouquet of pink stargazer lilies, white orchids, and pink roses. They were all so gorgeous I didn't know which bouquet to pick. But when she flipped to the next page, I just knew. I knew that *this* was the one. It was comprised of purple and fuchsia orchids and ivory calla lilies, all equally distributed in a teardrop bouquet about two feet long. I loved it.

"This is the one," I said, pointing to the image. "I want this one for my bouquet."

"Excellent," Lucia said, going behind her counter to write down my order.

"Oh, Anne, this is the most fantastic one yet. It's even prettier than my bouquet," Lauren squealed, clapping my hands in hers.

"I agree, it's absolutely gorgeous," Victoria said, giving me a hug. She hooked her arm through mine. "There's more decisions to make, but look how easy the first one was."

"Yeah, I enjoyed that decision, and I can't believe I'll be holding something as beautiful as that bouquet at my wedding."

"You don't deserve anything less," Lauren said. "And with that decided upon, I have to run. Stephen has been texting me and asking when I'm coming home, so I best get going. But, oh, I'm so excited, Anne! This is going to be fun! We'll set up a date to go wedding dress shopping and—oh, wait! You said you already have your dress, but there's still a lot of other things we can do together, and Victoria and I will need to go try on bridesmaid dresses as well. Oh, this is going to be fun! You should fly Leslie up, too, and the four of us can have a girls' day spa. We should then go out for dinner and discuss the bridesmaid dresses, hair, nails, jewelry—oh, I love this!" She was beaming; her smile stretched right across her face. "Okay, I really have to go now. Maybe next weekend we can do that—does that sound good?"

By now, Lauren was already halfway out the door. Victoria and I both agreed we were free, and as soon as she left, Victoria turned to me and asked, "Are you absolutely positive you want Lauren as one of your bridesmaids?"

"Of course, why do you ask?" I said, wondering if I had missed something.

"Just wanted to make sure. I don't want anyone taking over your wedding."

I laughed. "She's not going to take over my wedding. I just picked my own bouquet, right? Lauren just gets excited about things."

"Okay."

I could have sworn I saw Victoria and Lucia exchange a

look, but I ignored it. It was going to be fun having Lauren help plan the wedding. I wouldn't have it any other way.

When we got home, I called Leslie to keep her updated. Lauren's advice on flying her up seemed like a good idea.

"Hi, Leslie."

"Anne, it's good to hear from you. Just a second."

I heard Madison's loud voice in the background, then Leslie telling her she needed to pipe down because "Mom is on the phone." Then I heard a door close, and the kids' voices faded away.

"Okay, now I can talk," Leslie said.

"Where are you? I remember you saying you hid in a closet to talk, but you're not really in a closet, are you?"

"I'm in a closet. It's the only place the kids aren't interested in right now, so I know I have five minutes to talk to you before they come and find me."

"Oh." I bit my lip at the image that created.

"What's up?"

She sounded haggard, and I felt bad for calling, but since I was already on the phone with her, I said, "I wanted to keep you updated on the wedding."

"Oh yes, please do tell!"

The excitement in her voice made me hopeful that I wasn't completely bombarding her day with the kids. "I invited Lauren to be a bridesmaid, too, and she introduced me to her wedding planner, who I don't think I'll hire, but it was nice to meet her."

Leslie sighed. "I wish I'd had a wedding planner. There were so many details that I hadn't considered, and Mom was so opinionated—but sorry, not my wedding. Back to you. I'm so glad you called, because I've been meaning to ask you to come down so we can get a qipao made for your reception. I think it will go well with the colors you've chosen."

Did I share with Leslie what my wedding colors were? I must have if she knew. "Oh yes, I forgot to follow up about the qipao with you. I don't think I need one, Leslie."

"Oh, you definitely need one! When you come to try on your dress, we can get your qipao measured."

Hmmm. It was time to change the subject, and I decided now was the right time to ask her about coming next weekend. "I'd also like to fly you up to join us next weekend if that works for you?"

"Absolutely! I'll have to discuss the trip with Jonathan, but I'll make it work. I want to be there for you. As for the color of your wedding, I think you need to pick out stuff here in the Bay Area. You'll have a wider selection."

"Oh, I think I'll be able to find things here in Portland, but I'll keep that in mind. I was originally thinking purple and light pink with a dash of green, but we went to Lucia's today and I picked out another bouquet. Leslie, it's absolutely gorgeous! I'll send you a photo after our call. It's a mix of purple and fuchsia orchids and ivory calla lilies." I heard Madison then, and Leslie was distracted for a second.

"Did you say purple and fuchsia?" she asked when she came back on.

"And ivory. It's going to be—"

"You can't do that!"

I paused. "What?"

"The wedding needs to be red. Chinese Red."

I had to have Chinese red? This was a thing? I realized Leslie had stopped talking. "Leslie, are you still there?"

"Yes, I was just making sure Madison wasn't hurting Ryan, but they seem fine." After a moment, she continued as if we hadn't been interrupted, "Chinese red is the most important color to have at your wedding. You have to ward off evil. I can't believe I forgot to tell you. My mind these days is just mush."

A high-pitched scream came from the background, and I heard Leslie suck in a deep breath before she said, "I'm sorry but I have to go, Anne. Just look it up on the internet— Chinese red. I'll talk to you later, okay? Very exciting, though!"

Then she hung up, and I was left staring at my phone wondering what in the world she was talking about.

CHAPTER 9

"I swear, you are the worse Taiwanese person ever," Victoria said, sitting next to me while the both of us stared at my laptop.

"Don't say that! I know what Chinese red is! I just didn't know it was so important to have the wedding in that color."

"I was just joking."

"Wasn't very nice." Though, I did feel like I'd failed my culture by not knowing about this. But why would I? It's not like I went to any Taiwanese weddings growing up. And I'd assumed that the bride and groom at the wedding Sebastian and I attended in Taiwan just liked that color for their wedding.

"I'm sorry, Anne, I really am. It just popped out of my mouth. What does the site say?"

I looked back at my laptop screen. "It says Chinese red symbolizes luck, joy, and happiness, and it represents cele-bration, vitality, and fertility. It's the traditional color worn by Taiwanese brides and supposedly wards off evil."

"Goodness. Well, it sounds like you really should wear

red. You don't want bad luck following you into your marriage."

I turned to look at Victoria and was surprised to find she was serious. "When did you get superstitious?"

"Only right now."

"Why?"

"I want your wedding to be perfect. You just found your extended family, Anne, and they're all Taiwanese. I know you want to make them happy and feel welcome. I also know you, and, during these past many months, you've been discovering a whole new part of yourself. I know you want to incorporate as much tradition as you can."

I threw out a deep sigh because Victoria was right. Deep down, I knew I wanted to include as many Taiwanese traditions as I could, because I really didn't want to leave out this important side of me—a side I'd only just started to discover. "You're right. I already picked the flowers, so maybe I can integrate the purples and the reds together?"

"Eww! You know those two colors are going to clash."

"You're not helping Victoria!"

"Why not just get a new bouquet?" she suggested.

"But I really love the one I picked out."

"Well, it's just something to think about."

"Okay, good idea. I'll tuck it away as something to consider."

We heard the front door slam shut. We both looked at each other, wondering what that was all about. In the months I'd been living here, no one had ever slammed the door before.

We both ran to the top of the stairs and looked down to see Sebastian, one hand on his hip and one hand in his hair, pacing back and forth while muttering to himself.

Victoria gave me a tap on my shoulder and gestured

behind us to say she was going back to my room. I continued down the stairs.

"Sebastian?"

He looked up with a jolt, as if surprised to see me here. Then, realizing who he was looking at, he ran forward and pulled me into his arms. My brain instantly calmed down. Sebastian was just who I needed and only who I needed.

"What's wrong?" I asked after a moment of us just holding each other. "You look distressed."

"Obvious, huh?" he murmured, burying his face in my hair and hugging me tighter.

"Very. You might have worn a groove into the lobby floor."

Sebastian chuckled, which made me smile. At least he wasn't so distraught that he couldn't laugh.

"I need a bowl of ice cream," he said, pulling me in the direction of the kitchen.

"I'm game for that."

When we got to the kitchen, Cook took one look at Sebastian and shooed the staff out. She then gave me a questioning look, and I shrugged.

Once it was just the two of us, Sebastian headed to the freezer and found the largest tub of ice cream we had. It was coffee flavor.

"How many scoops?" he asked.

"I'll take two," I said, clearing a space at the table for us to eat.

Sebastian brought over our bowls, and we ate in silence for a bit until he said, "I called my father today."

"Oh, that's fantastic. You haven't talked to him in a long time."

"Yeah, about once a year we check in with each other, but otherwise, we live our own lives. I called him today because I wanted to let him know I'm getting married."

I frowned. "This is a good thing, Sebastian. Why is it making you sad?"

"It's not the act of calling my father that is making me worried, it's the domino effect it started."

"Domino effect? Are we still talking about your father?"

Sebastian seemed to be sinking into his own world, and he clearly didn't hear what I said, because he continued as if I hadn't spoken, "He loved my mother, and he fell apart after she passed away. That was when I graduated high school. He sent me to live with my Uncle Roger and Aunt Cassie. Father doesn't have any siblings, but Mother had Aunt Cassie. She's really nice and motherly, and if it had just been her, I think things would have turned out differently. But Uncle Roger is greedy. I learned things about how he treated Father when I interned that summer after graduation at Schuster and Schuster, amongst other things I'll explain in a bit. When I graduated law school and went back to work for Schuster and Schuster full time, I avoided Uncle Roger like the plague. I never wanted to be on the same case as him. If he requested me, I denied him. If someone put us on the same case, well, I left the case. I didn't care how high profile it was, I just didn't want to work with him."

"Okay—"

Sebastian held up a hand. "Wait till I'm done. I need to get this all out before I burst."

And Sebastian did look like he was about to burst. I nodded, which he took as a signal to continue.

"To get back to the point, Father always had a tender spot for Aunt Cassie because of what she did to help our family, as well as the love she had for my mother. So, Father called Aunt Cassie to tell her I was getting married. And, of course, he told her my bride is you. Aunt Cassie got so excited. Father swears that he asked Aunt Cassie to not tell anyone, especially Uncle Roger, but Father also should have known better, as Aunt Cassie doesn't keep anything from Uncle Roger. He can do no wrong in her opinion."

"Why is it bad that she told your Uncle Roger?" I was very confused about where this was going.

"Because he now knows we're an item," Sebastian said, as if this explained everything.

"And how in the world did he not know before? You two worked in the same company." Now I was really confused.

Sebastian stared at me. "I told you I avoided him. And I made sure I didn't hang out in the same groups that he did. It was amazing that Schuster and Schuster never kicked me out of the firm. But I had the Wilkens's backing, so . . ."

"You were untouchable," I finished for him. Then I laughed. "My fiancé is untouchable."

It worked to break his tension, but he still had a crease across his forehead. He pulled me into his lap and wrapped his arms around me. "When I proposed, it was only in front of your family, Anne. As they're not part of the elite world, word had not gotten out yet that we are marrying. It's one thing for us to be dating, but getting married is a different story. Although, I think Uncle Roger already knew I had a crush on you."

"Yeah, Sir Anthony wrote me a letter before he passed, and he said outright that he hoped you'd get over your shyness and ask me out already."

"He did?" His brows flew upward, and I couldn't help thinking Sebastian looked cute when he was surprised.

"Yeah. Andy brought me the letter when he came to find me at my mom's place. Told me you were smitten with me."

"He did?" Sebastian said again, running his hand through his hair.

I could see a slight flush rising on his cheeks. "I've never seen you blush," I said, putting my hand on his cheek.

"I'm not!" The outburst only made him blush more.

To save him, I prompted, "You were saying about Uncle Roger?"

"Yes. He now knows we're official—and, Anne, please forgive me."

"What is it? You're making me nervous, Sebastian." I pushed away slightly so I could look into his eyes.

"He's—I . . . Well, you know I worked for the Wilkens?"

"Yes, we know that well. Let's move onto more recent events."

He took a deep breath. "Remember how I told you about the Wilkens taking me in and paying for my education? Basically establishing me in their world as the go-to guy?"

"Yeah."

"Well, Uncle Roger never forgave me for taking that account away from him. I wouldn't be surprised if he's been scheming this whole time on how to get back at me for it."

My mouth dropped open. "He would never do something like that! You're family, Sebastian!"

"Not everyone's family is as forgiving, nor loves each other like yours does," he said, twining his hands through my hair.

"But that's awful to think about."

"Yes, but I want us to be prepared."

"Prepared for what? What could he possibly do?"

Sebastian looked at me as if I should know the answer already and said slowly, "You are very rich now."

"Yes. Say something that isn't obvious." I was getting irritated now. What in the world could be bothering Sebastian so much? What could his uncle possibly do to us?

"He was, or is, friends with—well, I never could figure out if he kept in touch with her."

"Sebastian, just say it already!" But I had a sinking feeling about what was coming.

He released a big sigh and said, "He was very good friends

with Geraldine—the same woman who tried to kill you."

My stomach dropped. "Oh. And if he's been mad at you this whole time . . .?"

"Yes, I'm worried what he'll do. I think he's capable of anything."

"Surely not!"

"Maybe not like Geraldine so much. Well, at least I hope not. But I wouldn't be surprised if we started seeing our wedding announced through the social circles. That would mean expectations will arise, and you might start getting bombarded with requests from vendors—people you don't usually hear from wanting an invitation, or the news crews wanting to come and publicize it or request interviews, you name it."

I started laughing. I couldn't help it. This was too absurd. Just because I had inherited all of this money didn't mean that I was well-known. Well, people did know me now in the sense they recognized my face after someone had plastered a photo of me in the article that came out shortly after the inheritance, but really.

"I think you're being extreme, Sebastian," I gasped out. "There's no reason to worry. We're just going to plan a small wedding with our immediate families and friends and that's it. Done and done."

Sebastian, as if realizing I wasn't going to give in to his worries, began to smile ruefully. "I love you. I wish my brain could be that simple."

"Are you calling me simple?" I gave him my best glare, but the giggles had taken over, and I couldn't stop.

"Your ice cream is melting," was all he said, a smirk now on his face.

That stopped my giggles quick, and I went back to eating. Sebastian looked at me the whole time as if he didn't want to let me out of his sight.

CHAPTER 10

THE NEXT MORNING I WAS DISGRUNTLED. NOW that I had picked my bouquet, I didn't want to change the wedding colors just because I was supposed to. This was my wedding after all, no one else's. I knew Sebastian would agree with whichever decision I made, and he had enough on his mind right now that I didn't need to discuss it with him. I still didn't think his uncle would go to the lengths Sebastian thought he would, but I knew my fiancé thought otherwise.

I was looking for a snack when my phone rang. I didn't bother seeing who it was before answering it.

"Anne?" a raspy voice said on the other end of the line.

"Who is this?"

"It's Mary."

"Mary!" I exclaimed, my mind immediately going to our last conversation.

"Why do you need to shout? I'm not deaf."

"Sorry, sorry! I hadn't expected to hear back from you."

"Silly girl. Of course, I would call back. I just needed some time. You gave me a big surprise that day you called."

Guilt flooded my chest. "I know. I'm sorry to spring it on you like that. I wish I could have told you in person."

Mary ignored that and got straight to the point. "I'm ringing because I want to talk to Harrison. Can you put him on the phone?"

"Um . . . he's not here."

"What do you mean? You said he is at your house."

"No, he was visiting with his family at the time I called last, but now he's back at his own home in the Bay Area."

"Ah yah!" I could hear her conversing with her daughter, and I waited to see where this would go. She came back on a moment later. "Give me his phone number, and I will call him."

"Um . . ."

"Stop umming. It's not ladylike."

"Sorry."

"And stop apologizing. We're family; there's nothing to be sorry about."

I didn't know what to say for a moment, then I remembered Mary had asked for Harrison's number. "I can't give you his number, Mary."

"Why not?" I could hear an accusatory tone in her voice, and I couldn't blame her. She was his mother and had been looking for him far longer than I had.

"He told me not to call you and . . ."

"And you did anyway," Mary finished for me. "Well, how do you want us to meet then?"

"Let me think about it. I want him to meet you again, but if I surprise him, he'll back away really fast."

"Yes, I know that all too well."

"Let me talk to him first," I suggested.

"Okay. But, Anne?"

"Yes?"

"I'm not getting any younger."

"I know."

"I'm going to Oakland," I announced to Victoria and Lauren.

"Why?" they both asked in unison.

I had called them up later in the day after deliberating over whether I should call Harrison about Mary. In the end, I decided a surprise visit might be better. I planned to be there, phone in hand, while I dialed Mary's number for him myself, and I wouldn't leave his side until Harrison said hi.

"I need to go see Harrison," I explained. "Mary wants to talk to him."

"But why couldn't you just call him?" Victoria asked.

"You know why. He'll never agree, and if Mary was to call him, he'd hang up on her and never pick up again."

Lauren, not really sure what was going on, was thinking of other things as she piped in with, "Anne, have you read the notebook Eda gave you? Have you decided if you're going to hire her? There's so much planning to do, especially if you want to get married soon."

"I haven't. It's really not high on my list right now. The wedding will be fine. We picked out the bouquet, right? And I got my dress already. The bride and groom will both be present. We can deal with the rest later. I need to see Harrison."

Lauren was about to protest, but Victoria spoke up, which I was thankful for. "Anne, I think you need to do what you need to do. Lauren and I are going to go bridesmaid dress shopping. Right, Lauren?"

At this, Lauren got excited again. "Yes! We decided that we're going to look for light purple dresses that will add a hint of color but not enough to overpower you. It'll go with the bouquet you found."

"That sounds great." A nagging thought that it wouldn't match the bright Chinese red—if I went that route—came to mind, but I pushed it aside.

Victoria seemed to read my mind. "We'll make sure it goes with everything, okay, Anne? Just in case."

"Yes. Thank you, Victoria." I sighed. Everything was going to be fine. The wedding was no big deal.

Lauren, on the other hand, had picked up on the 'just in case' statement. "What's just in case? We can't have any just in case. You need to plan every detail so there's no mess ups."

Thankfully, Victoria stepped in again. "Lauren, it's okay. I'll explain everything when we leave."

"Okay . . . but I don't like this. And Anne?"

"Yes?" I was getting antsy on leaving. But this time, I was going to take my own plane so I could go whenever I wanted to.

"You should consider inviting some of the people from your Christmas Gala."

"Why?" Victoria and I both said at the same time.

"To make a good impression. You want them to know you remember them, and that you liked them enough to invite them to your personal wedding."

Victoria cut in before Lauren could keep going, "Lauren, I think we'll discuss this later too. Anne, you have to go, right?"

I loved Victoria. "Yes, I do have to go. We'll talk about this later." *Maybe never. Invite strangers to my wedding? What was she thinking?*

CHAPTER 11

I GOT TO THE AIRPORT IN NO TIME, AND THE flight to Oakland was uneventful. This was going to be a one-day trip. All I had to do was get Harrison on the phone with Mary, and that would be the end of my involvement. I knew they both missed each other and yearned to heal the rift between them, they just needed some help to do so. I believed once they heard each other's voices and remembered what they were missing, it would all come together.

I hailed down a taxi and gave the driver directions to Harrison's shop rather than his house, as I didn't want to run the risk of having Grace invite me in for dinner.

Harrison's store was in the middle of San Francisco, and as the taxi drove through the city, I was amazed once again at the magnitude of people stuffed on the streets and in the stores—just everywhere. Where was everyone going? On all my travels I never got over the fact that so many people could be together in one place like a big city and never know one another—never know the story of the person next to you. It still baffled me, but I couldn't think about it for long because the taxi stopped in front of a store.

Except for a postcard taped to the front of the door, there were no other signs advertising what was inside. This had to be Harrison's store, but how did anyone find it? But then again, knowing Harrison and how he valued his privacy, maybe that was the point.

I pushed on the door, and it opened easily. The inside was immaculate if you didn't count the stack of boxes in the corner. The room wasn't that big, maybe six by eight feet. There were a couple of shelves holding library catalog drawers and a table in the middle of the room, but what grabbed my attention was the rows of postcards on the table. Pulling out one of the library catalog drawers displayed even more postcards to choose from.

I loved postcards. I couldn't help it, I started digging through them, and I was so engrossed I didn't notice the door on the other side of the room open.

"You like postcards?"

I jumped, then realized Harrison was standing in front of me with a bemused look on his face. "I do. I used to collect them when I traveled."

"Nice to know I'm not the only one who likes them."

"Do you sell them?"

He nodded. "It doesn't look like it because I just replaced my door, but the old door used to have a sign on it that said 'Harrison's Postcard Shop.'" He smiled. "It was very original, I know."

I laughed. "Did you get much business?"

"Less so now, but when I first opened there was a lot of business. These days, kids don't want to mail postcards anymore. I now sell them to art professors who are looking for inspiration for their students or to collectors like you."

"This is really awesome. I'd love to comb through your collection."

"Feel free to, but I'm guessing you did not fly all the way here to look for postcards."

"Oh yeah, I didn't," I said, a bit embarrassed.

He gave me another small smile. "Well, come on in. Mind your step, though. I haven't cleared everything out yet."

I watched my feet as I followed him. "This section looks really good, though."

"Yes, I cornered off this small area so it still looks like a store in here, but the inside is far from finished."

"I'm sorry the store was ransacked."

Harrison turned to look at me over his glasses. "It's not your fault."

He walked through the door, and my mouth dropped open when I saw the mess inside. Lots of shelves like the ones in the front room had been knocked over, and there were piles of postcards laying on the floor.

"Who would do such a thing?" I asked Harrison, my heart sinking.

"I don't know. I don't have any enemies that I know of."

"The surveillance camera was too fuzzy, wasn't it?"

He nodded. "I should have upgraded it many years ago."

"Do you mind if I take a look at it?"

"Sure. It's this way."

He took me past the debris and through another door that led into an office. A small monitor was sitting on a shelf in the corner, and it showed a view of the room we had just left. Harrison went to his desk and turned on his computer, which looked ancient. He brought up a saved video file, and we watched as the seconds ticked by. For a while, nothing happened. The timestamp said it was broad daylight, and I was starting to wonder if Harrison had pulled up the wrong day when I saw two men appear at the main entrance, both hooded. I watched them break the glass before a hand reached in and unlocked the door. They walked in through the main room with all the postcards but didn't show any interest in the merchandise.

Harrison cut to another feed, and I saw the two men now in the office, rifling through his paintings and drawers.

"Your office isn't locked when you're not here?" I asked him.

"It is; they broke in."

We watched as they went through every drawer, forcing some of them open.

"What were they looking for?"

"I have no idea. They didn't take anything."

After some shuffling around, one of the guys slammed his hand on the table, knocking a pile of paper and some pencils onto the floor. I gasped. *It couldn't be!*

"Rewind that, Harrison!" I urged him. "Not too far . . . just a couple seconds . . . right when he slams his hand down on the desk. Right there—freeze it!"

I stared at the perpetrator's hand, noting the inked hearts right above the knuckles. I knew that unique design and whose hand that was. *It was him!* But why in the world would he have done this to Harrison? Then it hit me—Isabella! Couldn't she leave well-enough alone? How dare she hire someone to do this to Harrison!

"Do you see something?" Harrison said, moving closer.

"I do, and I'm pissed off now. Those bastards!"

"We should call the police if you know who they are."

"No, I want to deal with them myself first."

"They could be dangerous, Anne."

"Not to me they won't be."

Harrison just looked at me like I was crazy.

"They destroyed your place!" I said, raising my hands to my hair and pulling the strands, hoping the pain could override my anger.

"Actually, they didn't."

"What?" I said, whirling around to stare at him.

"I wasn't there that day, so I didn't know about the break in." He gestured to the room. "There's nothing to steal in here except my paintings, and no one would steal those. I never bothered to put an alarm system in because of that fact. But those two left soon after and didn't touch anything else."

Then who made all the mess in these rooms? I stared at him, thinking on what he'd just said. Then it hit me. "Your door was left unlocked and broken for the rest of the day, wasn't it?"

He nodded. "And that night."

Harrison turned back to the monitor and fast-forwarded the video, pausing it at about one in the morning. We watched as a group of five men walked by the store. One of them beckoned the others to hold up as he reached out and tested the door. Realizing it was unlocked, he went straight inside, followed by his friends. They all wore dark outfits with hoods. No masks, but they knew to keep their heads down. I watched as they ransacked the whole place, going through the postcards and scattering them all over the floor. Two men went into the office, making an even bigger mess than what was already there. They weren't careful. They broke whatever they saw.

My heart broke watching the footage, knowing this shop was Harrison's livelihood. It was his safe place where he came to paint and be by himself. And for others to destroy it . . .

When Harrison stopped the video, I said softly into the poignant silence, "You must have been devastated when you came back."

"I was. Very distraught. But no one was hurt, and they didn't take much, just some cash in the drawers and some of my snacks. Guess they were hungry." He forced a laugh.

I stared at him. "I can't believe you can laugh about it."

"What else can I do? I cannot see their faces, and there's no identifying marks on them. The police are too busy in a big city like this to bother with a small store such as mine."

"That's awful." And it didn't make it right.

Harrison shrugged. "It is life. My family is safe. Besides, I do not think these people would have come in if the door wasn't already broken."

"Well, we can take care of the first two men who came in and caused this problem in the first place."

He squinted at me. "Who are they?"

"One of them is an acquaintance. I'll let you know after I talk to him."

Harrison stared at me for a moment but clearly thought better of questioning my resolve. "Okay, but be careful, Anne. We only just met, and I would hate to lose you again."

I looked at Harrison, surprised he would say those words. After being in hiding for so long and avoiding his extended family, this comment warmed my heart. "Harrison, that's the—"

"Don't say it—I have a reputation! I must not let them know I'm less grumpy after meeting you."

I smiled and gave him a big hug. "I'm so glad to have met you. I know Mom is as well."

"Since you're here, you should come home with me for lunch. Grace would be very mad at me if she knew you were here and didn't come over."

"Oh, I'd love to, but I was planning on going home today. And oh, I almost forgot! The reason why I came is because Mary called."

Harrison released a big sigh and turned away from me. "I just can't, Anne. I don't think I will ever be brave enough to call her."

"I know." I felt guilty for what I was about to say, but

Harrison and Mary really needed to talk. "I called her for you."

He whirled around, his eyes big. "You did? And?"

"You're not mad at me?"

"I'm mad at you, but I'm also curious. What did she say?"

"She didn't sound well, but she wanted to talk to you."

"No. I can't do that." He started picking up his things and walking toward the door.

"Harrison, just listen. It's just a phone call, you won't be seeing her. Maybe you could just say 'hi'?" I was following closely behind him as he marched to the entrance. He was about to pull open the door when I put my hand on his arm. "Please, I think you two owe it to each other to at least say hi."

He looked at me, face tight. "You don't understand, Anne. It's been too long."

"I understand perfectly well. If Ah Po was still alive, I would love to be able to say hi to her, even if she hadn't talked to me all these years." I started tearing up just thinking about all the times I'd wished I still had a grandmother.

"You are still young and have hope for change. I stopped hoping a long time ago. Come, let's not talk about this now. Grace will be waiting for me to come home for lunch."

"But—"

"I will think about it," Harrison interrupted me firmly. "Will that be okay?"

"Okay." Little did he know I wasn't going to give up that easily, though.

"Anne! You should have told us you were coming. I could have made up the extra room for you."

"No, it's okay. I'm planning on heading home today."

"No, you're not." Grace had that look on her face that Mom had when she wasn't going to take no for an answer.

I sighed, aware I had no choice but to relent. "Just one night. I do have to get back tomorrow."

"That's good. Now, sit, sit. I just got lunch done, and it's going to get cold."

I had to admit the smell was glorious. It wasn't anything fancy like Cook would make, but it was home-cooked Taiwanese food. There was pork belly with dry mustard greens in white puffy buns and a side of A-tsai, which was a leafy green. I was salivating just looking at it.

"Dig in, no need to wait for me," Grace urged. "I just need to clean this up first."

Harrison was already going for the food, but I felt bad that Grace was still tidying up the kitchen. In the end, my stomach won. I remembered Mom saying Ah Po used to feed the geese A-tsai when Ah Po was a child. No humans used to eat it back then, but we loved eating the greens now.

We ate in silence for a bit until the doorbell rang.

"I'll get it, you keep eating," Harrison said, waving at Grace to sit back down.

A few seconds later, I heard Leslie at the door with her kids, and I groaned inside. I really wanted to get to know her better, but this wasn't the trip I had planned for that. I hoped she wouldn't come in and see me, but it was too late— Harrison and Leslie were both entering the kitchen, followed by Madison and Ryan.

"Anne! You're here! Why didn't you tell me you were coming? We have to go get your qipao made."

"Auntie Anne!" Madison screamed, running over to climb into my lap.

"Hi, Madison, how are you doing?"

"Madison, get down from your aunt! You can't just jump into people's laps like that, especially while they're eating."

"It's okay. It's good to see you too, Madison." I had a soft spot for Madison. I had a feeling it was because she was the total opposite of me.

Harrison huffed. "I guess I've been replaced as the favorite person around here."

"Only when Auntie Anne is here!" Madison squealed.

We all laughed.

"Mom, this looks delicious!" Leslie exclaimed. "I don't know how you had time to make all these foods when we were young. I can't get around to making more than two dishes at a time."

"Practice, darling, and I craved the food. Who was going to make them except me? There weren't a lot of authentic Taiwanese restaurants around when we arrived here."

"It really is delicious, Grace," I gushed.

"Thank you, Anne. Are you two going to Ms. Lu's for the qipao?"

"Who else? She's the best," Leslie said through a mouth full of gua bao.

Ryan was sitting next to Grace, who was busy spooning meat onto a plate for him.

"I thought she only made American wedding dresses?" I asked.

"No, of course not!" Leslie laughed. "She makes American and Taiwanese wedding dresses. She just doesn't advertise the Taiwanese dresses, as it's all done through word of mouth. She usually has a couple hanging in the racks, but she must have sold them before we got there."

"Oh, well, there's no need to have her make the qipao."

"Why not?" Leslie said, stopping mid-bite.

"I already have one. I have Ah Po's, and it fits well. I wore it to the Christmas Gala last year."

"Oh no, it has to be a new one," Grace said. "You want to enter your marriage on a clean slate."

"Oh," was all I could think to say. I couldn't understand how I would need all these new things that I'd only wear once. "But then why didn't we order one when we were there before?"

Grace said, "I was going to, but Ms. Lu wasn't there that day. It's better to go when she's there."

"It'll be fun!" Leslie said. "She has so many different cloths you can choose from. I'll show you mine when you come over some time."

"That'd be great," I said. There was no way I was getting out of this, so I might as well play along. I told myself a new dress would be fun to have anyways.

"We can go this afternoon!" Leslie exclaimed.

"And more reason for you to spend the night tonight," Grace added with a smile.

"Oh, were you going to head home today?" Leslie asked.

"Well, yes. I only came down to see if Harrison could talk to Mary."

"I bet he said no," Leslie said, giving her dad a look.

"Don't look at me that way," Harrison replied. "I haven't talked to her in years. It would be very awkward."

"From what you said, she was as good as a real mom. She raised you." Leslie was not going to let this go, and I was glad it wasn't me pushing Harrison this time, but it was also getting kind of tense, and I was afraid Harrison would bolt.

Before I could say something, Grace spoke up. "Leslie, that's enough. You don't know everything about the situation."

"Because you two kept it from us."

"Not now, Leslie."

"I would like to get to know my extended family too," she pointed out.

"Leslie!" Grace shook her head.

I felt bad as this seemed to be all my fault. I was bringing up family history that had been kept secret for a long time.

"Your baba has a lot to think about, and he and I will discuss it later." The way Grace said the last part made Harrison's head pop up to look at her. The look Grace had on her face spoke volumes, and I suddenly wondered if she was the secret weapon we needed all along?

We finished up eating pretty fast after that, and I was whisked away by Leslie.

"You really should tell me when you're in town," she said to me while we walked to the car.

"Yeah, Auntie Anne, we miss you." Madison had the cutest expression on her face. I completely melted.

"I'm sorry. I was only thinking about getting stuff done, and it didn't even cross my mind to spend time with my new family. I'll remember to let you know next time I come, okay?"

"Okay!" Madison said, giving me a huge hug.

As Leslie strapped the kids into their car sets, I asked her, "Do we need to drop the kids at home?"

"Oh, goodness no. Jonathan isn't home, and the kids come with me everywhere anyways."

Madison piped up, "Yeah, Mom says we're her minions."

"Yeah!" Ryan said, clearly wanting to be a part of the conversation.

"Mom, can we listen to Frozen?" Madison asked.

"Yes," Leslie said, but I swear I heard her groan.

We listened to Frozen with Madison singing at the top of her lungs all the way to Ms. Lu's shop.

Once we were there, Leslie gave the kids explicit instructions to not touch anything; but, knowing Madison, I wasn't sure how long that would last. Ryan was different, he seemed to stay by his mom's side.

The bell rang when we stepped in, and Ms. Lu came out looking like a dignified grandmother dressed in her qipao of simple black with black trim. "Leslie, your mom called saying you would be coming in with your cousin. Is this Anne?" she asked, turning to me.

"Yes."

Ms. Lu inclined her head toward me. "I'm so sorry I was not able to be here when you came to pick your wedding dress, Anne."

"Don't worry about it," I replied. "The ones you picked out for me were lovely, and I had my whole entourage here with me. It was a lot of fun."

Before I could say more, Leslie said, "Ah Yi, we are here to get a qipao made for Anne for her reception."

"Of course, come with me."

We followed her to the back, and I saw shelves of red, pink, purple, black, and many other colored materials lining the wall.

"And while you're here, Anne, I have your wedding dress if you would like to try it on. Then we can get you pinned so that it fits even better."

"Oh, really?"

"That's so exciting! You came at the perfect time," Leslie said.

"Yeah, Auntie Anne, and I get to see it too!" shouted Madison.

"Yeah!" Ryan added, holding onto his mom's pants like he was afraid he would get lost.

"I forgot I would need to get fitted in my dress. Good thing you asked me to come today, Leslie," I said, bumping her with my elbow. Leslie turned to look at me, and I saw a smile spread across her face. It was a reminder that I really needed to make more of an effort to get to know her.

Ms. Lu pulled my dress out from a row of dresses at the

back of the studio. "Here we are. Let's get you pinned in your dress first, and then we can pick out your qipao material," she said, unzipping the bag and pulling out my dress.

"Oh, Anne, I forgot how beautiful it is," Leslie said, putting her arm through mine and leaning into me. But, just as quickly, she let me go and began walking toward a rack of dresses, yelling, "Madison! Don't touch it!"

Ms. Lu seemed unfazed and beckoned me to follow her to the dressing room. The space was as immaculate as the one I had used on my first visit. The plush velvet walls and the decorative mirror were welcoming, and I felt pampered just standing in the room. This time, though, the sound of Leslie's kids kept me from daydreaming too long. I changed into the dress quickly, then realized I couldn't reach the zipper on the back.

"You're going to have to help me zip it up," I said, walking out of the dressing room while holding up the front of my dress.

"Anne, you look stunning! Here, let me help you." Leslie came around and zipped me up. "Oh, it looks like we may need to pin it a bit tighter in the waist."

"Anne, please stand up here, and I'll see what needs to be done," Ms. Lu said, gesturing at a standing block in front of a floor-length mirror.

I stood where Ms. Lu directed and stared at my reflection. The dress was gorgeous, and I couldn't believe that in under two weeks, I'd be walking down the aisle to marry Sebastian in it. Wow—I'd be *married!*

Thoughts of Sebastian made me wonder if he was okay. I had left home early this morning in such a hurry. But Sebastian had equally rushed off to work before I left that we hadn't had a chance to chat, and I felt bad for not calling him.

"Anne," Leslie said, breaking into my thoughts. "You had

mentioned that you were doing purple for your wedding colors, is that right?"

"I am." I girded myself for what was to come.

"I really think you should change it to red, bright Chinese red. You want as much luck as you can get going into your wedding. Red roses, too, and we'll look for red hairpieces. Oh, and gold jewelry."

"Leslie—"

"Oh yes, and candy! We need to get candy, as you'll need to give it to your guests. It means that they'll have some of your good luck from your wedding day. Mom knows a great caterer that can do your reception. He'll do a full thirteen-course meal—"

"Leslie!"

"Yeah?"

"I'm not doing all that," I said as clearly as I could.

"But why not?" she asked, looking confused. "It's tradition."

"Not for me. It doesn't mean anything to me. Plus, it's a lot of extra stuff that I don't think is needed. We're just going to have a small wedding with family and friends. It'll be in the backyard of the mansion, and it'll be nice and quaint."

"Oh . . ."

I could see Ms. Lu eyeing us, but she knew when to keep quiet. She just kept pinning. I was sorry to burst Leslie's bubble, but there was no need for all this stuff. I had a dress, a bouquet, and a venue, and I had a feeling that Cook would be more than happy to cook for us. Besides, I wouldn't hear the end of it if I didn't let her do so. We would rent some chairs and—voila! We got ourselves a wedding!

"Well, will you think about it at least?" Leslie asked.

I looked at her through the mirror. She looked sad. "Yes, of course. I'll think about it."

"And we're done," Ms. Lu said, standing up and walking around me to take one more look. She fixed a couple of pins, then shooed me back into the changing room.

I heard her and Leslie talking in hushed tones, and I wondered if they were talking about me, or maybe it was just about family in general since they had known each other so long.

When I came out, Ms. Lu had laid out six different fabrics on the table. "Which one speaks to you?" she asked me.

The fabrics were stunning. There was a bright red swatch with gold lining, a light pink velvet one, a gold one with delicate gold lace flowers, a light purple one that I instantly loved because it had silk purple flowers with light blue leaves and a gold trim, and a second bright red one that had gold flowers stitched all over it that reminded me of Ah Po's. But it was the sixth one that really caught my eye. It was a textured white material, and Ms. Lu had put a bright red cloth next to it with red buttons. I loved the simplicity of it.

Ms. Lu pointed to the white cloth and said, "This one would be white on the outside and red on the inside. You will only see the red through the slit on your leg and the opening on your neck. The buttons would go where the floral pankous would usually go. But, in this case, they would start at the base of your neck, go over your collar bone, and end before your armpit."

Leslie spoke up in almost a whisper, "We thought that would be a good compromise between American and Taiwanese culture. What do you think?"

"I love it!"

"Really?" Leslie looked very relieved.

"Yes, really. I really, really love it. It's simple, and it incorporates both colors for a traditional American and Taiwanese wedding. It's also very elegant."

"I'm so glad you like it," Leslie said, giving me a big hug.

Ms. Lu just smiled and started shooing us away, saying she had a lot of work to do if she was going to be altering my wedding dress as well as making my reception dress before the wedding.

I stopped, remembering something. "Oh, Ms. Lu, how much is it? I can pay you now."

"It's already covered," Leslie said.

"What?"

"It's my wedding present to you," Leslie said, hooking her arm through mine. "And now I'm going to treat you to dinner."

"But . . ."

"I can afford things too, Anne. Let me do this for you."

I swallowed the sigh that was about to come out, then I smiled and nodded. It was still unusual to have extended family who wanted to gift me things. This was going to take some getting used to.

Leslie took me to a hot pot restaurant. She said it was a place where she knew the kids would eat. We ate ourselves silly, ordering every meat dish on the menu and helping ourselves to at least half of the sides. There was an unspoken agreement between us to avoid wedding talk, and it gave me the opportunity to learn more about what she did as a stay-at-home mom with Ryan. I also asked her about how Madison was doing at school—and Madison made sure to interject with her own stories from time to time.

I noticed the one person Leslie didn't elaborate on was Jonathan. The couple of times I asked how he was doing, she answered, "He's fine." Clearly, it was a touchy subject, and I started worrying about the two of them, but I also knew now wasn't the time to ask.

Leslie dropped me off at Harrison's home, and we set a date for her to come visit me in Portland in a week's time so she could get fitted for her bridesmaid dress and see the floral arrangements I'd decided on. I also invited her to join in on whatever else we were doing at the time. I could tell she was excited to get away, while I was happy to say goodnight to everyone that evening. It had been another long day, and I was keen to head home tomorrow.

CHAPTER 12

THE NEXT MORNING GRACE HAD A BIG BREAKFAST made before I even woke up. I walked into the kitchen to find she'd made pan fried radish cakes, dang bing, warm soy milk, lu niu jian—which she'd cut into thin slices, sao bing, and yu tao.

"Wow! Grace, did you wake up in the middle of the night to start cooking all this?"

Grace laughed and almost doubled over. "No. I went to the grocery store yesterday when you and Leslie went dress shopping. It's all reheated except for the niu jian, because that I always have on hand."

"Grace makes the best niu jian, better than any I had growing up," Harrison said, coming into the kitchen to join us. On seeing the spread, he exclaimed, "Wow, we never eat all of this at once. I've missed this food."

"Well, eat, eat," Grace said, gesturing at us to sit. "Don't let it get cold. I slaved away to put it on the table this morning."

We all laughed and didn't argue. I got one of everything and shoveled it into my mouth. I loved Taiwanese breakfast food, and I really needed to ask Cook to make this more often.

Harrison suddenly paused with his chopsticks halfway to his mouth. "Wait, what's the occasion?" he asked.

"You know what," was all Grace said, giving him a knowing look as she continued eating.

In response, Harrison slammed his chopsticks on the table. "Don't start again. We are not going. I am not setting foot on a plane."

"Then there is no need for you to eat any of this." Grace started to get up and reached out to take Harrison's plate.

Harrison put up a hand to stop her, protecting his plate with the other. "Wait!"

"You seem to have already made up your mind. What is there to wait for?" Grace said.

"Let me finish eating, and I will think about it."

Grace sat back down with a sly smirk on her face. "Okay, but we will talk after Anne leaves."

"Fine, fine. Just leave me be."

My head had been on a swivel the whole time they had gone back and forth, and I had no idea what they were talking about. "What—?"

"Anne, just eat. Don't worry about it," Grace said.

"Okay."

I ate and ate and ate till I was bursting at the seams. "Grace, I'm glad Cook doesn't make this for me every day. I wouldn't be able to fit into any of my clothes if I ate like this all the time."

"Then I'm glad I could give you a treat," Grace said, beaming.

I was also glad I had stayed. "You two should come up to visit from time to time. I'll do the same and bring Mom too."

Grace's face lit up. "I think that's a terrific idea. Our

house is not as big as yours, but we have plenty of space for you and your mom anytime you want to come."

"Thanks, Grace. Well, I better be going. Thank you for the stay and the wonderful food."

"No need to thank us. We're family; it's what we do. Let me get some food packed up for you while you get your things together."

Since I hadn't planned on staying, most of the things I had to get together included throwing the bedsheets into the washing machine. After doing that, I grabbed my purse and was set to leave. Grace gave me a full bag of food to go, and I could smell the yumminess wafting out of the bag.

"Harrison doesn't like goodbyes so don't expect him to come back out," Grace warned.

I nodded, denying the lump in my throat. I held Grace's hands as I confessed, "Grace, I really want him to talk to Mary."

"I know. I do too. We discussed it yesterday—or more like I talked as Harrison just looked at me with a grumpy face."

I laughed. "That's a bit harsh."

"But true. Don't worry about Harrison and Mary for now. I didn't prepare the breakfast this morning just because you were here. I will let you know how it's going soon."

"Okay."

She squeezed my hands and released them. "Have a good flight, Anne. We will see you soon."

"Yes, you two are always welcome, and your kids and grandkids, of course. I guess they're my cousins too."

Her face broke into a huge smile. "Yes, you have more family now, and we love you, Anne."

"Thanks." *All right, it was time to go before I started crying.*

Grace had sent me off with a bag full of green onion cookies, and I ate half of them before we even took off. The delicious food put me in a food coma, but before I could fall asleep with the droning lull of the plane, my phone rang.

"Hello?" I said, hoping my grumpy voice would deter whoever it was to hang up.

"Hi, love."

Except for him! I sat up straight. "Hi, Sebastian!"

He chuckled. "Someone's happy to hear from me. Where are you?"

"I'm on the plane, about to fly back home. I came down to Oakland to talk Harrison into speaking with Mary, but that didn't happen. But Grace is up to something and has told me not to worry about it, and that she'll let me know tomorrow. I'm not sure what that all means but I'm about to take off for the flight home." Then I remembered something. "Oh, and Leslie found out I was here, so she took me back to the shop where I got my wedding dress, and now Ms. Lu is making me a qipao for our reception." I released a breath, adding, "I can't believe this all happened in the last twenty-four hours."

"Is that all that happened?" Sebastian asked with a laugh.

It was then I remembered what had happened to Harrison's store. "No! There was something else!"

Sebastian was chuckling on the other end. "Yes?"

"Harrison's store was ransacked. It's a mess. Oh, and Nick was involved!"

He instantly sobered. "Nick? Isabella's Nick?"

"Yes! The one and only. I'm so mad about it."

"Well, that puts a twist on things."

"It sure does. I tried calling him, but it didn't go through. I'm going to try again when I get back to Portland."

I could almost hear him silently deliberating with himself over whether to let me do that or not. In the next moment, he said, "Okay. Let me know how it goes, Anne. I just can't believe Nick would do something like that."

"Well, technically he didn't destroy the place, but because he broke in, he welcomed other people to come in and ransack Harrison's shop, so it was still his fault."

"We'll call the police if we need to, but for Nick's sake, I hope he has a good explanation for this."

"It's Isabella, I just know it is."

"Let's not jump to conclusions."

"You're standing up for her?" I was aghast.

"I didn't say that. I just don't want you jumping to conclusions about anybody before we find out more information."

"Right . . ."

"Anne—"

"Okay, let's change subject," I cut in.

"Yes, let's." Sebastian cleared his throat. "I heard from Jack today. He found documents that Geraldine had saved. It looks like she took meticulous notes in case Uncle Roger double-crossed her."

"Wow, that's huge, Sebastian."

"Yeah, I know. It goes deep." He sighed, and I could hear a weariness about him. "Remember when I told you about being an illegitimate child of the Donaldson family?"

"Yes, what do the Donaldsons have to do with all of this?"

"The notes show that Geraldine and Uncle Roger were working together using the Wilkens and Donaldson's funds to wine and dine people in power. Now that we're digging all this up, it also looks like Geraldine took me in because she knew of my connection with the Donaldsons. It makes me feel used."

"Oh, sweetheart, I'm so sorry. Look, I'll be home soon. Why don't we have a nice dinner tonight with a movie?"

"That sounds like a grand idea, but I'm still in the office

and not sure when I'll get back. Jack managed to set up a meeting with Ms. Donaldson, so we're pulling together to bring as much ammunition as we can."

"Why are you going to meet Ms. Donaldson?"

"Because she might have enough clout to stop Uncle Roger before he does anything."

It sounded risky. "Are you going to question Geraldine too?"

"Geraldine, well . . . I don't think Jack has the heart to incriminate his sister."

"That's too bad."

I could feel Sebastian's agreement through the phone line, but he didn't reply. Instead, he said, "Fly home safely, Anne. I'll see you when I get home, okay?"

"Okay. I love you."

"I love you too."

CHAPTER 13

I SLEPT THE REST OF THE WAY HOME AND ONLY woke when the flight attendant nudged my shoulder. The ride home was uneventful, and I told myself that all these issues about Uncle Roger would be resolved in no time. Sebastian and Jack already had an appointment with Ms. Donaldson, so it would get sorted out. In the meantime, I had a wedding to plan, and I still had to figure out how to get Harrison and Mary to talk to each other.

I called Victoria when I was almost home and was glad to hear she was free and would be bringing lunch with her. I wanted to show her the cloths I had picked out for my qipao. I knew she wouldn't admit it, but I had noticed her taking notes for her own wedding.

I called Nick just as we were cruising up the driveway to see if we could set up a time to meet or even just talk on the phone, but the line went to voicemail. I left a message and sighed with relief when we pulled up in front of the house. I was home.

Entering the house, I picked up the mail on the side table and started glancing through it while wandering to the kitchen, not really paying attention to what I was looking at, as all I could think about was the carrot cake I was going to have. But one of the envelopes made me stop before I reached the kitchen door. It had my name on it, written in big, black block letters, as if whoever wrote it wanted to make doubly sure I didn't miss it.

Before I opened it, though, I wanted to see if Ben knew who it had come from. Approaching his office, I was glad to see his door open. A slight knock was answered by a "Come in."

"Ben, when you pulled the mail yesterday and today, was this envelope in the pile?" I asked him, holding the envelope up.

"No."

"Drats."

"What's wrong?"

"I was hoping you'd say you saw the person who gave it to you."

"Oh, no one came by. Someone had stuck it in the fence at the beginning of the driveway. I was heading out to do some errands and saw it."

"Oh."

"What is it?"

I could tell Ben was very curious, but I wanted to read this in private.

Ben cleared his throat. "Anne, I was going to come and see you when you got back. A couple of news outlets came by to see you while you were traveling. I turned them away. I hope that's what you wanted?"

"Oh yes! Definitely. Thank you, Ben." I couldn't help wondering if they had anything to do with Uncle Roger.

Ben nodded, clearly relieved.

"I'll let you know if there's anything to do after I read this letter," I said, moving back into the hallway to head back to the library.

"Of course." Ben went back to doing whatever he was doing, but I could feel his curiosity following me down the hallway.

I speed-walked into the library and tore open the envelope. Inside, there was a typed-up piece of paper titled "Anne Huang is Getting Married—How Will She Spend Her New Wealth?"

What in the world is this?

I flipped the piece of paper over to find a handwritten note was scrawled across the bottom.

This article is going to appear in the newspaper tomorrow. We know privacy is important to you. Legal matters should also be taken into consideration when getting married with this much wealth. Think about how you want your marriage to start off. It's time the Wilkens's wealth was spread around.

What? I stopped reading to check the envelope and the letter again. There was no name or contact information anywhere to be seen. I flipped back to the front of the letter and started reading again.

By now, we have all heard of Anne Huang—the Taiwanese girl who inherited the massive Wilkens fortune without lifting a finger. She swooped in and settled herself in without even caring if anyone else should have inherited the fortune, not even allowing family members of the deceased Sir Wilkens to have a say—his own flesh and blood kicked out without any notice.

. . .

My hands were shaking by now, and it was only the beginning of the article. I continued reading.

On top of that, she won over the family lawyer, who she is now engaged to. We were able to interview her ex-boyfriend, who has asked to remain anonymous.

What? Brian gave an interview?!

He said, "She was always good with getting what she wanted. If she had her mind set on it, she wouldn't back down." From this reporter's eyes, Miss Huang seems to have outsmarted the Wilkens clan and taken their wealth as well as the one person who could fight for them from right under their noses. We have valid contacts that say Anne would not even negotiate. What is she going to do with all this money, you ask? We can only wait and see.

This had Geraldine and Isabella smeared all over it! And Brian was interviewed? What in the world?! I wasn't going to stand back and just let it happen. The whole article was a farce. I had done no such thing—Sir Wilkens was the only person who could claim who he wanted to give his wealth to. And the only family members who had challenged my inheritance was Geraldine and Isabella!

I crumpled the paper in my hands and threw it in the fireplace. Grabbing the matches that were on top of the mantle, I struck a light and threw it on top of the paper, watching the letter burn into a pile of black soot. I had thought this whole debacle was over. Geraldine was in an institute, and Isabella was doing who knows what, but no news was good news with her—at least that's what I'd thought. But clearly, I'd been wrong. Were they plotting something against me? Should I be looking behind me from now on? Should I hire security? Was I in danger?

"Miss?"

"Ahhhh!" I screamed, tripping over my feet in a desperate attempt to turn around as fast as I could. I grabbed the arm rest of the chair behind me, just managing to not fall flat on my face.

"Sorry! Are you okay?" Ben asked, running over to help me up.

"I'm fine. I'm fine."

"Did you want to start the fire? I could have done it, but it's quite warm outside so—"

"No, no. It's okay, Ben. There's no need to start the fire. I was just burning the letter I got."

"Was it in that envelope?"

"Yes."

"Is there anything I can help you with?"

I looked at Ben and saw the concern etched across his face. There was no need to drag him into this. This was between Isabella and me, and I was going to end this once and for all.

"No, I'll take care of it. Thank you, though."

"Okay."

He turned to go, but I stopped him at a new thought. "Ben?"

"Yes?" He turned to look back.

"Did Sebastian see this note?"

"No. He came home really late last night. I think I heard the door open around four in the morning, and then he left just before Cook had breakfast ready."

"Oh." I knew Sebastian was stressed and busy working on the mess Geraldine had left behind, but this seemed extreme.

Was it really that bad? "Thank you, Ben. I think I'll have to make a call now."

"All right, miss. Let me know if I can help in any way."

"I will."

I followed Ben back out into the hallway to retrieve my purse and phone that I had put down when picking up my mail. I dialed Isabella's number before I could talk myself out of it. The phone rang and rang, and I was about to hang up when Isabella's voice came over the line.

"Didn't think I'd hear from you ever again."

"I can honestly say you are never my first choice when calling someone."

There was a sharp pause, then Isabella said, "What can I do for you, Anne? Let's not drag this out."

She didn't sound guilty, but when did Isabella ever show much emotion? I cut straight to the chase. "I received an article in the mail today, and I know you or your grandmother are responsible."

There was silence on the other end of the line, and then a peal of laughter came through, loud and strange. I had never heard Isabella laugh before.

"Why are you laughing?" I demanded.

"You . . . you think . . . you think *I* wrote an article about you? That I care enough to spend any time writing about you?"

"Well, no, it's obvious someone else wrote it. You just supplied the information."

"Anne, sweetheart, you might think you're the center of my world, but as much as I loathe you, you already got the house, the money, and the boy. I'm over you."

Well, when she put it that way . . . . She continued laughing as I mulled over what she had just said. Isabella was a lot of things, but wasting her time on something that probably wouldn't get her anywhere after she had already tried other tactics really didn't seem her style. She was also direct and hadn't been secretive about things in the past.

"Fine, it wasn't you," I finally said. *Then who was it?* I felt a rock hit the bottom of my stomach at the realization that this time it wasn't Isabella and potentially, Geraldine, but that it was someone else. And I had no idea who.

"Of course, I would never stoop so low!" she said coolly. "Now, goodbye. Please don't call me again—ever."

I released a breath, ready to end the call and never speak to Isabella again, but then a new thought came to mind. "Wait! How do I get in touch with Nick?"

"Nick?"

I could have sworn her voice just went up an octave. "Yes, Nick."

Did she know what he had done? She may not be behind the letter, but I was pretty sure she was behind the destruction of Harrison's store—or maybe that was Geraldine? Did Nick work for both?

"I can assure you Nick would never stoop so low as to write an article about you."

"No, it's not that. That's not why I want to talk to him. I visited Harrison yesterday. He showed me some footage on the surveillance camera of when his store was broken into. Nick has heart tattoos on his fingers, does he not?" The silence on the other end of the line was chilling, but I trudged forward. "I saw his hands in the surveillance video. I know it was him and his partner that broke into Harrison's store. For what reason, I have no idea, but I need to talk to him. You know him the best, Isabella. Could you reach out and let him know I need to talk to him? It's either that or I go straight to the police with the evidence we have."

"No!" There was heavy breathing on the other end of the line now. "Don't call the police. I'll have him call you." With that, she hung up the phone.

I stared at the phone for a solid five minutes before realizing I was in a waiting game now. I was waiting for Grace to let me know what she had planned with Harrison, waiting for Nick to call me to discuss why he'd broken into Harrison's shop, and waiting for whatever new item I didn't know I just had to have in my wedding. I hoped Victoria would get here soon or I was going to buckle under all this waiting.

CHAPTER 14

"It's already too late to stop him!" Sebastian said, slamming his hands onto the mantel above the fireplace as he stared down at the pile of ashes that used to be the letter.

I gaped at him. "What are you talking about? You really think the letter was from your Uncle Roger?"

Sebastian whirled to face me. "Who else would it be from? He's the only one who's hungry, greedy, and stupid enough to do something like this."

"Well, I thought it was Isabella at first."

"No, she would never stoop so low. She's too classy for that."

There he was again, defending her. Was I the only person who thought she was just evil?

"Tomorrow, we're meeting with Ms. Donaldson," he continued. "I need to put an end to my uncle's meddling."

"Oh, Sebastian, you need to get some rest. Ben said you were only home for a few hours last night."

"Yeah, but I must get this resolved. It can't hang over our wedding." Sebastian came forward and put his arm around my shoulder. "It's been one thing after another for months now, and I want our wedding to be carefree and fun. I don't want us worrying about anything on the big day, especially a family member who seems to think I'm the solution to all his conniving, small-minded—"

"I get it," I said, reaching up to give him a kiss—and maybe to make him stop talking. His arms came around me, bringing me in close, and I melted into them, feeling safe. I would be happy to remain in his arms forever and ignore what was going on in the rest of the world.

He broke away too soon for my liking. "I want to keep you safe," he insisted. "I want you to go back to enjoying your life."

"I understand." And I did. I would do the same for Sebastian. I lifted a hand to his cheek. "You do what you need to do. But is there anything I can help you with?"

He gave me a small smile. "Just keep planning the wedding and see if you can get Mary to come."

"I'm on it. Grace told me to wait till she contacted me. I know she's up to something."

Sebastian laughed, and it relieved my heart a bit. He was still capable of laughing, which meant that he wasn't too far gone down the rabbit hole that was his uncle. "Grace knows how to handle Harrison, as I'm sure you're able to do with me."

I playfully poked him in the chest. "I don't think so."

"Okay, then I relinquish my manhood to you," Sebastian announced, his smile wide.

"Stop it!" I couldn't help laughing now.

"Glad to see you laughing," he said, bringing me in for another kiss. "I must go to sleep now. Like you said, I need to be recharged for the meeting tomorrow."

CHAPTER 15

MS. DONALDSON

"Annabelle, are the snacks out?"

"Yes, Ms. Donaldson. There's sandwiches, scones, tea, and fruit. It's all in the front room."

"Thank you, dear. We must make a good impression today."

My grandson was coming, and everything had to be perfect, especially when I surprised him with the fact that I already knew who he was. Benny was the only one who knew my secret, but he was also the reason I knew who my grandson was.

"They must be coming soon. I'm so excited, I get to meet him in person for the first time," I gushed.

Annabelle gave me a worried look. "Ma'am, are you sure you want to meet him?"

"Why, of course I do. I've been waiting his whole life to meet him."

"It's just . . ."

"Annabelle, how many times do I have to tell you not to stumble over your words. Spit it out, dear."

"Yes, ma'am. It's just you don't know him," she started.

I was about to interrupt that I did when she held up a hand to stop me and continued, "I know Benny and you have always kept tabs on him, but you've never met him. You don't really know him. What if he doesn't live up to what you imagine him to be? I don't want to see you disappointed."

"Annabelle, I have lived with disappointment my whole life. Even more so since I married Bruce. I have kept my mouth shut for years, let my own daughter get kicked out of this house, and been forbidden to ever see her or my grandson again—all because of pride and image. But Sebastian has reached out to me now, and I will welcome him with open arms. So I will hear nothing more said about it, is that clear?"

"Yes, ma'am." She swallowed, then asked, "Can Benny and I be near, though? For support?"

"Of course, do whatever you would like," I said, waving a hand. "But I'm pretty sure I won't need help. Sebastian seems like a nice young man. I'm sure our meeting will be civil."

Annabelle still seemed worried, and I didn't blame her. After all these years supporting me and watching me keep my mouth shut time and time again, I would be wary too. And to tell the truth, I *was* scared. Scared that Sebastian wouldn't like me. That he wouldn't be open to seeing me again, and that this would be my one and only chance to be in the same room as he was. I wasn't getting younger.

I didn't even know where his mother was. Benny had found her, but he wouldn't tell me. Said he lost her trail, but he wouldn't look me in the eyes as he told me that. I didn't want to think the worst, but Benny wouldn't have kept such an important detail about my own child from me; Bruce already did enough damage there. He ran this family into the ground. Now he was gone. Gone. Gone. Gone. And I was in charge now. Why couldn't I meet my child and grandchild again?!

I needed to be cautious, though. I should let Sebastian and Jack lead the conversation. That way I could feel them out, see what they were up to. I was also curious to know why their sudden desire to visit me? Did Sebastian know who I was to him?

"Ma'am . . .?"

I only vaguely heard Annabelle in the distance, I was so wrapped up in the questions turning around and around in my mind. "Hmmm . . .?"

"They're here."

"Oh!" All my senses went on high alert, and I took a quick glance in the mirror to make sure I was well put together. This was it—my one chance to see my grandson and persuade him I was not a crazy person like the rest of his unknown family.

I walked to the door, smoothing my hands down my dress and taking a deep breath before opening it. I couldn't help smiling when I saw my handsome grandson standing there with a very dignified man. For some reason, I felt my heart speed up a little at the sight of this older gentleman. He couldn't be much older than me.

"Ms. Donaldson?" Sebastian said.

"Yes, that's me. Please, call me Joan. You must be Sebastian, and the man with you, I presume, is Jack?" I asked, holding out my hand to shake first Sebastian's hand, then Jack's. I felt like a schoolgirl as Jack shook my hand and gave me the nicest smile.

Realizing how silly I was acting, I quickly took my hand back and led them into the front room. I was happy to see that, sure enough, Annabelle had set everything up just like I had asked her to. There were even fresh cut flowers on the table.

I gestured to the table and chairs. "Please, sit and help yourself to whatever you would like to eat or drink."

I so wanted to go over and give Sebastian a hug. This was the closest I'd been to him since he was a baby. Darn my late husband for keeping me away from him. Darn him!

"Jack, have we met before?" I asked, looking at the older man.

"Maybe. I'm the other boy in the Wilkens household."

"Ah yes, I knew Anthony through school."

I poured some tea for everyone and decided that, since it was probably going to be my one and only chance, I would sit in the chair next to Sebastian. At least I would have this memory moving forward, especially once he found out how we had treated him and his mother.

"What can I help you two with today?" I asked to get things started.

"It's a long story," Sebastian began.

"Why not just start at the beginning? I don't have anything else planned for today, so take as much time as you need."

Sebastian and Jack both looked at each other, and I had to hide my smile at the quizzical looks they exchanged. All I could think was, *Please stay. Take as long as you'd like.*

"Okay," Sebastian replied.

He seemed nervous, so I reached out and patted his hand —a gesture I did with anyone who was uncomfortable. The action almost made me cry, as it felt like more given it was my grandson.

Sebastian gave me a smile and seemed to relax a little. "We're sorry to bother you today—"

"It's no bother," I said, cutting him off. "Don't be sorry. I don't go out much or meet many people these days, so a visitor is great entertainment."

"Oh, okay. Well, there's no good way to put it, but—"

"My husband was a shady character and egotistical, too, I might add," I said, cutting him off again. I had preempted the awkward start, and it made sense to cut straight to the chase. The two men looked so surprised I couldn't help but laugh as I asked, "What did he do this time?"

They silently stared at me, then looked at each other and then back at me. As much as I wanted them to stay, I decided to prod the discussion along. "He had his hands deep into something illegal I'm presuming?"

Jack decided to speak up this time. "We came to ask you for help."

"Help? What can I help with?" No one had ever asked me for help before. Not even my closest friends.

"There's a man by the name of Roger Cambell."

"Ah, yes. I know Roger." I saw Sebastian's face twist into intense dislike, and I ached for him, knowing Roger had likely hurt him in some way. "If Bruce had asked me for my opinion, which he never did, while pointedly telling me he didn't care even if I did voice my opinions, I would have told him never to trust Roger."

"He's been causing some problems," Jack said.

Sebastian added, "He's always caused trouble when it came to my family, but this time he's gone too far in threatening my fiancée."

He's getting married? My grandson is getting married? Oh, I have to think of a gift to give them. I'll see how today goes to decide if I want to include my name on it or not.

Sebastian seemed to have found his voice when it came to Roger, as he continued, "Roger is my uncle. His wife was my mother's sister, and I recently found out that, because of her, we were able to live a good life. She persuaded Uncle Roger to send money to us every month. This led to my father not having the best of experiences while working with him."

"Why didn't your father just leave his job?"

"I've learned that Father isn't good with change. He was probably too scared to look elsewhere."

I watched as pain, anger, and frustration crossed his face. I so wanted to go over and hold him, or at least hold his hand. Maybe I should tell him . . . but would that be too big of a shock?

Sebastian continued, "Uncle Roger has always been greedy and resentful that he had to take care of us. Jack and I have found that when I first started interning at Schuster and Schuster—where Father and Uncle Roger also worked—that Uncle Roger began plotting something with Geraldine Wilkens."

"Your sister?" I said, shooting my eyes at Jack.

"The one and only," he replied, looking sad.

Both men looked so uncomfortable I was wondering what in the world Bruce had done. Because there was no way Bruce was not involved here. He always had a finger in something that made other people's lives miserable, and it always ended in him being richer.

I saw Annabelle peeking into the room to see how I was doing, and I waved her away. At the same time, I nodded at Sebastian to continue.

"The reason for this visit is that the two of them were plotting to get money from your family because they'd unearthed some key information my parents had kept secret up until then."

Did he know? Is he about to admit what I think he is? My heart was pounding so fast I had to put a hand on my chest.

"Are you okay?" Jack asked, standing up and coming over to sit on my other side.

"I'm okay. I'm okay." I took some deep breaths and asked Sebastian to continue. The whole time, Jack didn't look away from my face.

"Father told me that Uncle Roger had learned I'm your grandson. I recently learned that Geraldine knew as well."

That word hung in the air, but my heart was now pounding with happiness. *He knows. He already knows!* I could feel tears starting to flow down my face, then I felt Jack's hand come over mine. I turned to look at him and gave his hand a squeeze. Turning back to Sebastian, I saw that he had slumped back in his seat. He also looked embarrassed and a little shy. It was time to tell him that I knew.

"Yes, you are my grandson, and I have loved you since the day you were born."

At this, he looked up at me, and I could tell the words were slowly sinking in. Incomprehension flashed across his features. This was soon followed by wonder, then anger. His voice was hoarse. "You knew?"

"Of course, I did. I love my daughter and to lose both of you at once was unbearable. Benny, my butler, would keep me up to date on what you were doing. Don't worry, he didn't follow you around. He would check in with your parents once a year on the pretext of the adoption center making sure you were okay."

Sebastian's face had lost all color. "If you knew, why didn't you come see me? Why keep me in the dark when you clearly wanted to know me—and I would have wanted to know you? What happened to my mother?" Another flash of anger appeared on his face, but it was gone as soon as it came.

The quickness of it startled me, as he'd looked so much like his grandfather. Bruce was always able to set his face back to neutral in an instant. Only the people who lived with him ever knew he had emotions, and usually the volatile kind.

I realized Sebastian and Jack were staring at me, waiting for me to answer. I composed myself and said, "Your grandfather was not a kind man, and he had a lot of power in this family and with others. Cecilia was forced to put you up for adoption and was then quickly kicked out of our home. I was forbidden to have any contact with either of you." I was really crying now, the tears splashing down my face. Jack hadn't let go of my hand the whole time, and I could tell Sebastian's anger had faded. I hoped he was warming up to me, even if it was just a little.

"Where did she go?" Sebastian asked, his voice now carefully neutral.

"I don't know," I answered honestly. "At first, Benny was able to find her, and I tried to give her money, but he always came back saying she refused any help. She was mad at me, too, you see. But not even a year later, she disappeared. I don't know where she went, and I've missed you two every day since." I looked at him, holding his gaze as I said quietly, "I used to hold you till you went to sleep, did you know that?"

"No," Sebastian whispered.

I knew this was a lot for him to take in, and I completely understood if he didn't want to see me again. But since we had already opened up the past, I wasn't going to let him go that easily. Now was my only chance to tell him how I really felt. "I used to sing to you and bathe you. You were so small. I watched you learn to walk and say your first words. Sebastian, I have loved you since the day you were born.

"I can't fix the past or wipe away what my husband did, but I'm here now. I'm sorry I didn't reach out to you myself, but I was so scared you would reject me. Despite all that, I'm here now, and I'm hoping we can get to know each other. What do you think?"

He swallowed. "I . . . I need to think about it. Like you said, this is a lot."

Jack, who had been quiet up to this point, chose that

moment to interject. He said in a soft voice, "We should get back to the topic of why we're here."

We both shifted in our seats to face him, and I could see that Sebastian seemed happy to think about something else. I felt sad to lose the moment, but I really hoped my grandson would give us a chance.

Sebastian blew out a breath before continuing with his initial story. "Yes, so Uncle Roger and Geraldine wanted to blackmail your family. When Geraldine, her daughter, Jacqueline, and her granddaughter, Isabella, took me in after Mother died, I thought it was a nice gesture, but it turned out it wasn't. It was a move Geraldine made to cut Uncle Roger out of her scheme. Jack has her notes if you want to read them in detail. But basically, Geraldine believed that since she now had me under her care I would be even easier to use in extorting your family. Well, I guess I mean my family . . ." He trailed off as he ran his hand through his hair.

I admired what a handsome young man he had turned into. His adoptive parents did good raising him. They probably made a better job of it than if he had grown up here—and that was hard to admit.

"I remember her asking me time and time again to take on the Donaldson account," Sebastian continued. "And that Uncle Roger was getting older and didn't need so many cases on his plate. She didn't know that I already knew about the family ties, and that I wanted nothing to do with the Donaldson accounts. This badgering lasted for about two years—with her trying to persuade me to take the job and me telling her no. It was hard to say no, because she paid for my law school fees and supported me in my career. I wouldn't be where I am now without her.

"But I just couldn't touch the Donaldson accounts. In the end, Uncle Roger kept them. Jack recently found out that Geraldine and Roger got back together and tried a different tactic. This time, they approached your husband . . . my grandfather." Sebastian paused, running a hand down his face as if he still couldn't quite believe what he was saying. "They made a deal with him that Uncle Roger would be his sole lawyer moving forward; he would use no one else. And Uncle Roger guaranteed that he would make any problem for the Donaldson family go away. I have no idea what that means as Jack won't tell me, but I'm sure Jack can share more on that if you're interested."

"I can, but it's really not something to talk about in polite company," Jack said.

"Oh, pish posh!" I said. "I'm hardy enough to hear about my husband's exploits. Goodness knows I lived with him all these years. But I do agree that we won't talk about that at this moment. I can talk with Jack about it on another day. Is there more you want to share, Sebastian? You mentioned your fiancée earlier."

"Yes. I'm engaged to Anne Huang, who—"

"Inherited the Wilkens fortune last year," I finished for him.

"Yes. It's a long story, but we're getting married soon, and we were hoping to keep it low-key. But Uncle Roger is now working in the background trying to make it a big deal and painting Anne in a bad light. I'm sure he's also thinking of ways to exploit money from us. We wanted to come to you to—"

"See if I can put a stop to him?"

Sebastian flushed but he didn't miss a beat as he replied, "Yes. I know you don't know us. Well, I guess you know me, kind of, but you have the most influence over him. From the documents Jack found in Geraldine's notes, the two of them were still working with someone in your family as recently as a few months ago. That means Uncle Roger is still banking money for jobs with the Donaldson family."

I knew immediately who that person was. "It must be Griswald," I said. "He takes care of everything financial. He's been with us since I married Bruce. Never liked the guy, he's sly and always kissing up to me. You know the type. He feels like an oily car salesman every time I interact with him. But my husband listened to everything he had to say. It was brutal. I tried at the beginning to persuade Bruce otherwise, but I quickly learned Bruce only married me for my connections and nothing more. Like I said, your grandfather was not a good man, and I learned that too late to get away. But . . . he's not here anymore, and I'm now head of the household."

Jack was still holding my hand. He said, "You don't have to do anything if you don't want to. I know this is news that you shouldn't have to deal with."

I shook my head. "No, I want to. I can finally see my grandson, and I have a chance to help him. Give me those documents you found, and I'll have a talk with Griswald. We'll get your Uncle Roger off both your and Anne's back. By the way, when is your wedding and where?"

"It's next Saturday. It will be at the mansion. Just a small wedding with friends and family."

Before he could feel guilty for wondering if he should ask to invite me, I stood up. "Come outside with me. I want to show you my place of serenity. Bruce didn't let me do much, but I had my garden. There is something I want to show you."

Due to polite convention, they followed me outside at my urging, but I could see Sebastian was a little hesitant. We walked into the garden where I had once hosted parties for Bruce, parties that had accommodated hundreds of people. I'd refused to host any more after he kicked Cecilia out. I had planted tall arborvitae hedges to divide off a section of the garden as my own private sanctuary. Bruce had never bothered me here. I was hidden and quiet, which was all he cared about.

I ushered them into the space and pointed at the plethora of roses scattered around the area. "I planted a rose bush every year on your birthday. It allowed me to tend to something living while also reminding me you were healthy and safe." I turned to look at Sebastian. He had tears in his eyes. "I want to get to know you better and to have you in my life. I won't pressure you, but I hope you'll think about it."

He nodded but didn't say another word. That was all I could hope for. Having not been in his life for the last twenty-eight years was not something I expected him to instantly forgive me for, but I hoped he would soon so I could be a part of his future.

CHAPTER 16

ANNE

T HE NEXT DAY A NUMBER OF VENDORS CALLED TO
see if I wanted to hire them for the wedding, and after
picking up the first two unknown numbers, I started sending
them to voicemail.

There was also another article stuck through the fence.
This message was very clear-cut. It was all about how I was
going to make people pay me money, even though I should be
the one paying others. It went on and on about how if I held
a traditional Taiwanese wedding, I would request everyone to
send red envelopes, and since it would be a big wedding—as
apparently that's what I'd always wished for—I would be
expecting people to be paying me big sums. It also went on
to say that I had always been greedy when it came to having
my way, and this included having a big banquet offering a
plethora of food—which, in all honesty, would happen even if
I wasn't rich.

The article also claimed I would change dresses multiple
times throughout the wedding and reception, and that there
would be lots of opulence that wasn't needed. Never mind
that most of what the article said was about traditions that

spanned thousands of years. Never mind that I had never said I was going to hold a traditional Taiwanese wedding. Clearly, whoever wrote the article had no idea that Sebastian and I were going to get married in a small ceremony in our backyard, with only our family and friends.

The author of these articles plagued my mind. I now knew Geraldine and Isabella wouldn't have gone to these lengths— they would have said this directly to my face. But Brian wouldn't have. He had given an interview in the last article. Was he the instigator of all of this because he was jealous I had received the Wilkens fortune? Or, was Sebastian right in thinking Uncle Roger was behind these articles and maybe it was he who had enlisted Brian?

Ahhhh! This was crazy. Why was this happening? The only worry I should be having right now was our wedding. But instead, I was worrying about people harming me or Sebastian. That saying people said—what was it? More money made more problems? Well, that was so true.

I suddenly realized dwelling on this problem was getting me nowhere. Victoria had gone to work, and I was just sitting here feeling sorry for myself. I decided to call Lauren.

"Are you up for lunch today?" I asked when she picked up in her usual bubbly way.

"You bet! I know just the place. Meet you at noon? I'll text you the address."

"Sounds good."

Easy peasy. No more thinking about the article.

"I saw an article this morning about someone claiming that you took the Wilkens fortune," Lauren said as soon as we sat down.

So much for that.

"It's nothing. Sebastian said he knows who's behind it and is taking care of it." I hoped what he said was true and it would get taken care of quickly.

"Well, if Sebastian says so then I won't bring it up again. But just so you know, I don't think it's Isabella. It's not her style to be so public about family matters."

"I already . . ." I started to say, but Lauren cut me off with a nod, and that was that. We moved on to the wedding.

"Have you thought more about hiring Eda?" she asked. "And what I said about inviting more people?"

"I have, and I decided I don't want either. We'd like to just have a small wedding with family and friends. It'll be in our backyard."

"Oh, well, I . . ."

"Do you have pictures of the bridesmaid dresses?" I asked, hoping this would change the subject for good.

"Oh, yes! Victoria and I picked out the prettiest dresses. You're going to love them."

Lauren flipped through her phone for a bit while I chewed on some pasta, wondering if she would really let the subject drop about having a big wedding. Because with the release of the articles, I wanted to dig my toes in even more about doing a small wedding.

"Here they are," Lauren suddenly announced. "What do you think?" She turned the phone to face me.

I took the phone from her in awe. "Oh wow! These are gorgeous."

"Aren't they?"

They were a soft shade of pink and were fitted in the chest and waist with a strapless heart-shaped neckline. From the waist, the chiffon flowed into a pool on the ground. It looked airy and ethereal, truly beautiful.

"I even got you one in white so we can do matchy-matchy photos," Lauren said, anticipation lighting up her features.

"Oh! Well, thank you."

There was a pause, then she slumped in her chair. "You don't like it, do you?"

I gasped. "No, I love it! It's just I already have a dress, and I also got the qipao with Leslie yesterday. I wasn't expecting another one, but I think it's gorgeous, and I'm really happy you got me one!" I scooted my chair right next to hers and gave her a big hug.

She hugged me close. As she pulled back, she cried, "You got a qipao? I want to see pictures!"

I took out my phone and showed her the materials, and she oooed and ahhhed. I loved the compromise we had made on the qipao, and I really did like the bridesmaid dress. It was just that all these dresses were going against what I wanted for our wedding.

After a few minutes of ogling at the phone, Lauren turned back to me. "Don't think for a second that I'm going to let you forget about what we talked about before."

"What's that?" There had been a lot of things thrown at me the last couple of days that I really had no clue what she referred to.

Lauren raised a brow as if it was obvious. "I meant have you thought more about inviting the people from the Christmas gala?"

Oh. "Honestly, no. I don't plan on doing a big wedding. I think it'll be nice to just have you and Steven, Mom, Victoria and Paul, my extended family, and Sebastian's dad and friends. It'll be a nice intimate wedding."

"Okay, but . . ." She didn't look convinced.

"Lauren, we already discussed this."

Thankfully, a lady came up to our table right then. "Are you Anne Huang?" she asked.

"Yes."

"I just want to say that you shouldn't give up on your tradition just because the money you got isn't from a Taiwanese family. You should do what you are comfortable with." She patted my hand, gave me a reassuring smile, and left.

I didn't know what to say. When was I giving up my traditions? My traditions were the same as hers—American! If I wanted to add Taiwanese traditions to my wedding, that was my problem, not anyone else's!

"Anne—" Lauren began.

"Don't. Say. Anything. Not a word. Let's just eat and wait for Victoria."

Thankfully, Lauren did just that while I brooded on what the lady said.

A moment later, Victoria rushed up to us. "I'm so sorry I'm late," she panted. "There was traffic, and I couldn't get through the tunnel fast enough. Oh, my goodness, it smells so good. Can I have some of those fries?" Without waiting for an answer, Victoria took a couple off my plate, sat down, and chewed like it was the most delicious food she had ever had in her entire life. "What did I miss?"

Lauren started speaking before I could. "I showed her the bridesmaid dresses, and she showed me her qipao—"

"You got one? Ooooh, I want to see!"

So ensued more looking at pictures, which I was fine with, because I didn't want to talk about the lady who had stopped by the table and what she'd said. The more I thought about it, the madder I could feel myself become.

But Victoria saw right through me. "Why do you look so uptight, Anne?"

Lauren answered for me again. "A lady stopped by and told her to not forgo her Taiwanese wedding traditions just because of what others think."

"Oh," Victoria said. "I saw that article this morning."

I put my head in my hands and shook my head. "Other people's problems. Not my problem."

"Except there are people who look up to you now," Lauren said.

I jerked my head up to stare at her. "Who? I'm nobody."

"You have the Wilkens family backing," she reminded me. "And the Wilkens have always had a lot to say in this town."

I sighed. "Can I just give it all back?"

Victoria chimed in before the conversation could go further down the rabbit hole. "You know that's not what you want to do, Anne. Look, I have an idea. Why don't we finish up here so that you can go on a walk in Forest Park. I'll even prep some ice cream for you for when you get back."

"That does always calm me down," I agreed slowly.

"That's a great idea! I think I'll join too," Lauren piped in.

"Great! You can help me with the food," Victoria said quickly, which meant she wanted me to have the alone time I craved. "We can talk to Cook about catering while Anne goes for her walk."

I loved Victoria.

CHAPTER 17

I TOOK MY DOG, LADY, FOR A WALK IN FOREST PARK. Even though there were quite a few people on the trail, it was nice to be outside and away from people I knew. Who would have thought wedding planning would be this overwhelming? In all honesty, I was starting to rethink the idea of hiring a wedding planner. As Victoria said, I could afford it, and it would also save a lot of stress.

I hated this feeling of helplessness. Was this even my wedding anymore? I had no idea. I was listening to Lauren and Leslie, but it wasn't their wedding. It wasn't anyone's wedding except Sebastian's and mine. And yet his uncle, who I had never heard of, was writing articles about it—and with the help of my ex-boyfriend, Brian. Was the sole aim of these articles to drive me crazy and make me feel guilty? It sure felt like it.

But what became abundantly clear as I walked along was that I was listening to everyone but me on the subject of my wedding.

Lady was sniffing around, and I could see she, too, was enjoying being outdoors. I made a mental note to do this more often. Looking at my surroundings with new eyes, I saw a car parked in the parking lot across the street. I'm not sure what made me look but I could see a guy sitting inside the car, staring at me. When he saw he had my attention, he waved. *What in the world?*

I decided to ignore him and continued walking. An engine started up, and next thing I knew he was driving past me, his hand waving again. A tingle of foreboding shot up my spine, and I contemplated turning around and walking straight home, but as the guy had driven off, I decided I wasn't going to let him ruin this time by myself.

I walked some more, lost in my thoughts, until the sound of music came from behind me. I turned to see a cyclist go by, speaker on the back of his bike, his upper body moving to the music while he pedaled. That was the way life should be —dancing to your own beat on your own time, not catering to everyone else's whims.

"That was pretty cool, wasn't it?" said a voice from my left, startling me, and I jumped before turning around.

"Um, yes?" I was at a loss for words, as it was the same guy who had driven past me and waved. How was he now standing right next to me? Up close, I could see that his hair was tied back in a ponytail, and he was dressed in baggy jeans and a long sleeve t-shirt with some sort of sport team logo on his shirt pocket.

"The guy with his music," he explained with an easy smile. "Great relaxing way to live, don't you think?"

"Uh huh." *Why was I still standing here?* Yet I remained frozen to the ground.

"I've lived in Japan, Korea, Taiwan, and other Asian countries, and I just love y'all," he continued, not fazed by my awkward responses. "You work together so well and get things done. Not like people here." He looked off into the trees, seemingly lost in thought.

I told myself to breathe. I couldn't make heads or tails of what was going on here, and I still couldn't move. My heart rate was also starting to rise. Thank goodness there were other people around.

He turned back to face me, and his face lit up as he burst out, "Wait! Are you Anne Huang? I saw that article about you this morning!"

I just stared at him. I wasn't going to admit anything.

"You are! You're just so beautiful. I didn't know you were Anne Huang, but I saw you walking down this trail, and I thought I'd come say hi in the hope that I would see you again."

What in the world? Did he just say he wanted to see me again? That woke me up. "No! Uh, I can't see you or anybody. I'm getting married soon."

This comment seemed to give him pause.

Thank goodness! You need to just leave now, Anne! But my body wouldn't listen to me. It just stood there, still frozen to the spot. This whole time Lady was looking at the man in the hopes that he would pet her. Maybe next time I would get a bigger, more ferocious dog.

The man seemed to come alive and recognize what I'd said because he replied, "Oh no! It's not like that. I wanted to see you again for other reasons." He actually laughed. "Can I give you my card?" And he took out an actual business card. "Here, just take it."

And I actually took it! *What was I going to do with his card?*

"I run a massage parlor. You should come and check it out. It would be great to see you again!" he said while walking back in the direction we came. Before he turned, he added, "And don't let those naysayers stop you from adding Taiwanese traditions to your own wedding. Red envelopes are the best!"

All I could think about as my feet finally found a way to

move forward was, *What in the world just happened?* All he had seen was that I was Asian. He'd associated nothing else with me. It was an epiphany—he didn't know me, just like all those people out there who had an opinion on my life didn't know me either.

Back at home, I showered, trying to wash off the encounter. I had heard about non-Asian guys hitting on Asian girls, that it was a fetish. But it had never happened to me before, and Sebastian had never given me that vibe. Just thinking about him made me wish I could be in his arms right now.

While showering, I decided I would hire the wedding planner. I truly felt like I was in over my head planning this wedding, with no idea what to do. I took my phone into the sitting room, but before I could dial Eda's number, Leslie called.

"Anne, I just found a great deal on ordering the candy bags, and I thought we could ask Cook to make chocolate-shaped blossoms to put in the boxes. It'll be special to you and Sebastian. There are also the tablecloths to organize, and have you decided where you're going to rent the tables, chairs, and dance floor?"

"What?"

"You said you were having the wedding at your place, so we need to rent tables, chairs, and a dance floor, and we'll also need to interview live bands. Oh, and you wanted an open bar, or you said something about Sebastian wanting one. Did I remember that right?"

Oh my goodness, I was in way over my head. "Leslie, let me call you back. Okay?"

"Anne, just one more thing—"

"No, I'll catch you in a little bit, okay? I'm in the middle of something."

"Okay, but don't wait too long. This deal is only going to last for a couple more hours."

I sighed. "Okay, Leslie."

"Oh wait! Anne, Mom wants to talk to you."

What now? But Leslie was gone before I could get an idea of what Grace wanted to talk to me about. There was the sound of the phone changing hands, then a voice came on the line again.

"Anne?"

"Hi, Grace."

"You sound so tired."

"I am. It's been a whirlwind couple of days."

"I wanted to let you know that Harrison and I are going to Taiwan tomorrow."

I woke up at that. "What? What do you mean? How?"

Grace laughed. "I tried talking to him about speaking to Mary, but he is so stubborn. So, I bought two plane tickets last night and gave him no choice. He is frugal, so he will not want to waste the money I've spent on the tickets."

"Wow, Grace, that's bold." And it was. I was so thrilled she'd done that.

"We're not getting any younger, and I would like to visit my hometown."

"I don't blame you. I wish I could go along. I would love to visit Taiwan again." I really did.

"Well, why don't you come with us? Mary would love to see you again."

"I don't want to be the third wheel on this trip," I said quickly, suddenly feeling guilty for imposing on an important occasion.

"You wouldn't be," Grace replied, just as quickly.

"Thank you for the offer, Grace, but I should probably

stay. There's a lot going on right now that I need to take care of." *Like my own sanity.*

"Okay, Anne. You take care of yourself. I'll let you know how it goes, okay?"

"Yes, please do. Say hi to Mary for me."

"I will. It has been a long time, but I am looking forward to finally seeing her again."

My heart felt happy for them. "Have a safe trip."

"Thanks, Anne, and we'll see you at your wedding."

"Yes."

"Don't stress over everything Leslie is telling you. Just hire that wedding planner. You can afford it, after all."

Little does she know I'm trying to do just that. But all I said was, "Very true."

"You know I'm right."

I laughed. Grace was like a second mom to me already. And just like Mom, she was good at prolonging phone calls, because she then asked, "Oh, Anne?"

"Yes?"

"Did you find out any more about who you suspect broke into the store?"

I groaned. "No, I can't get ahold of him. But I will."

"Okay, just keep us updated."

"Of course."

CHAPTER 18

FIRST THINGS FIRST, I WOULD PAY ISABELLA A VISIT. Lauren had said Nick followed Isabella everywhere, so if anyone knew where Nick was, it'd be her.

"Anne?" A familiar voice called out.

"Sebastian?" *He's home early.*

"Hey, do I have news for you," he said, entering the room.

"How did your visit go?" I asked, patting the empty seat on the sofa next to me.

"It went better than we thought. Ms. Donaldson, otherwise known as my grandmother, is being very cooperative and loves what we're doing. She said she also kept tabs on me throughout the years but was never able to meet me once I got adopted." He settled into the sofa and tucked me into his arms as he added softly, "I kinda now know what you feel like, knowing a stranger was keeping tabs on you. I'm sorry."

"Yeah, it's creepy, isn't it?"

"It sure is."

"I'm glad it turned out to be you, though, because I love you."

Sebastian pulled me closer and gave me a satisfying kiss. "Just what I needed to hear after a long day."

I smiled and stroked his chest. "What else did she say?"

"That my mom got kicked out of the family home at the same time I did, and Ms. Donaldson has no idea where she is."

"Oh . . . But wait! I have to find Nick—I can ask him to find your mom?"

Sebastian's eyebrows rose. "You haven't been able to get ahold of him yet?"

"No, he's not returning my calls, but I'm going to pay Isabella a visit soon."

He shook his head and said he'd come with me to visit Isabella, but I could tell he was already overwhelmed by the day's happenings, so I laid him down, put a blanket over him, and told him to take a nap. He was asleep before I stood back up. I tiptoed out of the sitting room and got ready to visit Isabella.

"What in the world are you doing here?" Isabella asked.

She stood at the entrance of her house, looking down at me while tapping her fingers on the door frame. I couldn't help but stare at her. I had never seen Isabella look so disheveled. She had no makeup on, and she was wearing flowy cotton pants. Nice ones, but still not going out pants, and was that a sweatshirt she was wearing?

"Well, are you going to answer me or just stand there wasting my time?" she pushed.

Oh yes, but her attitude was clearly the same. Why couldn't Nick just pick up his phone? Lauren better be right that Isabella knew where he was. I could do without ever seeing her again. I began in a neutral voice, "I'm here to ask for Nick's whereabouts."

"And why would I know a thing like that? Nick is his own person. He can go wherever he wants."

"You said you'd have him call me, and he still hasn't called."

"And why is that my problem?"

"Because he's attached to you."

"Attached to me? What do you think we are, Siamese twins?"

This was going nowhere! "Isabella, I know you know where he is. I also know he's not calling me back when he is usually very prompt."

Isabella put her hands on her hips. "Anne, please leave. I have enough going on in my life right now without you barging in again. You got the house, you got Sebastian, what else do you want?" she almost screamed at me.

"I want Nick to take responsibility for what he did to my uncle's store! And I'm trying to be nice and not go to the police about it." I was seething by this point. What was it going to take to get Nick to talk to me?

My last comment seemed to get her attention. Her lips became a thin line, and I saw one of her hands ball up into a fist. If her eyes could shoot daggers, I think I'd have many covering my whole body right now.

"Wait here." She barely got the words out of her mouth before slamming the door in my face.

I was so stunned I didn't move for a minute, just stared at the shiny door knocker reflecting my startled face. Why was I so surprised by Isabella's actions? I should be used to her already—but, oh wait, she wasn't normal, and this wasn't how people treated each other.

I took the door knocker and rammed it against the door. Who did she think she was slamming the door in my face? I heard footsteps approaching. They sounded heavier than Isabella's, but maybe she was stomping? I felt a sense of satisfaction that I wasn't backing down. She wasn't anybody special, she was—*Nick?!*

He stood on the other side of the now open door. "Anne, I will be right with you. We are in the middle of a fight because of you, so . . ." He shrugged. "Oh, do whatever you want, Anne." He turned and walked away.

The door was left ajar, and I stood there, stunned. Nick was here! Lauren was right—interacting with Isabella was taking up all of my energy, and I knew I was going to take Cook up on trying some cake samples for the wedding as soon as I got home. I might even eat all of the samples, every last bite, no matter what flavor they were.

Feeling peeved, I pushed the door open to an immaculate foyer. It had bright, airy, and large windows, with modern lights, white walls, and marble floors. It was exactly the type of look Isabella had wanted for my place, and I had to admit, it looked really nice. If I ever got tired of all the wood carvings, I might think about modernizing the place just like this. But for now, I liked how much character the mansion had. Plus, I bet the house held even more secrets just waiting to be discovered.

"So, you think you can just invite yourself in?" Isabella said, appearing out of nowhere; barefoot, hair still disheveled, and with bloodshot eyes like she'd been crying.

"I didn't—"

"Oh, forget it," she said, swinging an arm out. "You're just like Brian. Barging into my home thinking you can demand things from me. I'm so sick of you Asian people."

I was rooted to the floor at what she said, but when I looked at her, she wasn't even looking at me. She was leaning against the stairs picking at her nails. This was not the

Isabella I knew. Not the put-together woman I had grown to expect.

"Isabella . . ."

"You know, I've seen the articles showing up in the news. I told you before, but you just don't listen. If you want to sway people to your side, you invite the people Anthony used to invite. You make them feel welcome. If you did that, they might actually stand up for you instead of standing to the side and watching you fall."

I could only stare at her. "Why are you sharing this with me?"

"Let's just say I'm tired of hearing your name everywhere. Even my own family members are talking about you. Wondering what you're going to do with all that money, and if they'll ever see the inside of their family home again."

"But it's not—"

"It's not their home anymore, I know. You've made that abundantly clear," she scoffed. "But it doesn't change the fact that my family built that house and lived in it and ran it for generations. It's where family get-togethers happened. Then, all of a sudden it's gone, all because my great uncle couldn't keep his hands to himself."

"Now—"

"You really need to stop interrupting me," Isabella said, giving me a stern look. "I'm giving you advice, and you need to just listen for once." She released a breath. "What Anthony did was wrong on many levels. What he did by giving you the money and the house was wrong." She held up a hand to stop me. "But I'm not going to fight it anymore."

I could see her defeat. This wasn't Isabella. This wasn't the woman I had known over the last many months, the woman Lauren looked up to.

I held up my hand to let her know I wanted to talk, and she didn't stop me this time.

Very slowly, I asked her, "Isabella, are you okay?" She didn't say anything so I pushed onward. "I know we haven't seen eye to eye, and we really dislike each other, but is there something I can help you with?"

At this, she looked up at me for the first time, and I saw there were genuine tears in her eyes, threatening to roll down her face.

"*You* want to help?" She laughed. "As if there's anything more you can do. Anne, have you ever looked up to someone so much? Thought they were the best thing that could have happened to you, only to find out they were probably the worst person you could have looked up to? Have you been left wondering what evil things you've done on their behalf? Started questioning what type of person you are and who you can really trust? Have you, Anne? Have you ever felt such loss?"

I didn't know what to say to this. The look in her eyes scared me. What had happened? "Who was this person, Isabella?"

"You really can't guess?"

After her speech, it could only be one person. "Geraldine?"

She only smiled. But it wasn't a nice smile or one a person would have after getting something off her chest. It was filled with anger and betrayal. For once, I realized Isabella's anger was directed at someone else rather than me, and I felt bad for her. I ventured, "Why are you being nice to me?"

"Is this being nice?"

"Um . . . yes . . ."

She shrugged. "Like I said, I'm tired of hearing your name everywhere. Maybe this will get you to blend in more, and then I can pretend you don't exist."

I realized that was probably the best I'd ever get out of Isabella. Turning back to the advice she'd given me, I asked, "But why invite people I don't know to my own wedding?"

"Why not?"

"Why not? Weddings are intimate. You don't invite people to make connections—you invite those you've already connected with."

"Huh, then I've been going to all the wrong weddings," she muttered.

"You don't go for the couple?"

She looked at me as though I was crazy. "Why would I? I don't have a lot of friends. The only reason I've been to weddings was because I used to be Lauren's plus one. She knew all these people; but, by the end of dinner, there would be at least ten party crashers who no one knew."

Had she ever known happiness? Suddenly drawn to Isabella, I began to walk toward her, but then Nick appeared on the upstairs landing.

"Well, that's that," he announced. "Anne, let's go."

Nick didn't wait for an answer. He came down the steps, gave Isabella a hug and a kiss on the forehead, murmured something about fixing it, and then turned to walk out the door. Not once did he look my way. The moment between me and Isabella was gone; she had already left the room. I didn't know what else to do, so I turned to follow him.

"Nick—"

"Wait till we get further from the house. She'll be watching from the window."

I started to turn around.

"Don't look!" he cried. "Really, Anne! I wonder, some-times, about whether you have any social cues."

I rolled my eyes and decided silence was the best option at the moment. Nick steered us toward the nearby park and over to a private bench situated well away from the parents and children scattered around the playground. We sat down, and I was about to launch right into the video footage I'd seen when Nick started talking.

"Isabella said you saw the surveillance video."

"Yes. What kind of person breaks in knowing there's probably a surveillance video in there?"

"Me, apparently."

"So, you admit it was you?" I was shocked. I thought he would put up more of a fight.

"Well, I guess now you know." He sighed.

"Why'd you do it?"

"Because I love Isabella."

Okay . . . that was not the answer I was expecting.

"I need her, Anne. She's all I think about. But I know she doesn't feel the same way. I'm solidly in the friend zone, have been for a very long time. I should have never let her go when we went out the first time."

I watched as Nick put his head in his hands . . . and were those tears coming out of his eyes? Were they real? I immediately admonished myself for that thought, reminding myself that I was here to see what the heck was going on, not to hurt the guy more. But what he'd done to my uncle's place still needed to be addressed.

"That doesn't explain about the store," I reminded him quietly.

He released a very big sigh. "You know Isabella was also looking for your uncle." He turned to look at me in question, and I gave him a nod. "Well, I paid him a visit. I lost my temper, and it didn't go so well."

Puzzle pieces started slotting together. "Were you the one Erik threw a vase at?"

He grimaced. "You know about that, huh?"

"Of course, I do! It's my family!"

"Okay, quiet down. I don't want to cause a scene."

"That's why we're sitting in a park with families nearby? So I don't start yelling at you?" He just looked at me like he couldn't believe I had finally caught on to that fact. "Oh, fine! I admit I'm a little slow at picking up social cues. Are you happy now?"

"No, I'm not," he snapped back. "I expected a lot more from you."

"Why?"

"Because Isabella spent so much of her energy on you. Because you're Asian. Because you're the reason Isabella's whole world is turned upside down right now, and hence, mine is too. You're not supposed to be such a big problem, and yet you have managed to become one. I expected you to stand up to that image I made of you."

"Well then, that's your fault."

"No kidding." He sat back and released another big sigh. "Anyways, I went to pay your uncle a visit at his store, thinking I could catch him there and persuade him to sign in writing then and there that he'd give up any claim to the Wilkens wealth. But you saw on the video that he wasn't there, right? And 'my partner'"—he said, using air quotes—"broke his front door and made a mess of his office. Trust me, it was the last time I used him. I'm not the 'go in and break things or mess people's places up guy.' I just wanted to talk to Harrison, and I can be persuasive without hurting anyone."

I so didn't want to believe him. I wanted to stay mad at him, but I could tell he was genuine. It also explained what I saw in the video.

"Please don't spread the word that Isabella is in a frightful state," he said, looking at me sideways.

"Why would I do that?"

"Anyone else would to make her look bad."

My stomach flipped. "You really love her, don't you?"

He nodded. "With all my heart and soul. She's the one for me. I'll never love anyone else."

I sighed. I couldn't stay mad at him, but I still needed to take care of Harrison. What Nick had done was wrong. "Well, I can't just let you go scot-free."

He froze. "You could, you know."

"Um, nope. You broke into my uncle's place of work and made a mess of it. He's still cleaning up the mess."

"My partner didn't make that big a mess, and I can wire your uncle some money for a new door," Nick suggested quickly.

I shook my head. "It's not just that. What you don't know is that you and your 'partner,' as you called him, broke the door and left it like that. This allowed a gang of men to come in later in the night and ransack the whole place. They destroyed his store, Nick!"

"What?" He looked startled to hear this. "I didn't know." He put his head back in his hands.

"So, you see, I can't just let you go scot-free."

"Why is this happening?" I heard him whisper, but then he sat up so fast I scooted away from him. "Okay, what do you want?" he demanded.

I stared at him. "Ah, I'm not sure yet. I just wanted to talk to you first to see if you were really who I saw in the video."

"You seem a lot calmer than I thought you'd be."

"Well, the interaction back there with Isabella has thrown me," I said honestly. "I've never seen her like that, and she was being nice. It was really not the Isabella I know."

"Yeah, I'm worried about her. Your ex won't leave her alone."

"Brian?" I exclaimed, almost shouting the name.

"Yes, the one and only. Greedy, sniveling—there are a lot more words I can use about him, but I won't say them in front of you." I saw his hand curl into a ball so tight his veins were starting to pop.

I sighed. "I'm sure I've used the words you're thinking of already about him. What has he done now?"

"Nothing I can't handle at the moment."

"Okay . . ."

Nick swiveled back to face me. "Don't butt in, okay? I'll come to you if we need help."

"Okay," I said again, more quickly this time. "On a different note, can I ask you about Geraldine?"

"What about her?"

"Isabella made it sound like Geraldine's downfall is really messing with her."

"Geraldine? Well, she's a work of art. I've never met anyone else like her. I've always been petrified of her. But Isabella, she adored her, and I can't blame her. Geraldine was more a mother to her than her own mother ever was. Geraldine could do no wrong in Isabella's eyes. She was very family focused, as you know. Isabella latched onto that instantly and never let go . . . until Jack called last month during Lauren's bachelorette party. We've since learned Geraldine had a twisted way of loving Isabella while still using her in her schemes. Isabella has made Jack keep her updated on what he's found about Geraldine, and with every new finding, I see Isabella retreating more and more into herself. There's nothing I can do." He wiped away a tear that was flowing down his cheek. "I hate that there's nothing I can do, Anne, and I'm breaking inside."

I didn't know what to say. Geraldine and Rose were two totally different people; yet, they had left such a big impression on their descendants that we were feeling their impact even now.

"Anne, I'm not a bad person," Nick continued. "Neither is Isabella. Whatever you want me to do to make up for what happened to your uncle, I'll do it. You know how to contact me. I'll make sure I answer your call next time."

"Okay." I was about to demand that he should pay for restoring Harrison's store, but now didn't seem the right time to discuss it.

Nick nodded and then stood. "I need to go back to Isabella. You know where you are from here?"

"Yes, I'll get myself home."

"Good." And with that, he started back the way we came.

I sat there for a long time, just looking at the kids running around their parents, like they had not a care in the world. Today had not gone the way I had thought it would.

CHAPTER 19

I WENT BACK HOME AND SAT IN THE SITTING ROOM, just staring into space as I contemplated what was happening in my life. I felt out of whack, and my thoughts were all over the place. Grace was leaving with Harrison for Taiwan tomorrow, but I'd believe it when they got on the plane. Leslie and Grace were wanting the wedding to have Taiwanese traditions incorporated throughout, and, apparently, total strangers wanted me to have them too. Lauren wanted me to invite total strangers to my wedding out of goodwill and camaraderie, and if I thought about it more it would probably be good for business seeing how I represented the Wilkens brand now. But for goodness sakes, I couldn't believe that even Isabella was giving me advice!

The thought of Isabella unnerved me, and I sank deeper into the couch, grabbing a blanket and wrapping it around myself. The look in her eyes haunted me. What her grandmother did to her . . . yeah, I would be messed up too. But Nick had also mentioned Brian. What had he done?

The thought of him terrorizing Isabella to the point she looked distressed and unkempt rattled me more than I wanted to admit. Was there anything I could do? But Nick told me not to help. Plus, Brian wasn't anything to me anymore, and I hated Isabella. But I couldn't get the sight of her out of my mind. She was a ghost of her former self, and that terrified me. I couldn't imagine someone as polished as Isabella becoming so disheveled by a person like Brian.

The more I thought on it, the more it became clear that there was one difference between Isabella and me—I had friends and family who cared. The thought of Mom, Sebastian, Victoria, Lauren, and Leslie made me smile. They cared about me and wanted the best for me. None of them were malicious, and there was no reason for me to be so overwhelmed by the wedding when Lauren had arranged the services of her wedding planner. I was silly to have dismissed Eda. Why let others manage me when I could hand them off to Eda and have her manage them all for me?

My thoughts were cut off by the sound of footsteps in the foyer. I walked out into the hallway to see it was Sebastian. He looked bedraggled, but he smiled when he saw me. Boy, did I love this man. I walked toward him and sank into his arms.

"How was your nap?" I asked.

"Short. Couldn't go back to sleep after waking up and thinking about my mother."

"You want to talk about it?" I asked as I led him into the library.

"I tried looking for her," he admitted, taking a seat on the couch.

"Oh?" I sank down next to him.

"She could be anywhere, but I figured there must be some sort of trail; she shouldn't be that hard to find, and maybe my grandmother just hadn't tried hard enough? But there's really nothing. I'm also not an expert, so I'm not sure where or how to look further. I have her locket and her name, but that's it."

That reminded me. "I can ask Nick. I forgot to ask him amongst the chaos today."

"I thought about that, and I'm glad you haven't asked him yet, actually. I'd rather not get Nick involved in my life. That guy can find details out of the trash you threw away last night."

"Exactly! He'd be able to find your mother. He found Harrison, didn't he?"

"And then got his place ransacked and accosted his family," Sebastian pointed out.

"Well, yes, but I think this time he won't go to that extent."

"How so?"

I sighed, leaning back into the couch. "We had a talk."

Sebastian swiveled round to face me. His eyes had gone big. "You saw him? Where?"

"At Isabella's. Just like Lauren suggested."

"Well, I guess that doesn't surprise me. He'll follow her anywhere."

I put a hand on Sebastian's arm. "Let me ask him. It would be so good to have some closure. Maybe she'd even want to come to our wedding?"

"But we don't even know if she's still alive!" Sebastian said, throwing his hands up.

"Well, let me ask Nick to help. He'll find her, I know he will, and he'll be discreet. None of this breaking into people's places. Besides, he knows I'll come after him if he does that again."

Sebastian stared at me. "You threatened him?"

"No, but I can get really mad."

Sebastian started laughing, and it was so good to see him smiling and happy for a change. He laughed so hard I started laughing too. It was the most cathartic feeling, and I was conscious we both needed it.

Sebastian's smile was still on his face when he said, "Okay. If you insist."

"I insist. I really think this is a good idea."

He sighed, clearly resigned. "Okay then."

I gave his hand a squeeze. "I'll call him right now." And I took out my phone and dialed then and there.

"What do you want?" Nick grumbled into the phone.

"Well, hello to you too," I said. Sebastian raised an eyebrow, but I waved him off. "I'm calling because I've thought of two things that you can do for us to make up for your misdeeds."

There was silence on the other end of the line, but then I heard loud whispering as if he had muffled the receiver before coming back on. "How can I help?" His tone had changed completely, as if he was accepting his fate.

"We need your expertise to find Sebastian's mother."

"That's it?"

"Too easy for you?"

His voice was smug. "Absolutely."

"Then you should have no trouble in letting us know where she is by tomorrow."

"Well . . ."

"You just said this was too easy for you," I pointed out again.

"But tomorrow is too soon," he said, now sounding irritated. "I do have other things I have to do, you know."

I heard some commotion, and next thing I knew, Isabella was on the line. "He'll do it, and then he'll be free. But not in a day. Give him a week. After this, I don't want you and I to have any more interactions ever again."

My feathers were ruffled, especially because Isabella was setting the ultimatums. "No," I disagreed. "This is easy for him, and it will take more than that before he is pardoned for what he did."

"Fine. He'll cover all the renovation costs for Harrison's shop then."

"It has to be pristine," I said firmly.

"Fine. Pristine then."

"And a better security system needs to be installed."

I heard Nick complaining in the background, but Isabella must have shut him down quick because the line went silent. I let them think on my proposition while Sebastian gave me a questioning look.

Isabella came back on the line. "Fine. We agree to your terms, but that's it."

"I can agree to that," I returned calmly, relieved that this was going easier than I'd imagined.

"Good. It's done. But before I go, I recommend you take a look at today's newspaper," Isabella said snidely, then hung up.

Sebastian leaned forward and grabbed the hand that wasn't holding the phone. "That seemed to go well."

"Yeah, better than I thought. Nick barely protested at all. He agreed to look for your mother and get back in touch with us before the end of next week. And Isabella seemed very shaken up and determined to resolve what happened to Harrison's shop."

"Nick will always do what Isabella says. That's never changed, even though it was always a source of tension when she and I were together. She couldn't ask for anyone more devoted to her than Nick. If only she'd open her heart to him."

I agreed, but I was done talking about them. "Well, that's enough about Isabella and Nick. I'm going to get the newspaper."

"Why don't I get it?" Sebastian said, standing up and walking to the door before I even had a chance to push off the sofa. He came back a few minutes later, reading one of the articles on the front page.

"What does it say?" I said, almost too scared to ask.

"The same old stuff," came his careful reply.

"Let me see!" I reached out for the paper, but he was too fast as he walked away from me, folding it up and tucking it under his arms.

"There's no need. You just keep doing you, Anne."

My heart sank. "I want to see," I insisted.

"Why?"

"Because I want to see what people are saying." *And because it will also affect you.*

Sebastian assessed me closely. "Do you care about what they think?"

I looked at him for a second. My gut reaction was no, I didn't care, but if I let my walls down a bit, I knew I did care. I cared a lot. I wanted people to like me. I wanted them to understand that I wasn't just throwing Anthony's money around willy-nilly, that I would continue his legacy. *Wait—his legacy? Ahhhh! I needed to carry on his legacy!*

I released a breath, imploring, "I do care, Sebastian. I've tried not to, but I'd be lying to myself if I did. I do care what others think, and I'm not going to change who I am to please them, but I can do things differently. I can be a bit more open to how traditions were done for the Wilkens family as well. They were—and are—a big part of this community, and I don't want it to all go away just because I'm petty or lazy."

"Anne—"

"I know I'm not petty or lazy, but others have to see it to believe it. People don't know me. Isabella was right, no matter how much I don't want to admit it."

Sebastian froze. "What did she say?"

"She agreed with Lauren that I need to invite all the people who I invited to the gala. Make them feel like family and welcome them. I think people are feeling left out right now, whereas they were always welcomed by Anthony."

"You don't have to, Anne. You know that, right?"

"I know, but I'm starting to think that Isabella and Lauren are right. Lauren's wedding planner seems capable of organizing a fabulous event, and you've reminded me time and time again that I have the money. I should spend it to simplify my life, so I can focus on the things I want to do. So, now can I see the article?"

Sebastian hesitated, but I saw the exact moment he decided it was futile to keep it from me. He handed me the paper, and I read the article.

"I am miffed that Anne hasn't invited me or my family to her wedding, or anyone for that matter," says Gertrude Forsaken. "She really is greedy and keeping to herself. That's not how the Wilkens used to be, and I'm worried Anne is going to destroy the Wilkens's legacy of being open, inviting, and giving. It just isn't right. What about the common folks? They used to be invited for a party in the garden once a year, given the opportunity to experience the finesse they don't usually get to experience."

Gertrude isn't one to mince words, and usually that turns away a lot of people, but right now, I think everyone is feeling the same. Is the town going to lose the family that was so philanthropic? As she said, the Wilkens family were very inviting and giving. And this is a true impression of what we've come to expect of our precious Wilkens family. . . .

Sebastian said, "You see, it's just a bunch of fluff. Gertrude is known for saying anything to appeal to the public. She lives to shock people, but most people don't listen to her, Anne."

I was deep in thought and didn't hear the rest of what

Sebastian said. I was too busy thinking that if there were a lot of people like Gertrude and the lady at the restaurant out there—many who thought they needed to tell me what to do —then they would never stop. Why make my life more diffi-cult than it had to be? I had already decided to hire Eda. She could deal with all the input coming in—everything from my close friends and family to the community at large. Besides, it's not like I *wouldn't* like a wedding that was a mix of Amer-ican and traditional Taiwanese culture. Combine that with the pizazz of a Wilkens wedding, and it would be fun—so much fun. A party for the masses.

"Anne! Anne, you still there?" Sebastian asked, his brows pinched together.

I smiled at him. "Yes, I'm good. I'm going to hire Eda, the wedding planner. Take this whole thing off my plate. Why should I have to field everyone's opinion? She'll do a much better job than me. Though, are you sure your uncle was behind these articles? Or at least the earlier ones? I feel like it's taken on a life of its own now."

Sebastian's lips thinned. "I know he was. I just have a feeling, but I'm going to follow up with Ms. Donaldson and see if she's been able to do anything. Clearly, someone's still behind this one, and I bet it's Uncle Roger."

"Okay. Well, I'm going to put this behind me for now and call Eda to see if she can still fit me in, then I'm going to fly to Taiwan."

Sebastian was nodding, but then he stopped. "Wait, what?"

I had the biggest grin on my face. I realized this is what I should have done to begin with. I explained, "Grace was able to convince Harrison to go to Taiwan, so they're headed there tomorrow. Grace invited me, but I had so much going on and hadn't even spoken to Nick when she asked me. But now that's all sorted and I've decided to engage Eda, I'm free to go. So, I'm going to go with them to meet Mary. My whole goal was to get Harrison and Mary together, and I lost sight of that amongst all this chaos."

But as I said that another plan came to mind, and I excitedly reached out for Sebastian's hand. "Wait! Why don't you come with me? We could get married in Taiwan! I could ask Mom and Victoria to come too. Then, we can all come back for the big wedding, which I'm going to think of as another party. What do you think?"

I knew my grin had gotten bigger the more I kept talking. Sebastian was standing there chuckling and shaking his head, no doubt amused at my sudden change in plans. He enveloped me in his warm arms, and I rested my head on his chest without hesitation. He was my world and always would be.

"All I want is to be married to you, Anne," he said softly, his chest rumbling under my cheek. "But I do know we're not going to fly to Taiwan to do it. I don't want to disappoint you, but I know my father won't be flying to Taiwan, and my only request is that he be present for our formal union. Can you live with that?" He raised his hand and ran his thumb across my cheek.

I breathed him in and held him tightly. I wasn't hurt by his curbing of my impromptu idea. In the end, Sebastian was all I wanted. Everything else was just fluff. "Then we'll do it here in front of hundreds of people."

"Yes, I'm beginning to think we don't have any other choice. But let's make it ours by ensuring we have our immediate family and friends sitting right next to us. That way, it will still feel like we know everyone."

I laughed. "It'll be a nice illusion."

Sebastian's phone rang, breaking the moment, and we saw it was Jack.

"You go and talk to Jack," I insisted. "I'm going to give

Eda a call."

Sebastian gave me a gentle kiss on my forehead before walking out of the library, and I settled into the couch in a much better mood. I had a plan now, one that I not only could carry out but that I also felt great about.

Eda's phone went straight to voicemail, but instead of leaving a message, I decided to give Lauren a call. I wanted things to start moving immediately, and I knew Lauren would be so excited she would get the ball rolling in any way she could.

She picked up on the first ring. "Anne! Oh, I just had the most wonderful idea."

"Lauren!" I exclaimed excitedly, then I laughed because she kept talking. I tried again. "Lauren!"

"Yes, Anne?"

"I'd like to hire Eda to plan the wedding."

"Really?" she squealed.

"Yes, really. I want to put the whole thing into her capable hands."

"That's wonderful news! I'll call her up right now. Are you free today? She'll usually fit me in as soon as possible, so I can try to get you in today. We have lots to do to get things ready. Oh, I'm so excited, Anne. You won't be disappointed. She can pull off the littlest detail without you even realizing you needed it. Eda's worth every penny, I assure you. Oh, and there should be a contract in the folder she gave you. You could get that all signed and ready, so when we meet with her it'll be done. We don't have much time—lots to do! Okay, I'm going to go now. I'll talk to you later."

After I hung up, I sat there on the couch, just smiling. It was nice to hear Lauren so excited, rambling on in her usual way. This wedding thing was more her jam than mine, and it felt good to see her so happy to help me out. It also didn't hurt to know that I wouldn't be the one planning it anymore.

CHAPTER 20

LAUREN SET UP A TIME TO MEET WITH EDA. I
decided they would meet me here at home so I could show
Eda the mansion and discuss my ideas for a garden wedding.
Following that, she was free to embellish as much as she
wanted.

This morning, I had finally opened the wedding folder Eda
gave me to see if there were any details I should have been
thinking of before she showed up. I gawked at her price—she
took twenty percent commission! The next many sheets gave
examples of weddings that cost anywhere between thirty
thousand and all the way up to five hundred thousand or
more. There were images of weddings in numerous locations,
illustrating an abundance of beautiful flowers and huge
numbers of people.

The more I looked through the images, the more fasci-
nated I became with the enchanting look of them. It was like
entering into another world. A fantasy world where dragons
and creatures could pop out at any time—a safe place for the
imagination to run wild. I instantly knew this wedding could
be much bigger than the Christmas gala. It would be a party

for the masses. The more I thought on the idea, the better I liked it.

A recent memory popped into my head. It was of Lauren saying a wedding wasn't really your own, that it was for everyone else. At the end of the day, being married was all I cared about; therefore, all these other decisions were what a wedding planner could accommodate. A smile curved my lips. The idea of employing Eda was looking more and more to my liking.

"Miss Anne?" I looked up to see Ben hovering in the doorway to the library. "Lauren and Eda are here."

"Excellent." I stood up and gave the paperwork a once-over to make sure everything was completed and turned back to Ben. "Please invite them into the sitting room."

Ben gave me a sharp nod and went to do my bidding. I took a deep breath and walked over to the sitting room. No sooner had I made myself comfortable than there was a squeal and Lauren was running over to give me a big hug.

"I'm so excited you've decided to work with Eda!" she said.

Eda walked up to me with a warm smile and held out her hand. "Yes, I'm very excited to be working with you, Anne."

I clasped Eda's hand warmly, giving her a smile in return. "I am too! Let's all sit down. Do you want anything to eat or drink first? Cook made some cakes for me to try for the wedding. Would you two like to try some too?"

"Yes, I love cake tasting!" Lauren exclaimed.

Eda was much more professional and just nodded. She was busy pulling paperwork together, and I noticed it looked like the contract she had given me. I pulled the papers out of the folder I had brought with me and handed them to her, saying, "I already signed everything."

She looked at me with wide eyes. "Wow, you really did sign everything," she said, flipping through the paperwork.

Lauren smiled. "I told you Anne is the best. You two are going to work so well together. In fact, Eda, you might end up liking Anne more than me by the end of this."

"Hey, don't say that!" I said.

"I'm just kidding," Lauren said. "But I know Eda is going to take care of you so well you're going to want to hire her for other parties after this."

"Lauren is being too nice," Eda said. "Now, how about we taste some of that cake while we talk further?"

"Oh yes, I'll be right back."

I walked to the kitchen to find Cook huddled over a big pot on the stove. "Hi, Cook."

She looked up at me while in the act of raising a spoon to her mouth. "Anne, come here, you should try this."

I walked over and tasted the broth and made a soft moan. "That is so good. What is it?"

"A lamb soup I'm making for your wedding."

"Oh, everyone will love that."

"I know they will," she said in a very matter-of-fact tone.

I hid a smile. "I can't wait to see what else you make. Speaking of food, though, could we have some of the cakes you made for the wedding brought to the sitting room? Lauren, Eda, and I would like to taste some."

"Of course. Lavender and I will be right up with them."

"Thank you, Cook, but I can stay and help you bring them up. I'm not taking no for an answer, either. I'm perfectly capable of holding and carrying cake, and I'm hungry, so to ask me to leave and wait would be torture."

Cook just stared at me with a look in her eyes that told me she was aching to throw me out of the kitchen, but, thankfully, she turned with a huff and headed to the refrigerator without another word.

I quietly waited as she got everything together, knowing that Cook was only agreeing to my assistance because she wanted us to taste her delicious concoctions and also because she wanted to see Eda. She had mentioned a couple of times today that she hoped Eda knew she was the one that would be catering my wedding. She'd announced quite firmly that she wouldn't tolerate anyone else doing so. I had tried to sooth her, telling her I would never hire anyone else for the job, because at the end of the day, it was still mine and Sebastian's wedding, and we wouldn't think of using anyone else. That seemed to placate Cook, but it didn't stop her from wanting to meet Eda in person. It made me smile.

We brought five cakes into the sitting room. There was German chocolate, carrot cake, plain vanilla with strawberries in the middle and on top, dark chocolate with multiple layers of coffee icing, and a rum cake with icing drizzled all over it. I'd had to beg Cook to make the rum cake. She said it wasn't traditional, but I told her she could decorate it however she liked. I also made the point that we would have other cakes there that were more traditional.

"Cook, these look divine!" Lauren said. "Eda and I were just saying that Anne is so fortunate to have you cater her wedding. I know so many who would pay you top dollar to cater their parties."

I couldn't have set this meeting up better!

Cook was beaming and trying not to show it. "Well, I only cook for Anne, but thank you."

I'm sure she had a whole speech ready for Eda, but with what Lauren said, she obviously decided to forego it and instead gave a big smile and a little curtsy—which I had never seen her do before—and walked out of the room.

"Wow, I've never seen Cook speechless before," Lauren said.

I let out the laugh I had been holding in. "She was going to make sure she was the one catering my wedding, no matter what anyone said. I'm sure she had a whole speech ready to prove otherwise, but Lauren, you threw her off her game. I think she's very happy."

"Well, good. There's no one better than Cook. Now, let's try these cakes."

We ate all five of them and couldn't decide, so, in the end, Eda said we could have them all. "I can work with Cook on making them into a traditionally tiered cake with different layers, or we could do multiples cakes, one of each flavor, all decorated differently," she suggested.

I couldn't have been happier. "That all sounds wonderful; either option works for me. I'll leave the final decision up to you and Cook."

She nodded. "Sounds great. I've made a note of that. Why don't we move on to the wedding itself? Can you tell me what you had in mind?"

"Well, I had wanted something small and intimate, just family and friends. It was going to be about twenty people, and I was thinking of having it here in the garden. The only florals would be the ones me and my bridesmaids would be holding. The rest would be organically decorated by the garden itself. I was going to get Anders Printing to make the invitations, but now that I'm saying this, I realized I dropped the ball on that." I sighed. "I had no idea a wedding could get so out of hand."

"It doesn't have to, but it tends to become that way more often than not," Eda said. "But that's what you have me for. The last time I saw you, you mentioned you wanted purple and light pink with a dash of green for your colors. Is that still the case?"

I laughed. "Do brides change their wedding colors all the time?"

"More than you think," Eda said, smiling.

"Then, as a matter-of-fact, I have too. Though, I'm not sure which to pick."

"What do you mean?" Lauren asked.

"I had light purple and pinks picked out for my bouquet and was going to center the wedding colors around that, but my cousin, Leslie, said that I had to have Chinese red. There was no exception. Except, I'm not sure I want an all red wedding."

But Eda was nodding. "I can work with that."

My brows flew up. "You can?"

Lauren piped in with a grin, "I told you she can make anything happen, even on a tight deadline."

I looked at Eda, wondering if she was cringing at what Leslie said, but she didn't even blink an eye. What a wonder it must be to have a demeanor like hers. Every challenge seemed to roll right off her shoulders.

"You said you had wanted something small and intimate. Is that not the case anymore?" Eda now asked.

Lauren started talking before I could get a word in. "It's like I've been telling her, it's pertinent that she invites more than just the people she knows well. Sir Anthony was generous, she'll want to continue to spread that goodwill."

"Ms. Lauren?" came a voice at the door.

We all turned to see Cook standing there. Had she been standing there the whole time?

"Yes, Cook?" Lauren asked.

"Can you come and help me with tasting some of the food? I need a taster, and you seem the best option, as Anne needs to keep talking to Eda."

"Oh, I'd love to!" Lauren was out the door before we knew it. It made me happy to know she loved food as much as I did.

"Your cook is indispensable," Eda said.

"I know, I love her. Her daughter is just as feisty and professional."

"Well, now that it's just the two of us, can you tell me why the change to a big wedding?"

I gestured at Lauren's vacant seat. "It's what Lauren said. Her cousin, Isabella, also said the same thing."

"But it's not their wedding," Eda said gently. Her face was sincere, and I could tell she wasn't trying to persuade me but instead was trying to remind me that it wasn't anybody else's choice.

I was very close to capitulating and going back to a small wedding, but then I remembered the look in Isabella's eyes and what she had said to me. There was also the fact the wedding itself was never a big deal to Sebastian and me. We would be happy getting married at city hall. But I was in a different position than what I used to be in when it was just Mom and me. I'd inherited the Wilkens's fortune, and I had a legacy to continue. So, since I had the means, why not provide the wedding that everyone was expecting and invite more people? It would be an ode to Anthony in its own way —an opportunity to have the wedding that he and my grand-mother, Rose, should have had.

"I've thought about it, and I think they're right," I said to Eda. "It's a celebration, and it would be fun to have more people. We can have a live band, the open bar that Sebastian wants, a few photo booths, appetizers, full course meals, and anything else people usually have at a wedding. Sorry, that sounds like I don't know much about them, and it's true, because I haven't been to any weddings before, except for a traditional Taiwanese one in Taiwan. Oh, which reminds me, I wanted to do red envelopes as gifts. I already have every-thing I could ever need, so I wanted the money to be donated to charity. But a lot of people are upset about all this opulence and the red envelopes, not really understanding what it's about, so I'm not sure what to do about that. We don't need more stuff. Would that fall under something you can mitigate?"

"Absolutely," Eda said, jotting something down. "I have plenty to work on from here. I'm assuming Lucia is still your florist?"

I nodded.

"Great, well, with these notes, the florist decided upon, Cook doing the catering, and your bridesmaids and their contact information confirmed, I have everything in hand. So why don't we go see if Lauren needs some saving, and we'll call it a day? I'll take a look at the garden on my way out and get back to you at the end of the week with some updates and choices."

"That sounds like a great plan."

I breathed a sigh of relief while following Eda out into the hallway. I could already feel the weight falling off my shoulders.

CHAPTER 21

Now that the wedding was rolling on its own with the help of Eda, I felt a lot better. I called Grace and told her I would take her up on going to Taiwan with them, and she sounded so excited I felt bad for saying no in the first place.

"You sure you don't want me to come with you?" Sebastian asked, watching me pack. "You're going for a couple days, right?"

I nodded. "Yeah, it's just to see Mary and make sure Grace and Harrison are able to see her too. Plus, I want to see her for myself, as I don't think Mary is doing so well. I'd love you to come along Sebastian, but I know you've got plenty to take care of here without worrying about another trip."

"That's true, but I like traveling with you."

"That's sweet," I said, turning to find him watching my every move. "But it's creeping me out that you're staring at me like that."

"Well, what if I sauntered over and pulled you up close to me?" he said, walking over and doing just that.

"I'd welcome it."

Before I could lean in for a kiss, he had thrown me on the bed and was tickling me without mercy. I couldn't get away and was laughing so hard I kicked the pillows and blankets onto the floor.

"I'm going to miss you while you're gone," Sebastian said against my hair as we lay there quietly, cuddled together.

"It's only for two days. Well, plus travel, but still!"

"I'm nervous about Nick finding my mother," he admitted softly. "What if he really does? I'm not sure I want to see her."

"Oh, sweetheart." I rolled onto my side to face him. "I told Nick to call me when he finds her so I can screen his call."

"I know. You said you'd do that."

"Then that means you'll have time to decide if you want to meet her. We don't know what she wants out of all of this either. It's been so long."

He was quiet for a moment, letting that sink in. "You're right. I've got to stay here, anyways. Jack and I need to finish pulling together all the paperwork Geraldine saved. She didn't have a good filing system, just stuffed everything into drawers—and I mean *drawers* of notes. There's probably a whole room worth of files that are not categorized or sorted in any fashion." He ran his hand through his hair and let out a deep sigh. "Can we agree that, once we get married and all these mysteries are solved, we can just live a quiet life? No more surprises?"

I laughed. "Yes! Yes to all of that. I can fund a charity and run the ones that the Wilkens Foundation already run, and you can keep doing your lawyering stuff."

"Lawyering stuff?" Sebastian guffawed. "I'm going to miss your words."

"It's only two days!"

"Anything with Harrison usually takes a lot longer, so I'm not expecting you back in two days."

"I will be back as soon as I can, and it won't be that long, I promise. We still have a wedding to plan, remember?"

"Have I told you how proud I am of you for hiring Eda? You never let things go."

"Was that a compliment and a diss at the same time?"

"I'm talented like that." Sebastian gave me the softest kiss, and I started thinking that I didn't want to leave for Taiwan. I could just let Grace and Harrison figure it out with Mary on their own. But then Sebastian pushed back to look at me, his hand on my cheek. "I'm going to miss you, Anne, but I know you need to go to Taiwan to talk to Mary and Harrison. Make sure you get them all back here to the States so they can be at our wedding."

He suddenly rolled off the bed and went to my desk. He came back holding my little red journal—the one he had given me.

"What's this?" I asked, looking between the journal and his face.

"You should start writing in it. Maybe your granddaughter will read it one day," he said, handing me the journal.

I held it for a moment, contemplating what he said. "I had meant to start writing in it a while ago, but you know, life happened." I shrugged.

"And life will always get in the way, so why not start now? You could start by writing about how Harrison came over to meet you and then disappeared, or you could start when you met your whole extended family for the first time. Or you could start today. There's really no rule to writing in a journal."

"Well, I'll put it in my backpack and think about it on the plane."

He nodded, smiling at me. "Good, and on that, we better get you to the airport."

"Yes, let's go. I'm excited about traveling internationally again." I sprang off the bed and swung my backpack on and we headed outside to the waiting car. The driver would take me to the airport. From there, Grace, Harrison, and I would fly out altogether.

I could have flown direct from Seattle to Taipei, but this journey to find my family had started out with me on my own. I had family now, and this final meeting didn't need to end the way it had begun. We would do this together.

Harrison groaned. "You two ladies are going to be the death of me."

Grace and I exchanged smiles.

"This is for your own good, dear," Grace said, patting Harrison's leg.

We had taken off about thirty minutes ago, and Harrison had been gripping the arm rest since the wheels left the ground.

"Harrison, it's going to be okay. We'll both be there with you," I said.

"Yes, but she's never going to let you two be there while she berates me. I'll be by myself."

"Well, who said for you to wait this long to go see her?" Grace said.

"I may never have gone back. We still don't even know if she wants to see me."

"She does!" Grace and I both exclaimed.

But Harrison wasn't listening. "You know what? I'm going to go tell the pilot to turn the plane around. I can't believe you talked me into this." He started to stand, and we each took one of his arms and pulled him back into his seat.

Grace said, "First of all, the seatbelt sign is on; second of all, they'll never let you into the cockpit; and thirdly, we are going to Taiwan to see Mary. That's final. Now sit back and try to relax. Or at least let Anne and I relax. Here, watch a movie. There are even Asian ones on here. You can find one you like. Catch up on those films Leslie wanted to watch with you that you still haven't gotten around to seeing."

"Because they're all kid movies!" Harrison grumbled.

"Who cares what they are. Your daughter wants to watch them with you. Anyways, just do whatever you want. I'm going to watch a movie, and you are going to leave Anne alone. We're going to go see Mary, and that's final."

Harrison leaned over to look at me. "Do you have anything you would like to say?"

"No," I said, trying not to laugh. It was fun to see Grace putting her foot down.

Harrison let out a loud "humph," tilted his head back, and closed his eyes.

Grace and I just chuckled, which elicited another "humph."

The rest of the flight was uneventful, and I even enjoyed the food. I was so happy to be back on an airplane and going somewhere.

We disembarked at Taipei to a sea of people going through immigration. I had expected Grace and Harrison to go through the citizen line, but, apparently, they were no longer citizens because they hadn't come back in so long. I breathed a sigh of relief that my American citizenship wasn't like that. The three of us stood in line behind what felt like a hundred people, all looking just as miserable as we were waiting in line for who knew how long for the person at the front to stamp our passports.

By the time we exited, we were all starving. It didn't take much persuasion from Harrison to convince Grace and I that we needed to eat first before meeting Mary. The bus ride was thrilling. I had forgotten how pretty the view was of the city with the mountains in the background. I had also forgotten the thrill of going to a different country and losing myself in its scenery and culture. I really missed it.

Everything smelled so good when we got to the underground mall part of the terminal. Grace was like a kid in a candy shop. Taiwan had changed so much since she had last been there and she wanted to go into every store. We finally settled on a restaurant that offered small plates of every kind of food we could ever want. It was like Taiwanese tapas, and we ordered almost one of everything, gobbling it all down like we hadn't just eaten a few hours ago.

With our stomachs full, we wandered around some more before Grace finally put her foot down. "Okay, we cannot stay here forever. I told Ming-Yue we were grabbing some food to eat and would stop by their place soon after. Mary will be waiting."

"You think Ming-Yue told her?" I asked.

"She said she would so Mary is not surprised," Grace said.

"I guess we'll find out when we see Mary's reaction."

"I bet she doesn't want to see me," Harrison grumbled.

"That's not an option," Grace said. She dragged him upstairs and out of the terminal and into a taxi. "But first, we need to go to our hotel and offload our things so we don't show up with all this luggage."

CHAPTER 22

WE ARRIVED AT MARY'S COMPLEX, ONLY TO SEE Ming-Yue waiting for us at the main doors.

"This doesn't bode well," I said.

"She's probably just here to invite us in," Grace said, but her voice gave her away, and I knew she was nervous about the situation too.

"I think—" Harrison began.

"You don't get a say right now," Grace said, hooking her arm into Harrison's and dragging him toward Ming-Yue. I followed close behind.

"Harrison . . ." Ming-Yue started saying, but Harrison wouldn't look at her and stood off to the side, looking grumpy. Ming-Yue also decided to ignore him, but I could tell she was nervous at seeing Harrison. I didn't blame her, though. She hardly knew him before he ran off. She turned back to Grace and I. "I'm sorry to say that Mary isn't up to seeing you today," she said.

"See!" Harrison exclaimed, startling some of the people walking by. "She doesn't want to see me. This was a waste of time."

"Hush!" Grace said.

Thankfully, Harrison listened and kept quiet as Ming-Yue continued, "I know she wants to see you, but she's nervous, and she hasn't been well. It's all too much right now. I have made lunch reservations at Din Tai Fung for tomorrow. It's her favorite place to eat, and we can meet there. I will make sure she comes."

"That sounds like a good plan," I said. "She must be so overwhelmed."

"She is. It's been so long, and she keeps saying how mad she is at you," Ming-Yue said, looking at Harrison.

To Harrison's credit, he hung his head in shame. We all knew it was his fault all this time had passed. He didn't say anything this time, and Grace put an arm around him.

"Why don't we go see some sights before going back to the hotel to rest? We can be well rested before meeting Mary tomorrow," she suggested.

Ming-Yue nodded in agreement. Then she held out a hand. "Here, Mary wanted me to give you this."

Ming-Yue had three red envelopes in her hand, and we took them, thanking her. I felt embarrassed that I hadn't brought one. It hadn't even crossed my mind, but Grace hadn't forgotten. She pulled out one from her bag and handed it to Ming-Yue, saying it was from the three of us.

We got back into the taxi, and Grace said she wanted to go see Taipei 101. Harrison didn't even mutter a sound. He sat quietly the whole way there.

I left them on the first floor. Grace was rubbing Harrison's arm while I went up to buy tickets. In hindsight, we should have settled into Taiwan for a couple of days before forcing Mary and Harrison to meet with each other. But it was too late now.

As I was paying for the tickets, another idea came to me. I bought the tickets and rushed back down to the first floor.

"Here are your tickets. It's an amazing view up there. I'm going to go run an errand while you two go up. I'll meet you back here once I'm done."

"Where are you going?" Grace asked, still rubbing Harrison's arm.

"Just an errand. I'll see you soon." I rushed out and headed off before Grace could ask any more questions. But I could feel both of their eyes boring into my back as I left the mall.

I hailed the first taxi I saw and asked the driver to take me to a place that sold the best pineapple cakes. After picking up twenty boxes—for Mary, Ming-Yue, Harrison and Grace, Leslie, Erik, Vanessa and Paul, Sebastian and me, and some for the staff—we headed to the hotel where I dropped off my impulsive buys. Grabbing the bag for Mary and Ming-Yue, I then headed over to Mary's.

I stood on the sidewalk looking up at Mary's complex in awe. Not that long ago, I came here for the first time to meet a relative I had no idea about. My life had expanded so much since then, and I really wanted Harrison to have that same connection with his family, too, no matter how stubborn he was—or how stubborn Mary was.

My phone started ringing, and I saw it was Ming-Yue. "Hi, Ah Yi."

"How are you, Anne? You called?"

"Yes, I'm actually downstairs and was wondering if I could come up to see Mary? Harrison and Grace are at Taipei 101, so it's just me."

I waited in silence for a few seconds before I heard Ming-Yue put down the phone and shuffle away, hopefully to relay my request to Mary. I crossed my fingers and toes and everything else I could think of. She had to see me. Well, I guess she didn't have to, but I really wanted her to.

I heard the sound of the phone getting picked up before

Ming-Yue said in a happy tone, "Come on up. Mary is excited to see you."

"Excellent. I'll be right up."

This time I took the stairs instead of the elevator. No claustrophobia for me, even if I was the only one in the elevator. Ming-Yue was waiting for me at the door, and I paused for a second, wondering if she was going to shoo me away, but she was smiling as she welcomed me in.

"I'm glad you came. Mary was ready to see all of you this morning when she woke up, but she had a sudden change of mind when I reminded her Harrison was arriving soon. I have been trying to persuade her to let you all come back, but I'm glad you came back anyway. She is very happy to see you."

"I'm right here," Mary said, leaning on a cane and hobbling over to the couch. It had only been two months, but Mary looked like she had aged years. A part of me wanted to reach out and help her, but, knowing Mary, I knew she would be too proud to allow my assistance.

"Sit, Anne. Sit right here," she insisted, tapping the seat next to her. "I know why you are here."

"Really?" I was curious what she would say about not letting us up earlier. I placed the pineapple cakes in front of her, hoping they were a good peace offering.

"You are disappointed that Harrison has finally come and I won't let him see me, no?"

"I am, but that's not why I came."

"Oh?"

Ming-Yue had taken the cakes away, and I saw she was opening some to place on a tray as I said to Mary, "See, I understand that you and Harrison are both nervous. I was super nervous to meet you for the first time myself. You raised Harrison and he ran away, leaving clues for you to find him all these years but never showing his face. I get it. I can tell you Harrison is just as nervous as you are, if not more so because he knows he should have come earlier. Much earlier."

"If you understand, then why are you and Grace forcing us to see each other so quickly?"

Ming-Yue placed the cakes in front of us, and we both took one, needing something to do with our hands.

"Yes, I realized that we were forcing the issue. So, I have an idea, and I wanted to run it by you first."

"Does Harrison know?" Mary's voice was sharp.

"No, you're the first I'm telling." That seemed to make Mary happy as she sat up a bit straighter and looked at me expectantly.

"Bettie has asked Harrison to do a meet and greet at the art gallery," I began. "He finally agreed, and Grace and I are holding him to it this time. It's going to be tomorrow morning at ten, before our reservation for lunch." I held up my hand, knowing what Mary was thinking. "You don't have to make an appearance. But I thought it would be a safe place for you to come and see him without him seeing you—if that's what you wanted. I know you're curious to see what he's like, and you want to see Grace too. I thought you could just hang out in the back and listen and watch him from a distance. Then, if you're comfortable, you can text me, and I can bring him over to you. What do you think?"

Mary stared at me for what seemed like hours, but a small smile had appeared at the corner of her mouth. She liked the idea, and that made my heart soar.

"I get to say when Harrison can meet me? Even though he's made me wait all these years?"

"That's right." Whatever it took to get her to the art gallery. And she wasn't wrong with her estimation either. Harrison *had* made her wait a very long time.

"I will think about it." Mary took a bite of her pineapple cake, but I saw a small smile spread across her face.

"That's all I ask." I took a bite of my cake, too, savoring the sweet, chewy taste.

After eating her cake, Mary looked at me, a determined glint in her eyes. "Now, about your wedding."

"You heard about it? I'm sorry. I keep meaning to ask you to come, but it's been one thing after another."

"Anne, of course, I know about it. Grace told me."

The relief was sharp. "Oh, good. I would love it if you could come, Mary—you and Ming-Yue and the others, but I don't want to put pressure on you about traveling all the way to Portland."

"That's up to me, isn't it?" I could see some of the Mary I had met two months ago coming out of her shell.

"Yes. Yes, it is."

"It's with that boy I met last time, isn't it?"

I tensed up. "Yes."

"I like him." She gave a sharp nod. "Good, I will think about attending the wedding."

I hadn't known I had wanted her approval until I felt a weight slide off my back. "Don't tire yourself out. It's okay—"

Mary held up a hand to stop me. "Speaking of tire, I'm going to go take a nap now. Ming-Yue will show you out." She stood up and started shuffling back to her room.

As Ming-Yue escorted me out, I watched as Mary disappeared into her room. "Do you think Mary will come?" I asked her daughter.

"I don't know. She's irritated more and more lately. But especially since you called her saying Harrison had visited you. I think she feels a bit spiteful that he would show up at your house unannounced when he never knew you, but he didn't come to visit her."

"I hadn't thought of that. I can see how she's upset by that. Try to get her to come and see Harrison from a distance tomorrow. Maybe if Mary sees him, she'll have a change of heart. I know the two of them miss each other and really want to see each other again."

"We all know that, but it's up to them."

My only thought as I descended the stairs was, *Not if I have anything to do with it.*

THE NEXT MORNING HARRISON WAS NOT IN THE room when Grace and I woke up. We both dialed his phone to no avail. It kept going to voicemail.

"I can't believe he's doing this right now," Grace said, sitting on the couch with her head in her hands.

"I'm sure he just went for a walk." Well, I sure hoped he only went for a walk and would come back to the hotel any minute now.

"He's been running for so long I don't know if he even knows how to stop," Grace said.

"He wouldn't leave you alone." I was sure of it.

"You're with me—I'm not alone," Grace spit out. "Sorry, I'm so frustrated. He promised me he would give this a chance, after all these years. And I'm so happy to be home again. I want to explore our country and see how it's changed in all these years. And it's changed a lot. But he's still running."

"Look, I—"

The door opened, and we both turned to see Harrison

come in carrying bags of what smelled like delicious break-fast food.

"Where have you been?" Grace yelled, marching over to the door.

"I bought food," Harrison said, holding up the bags for us to see.

Yup, definitely food. And my stomach was growling, but I didn't dare walk between Grace and Harrison.

"It took you two hours to get food?!"

"I needed to clear my head. You don't know what it's like for me to come back here and see Mary."

"I don't? Is that what you think? I've missed her, too, you know. I've stuck by your side through all these years, not going to see her when I could have jumped on a plane by myself and flown over at any time. I stayed by your side for you, Harrison!"

"Well, you should have!" he cried back.

Grace thrust her hands on her hips. "You could have left a note. I thought you had run off again."

"Why would I do that? I promised you I wouldn't." Harrison looked hurt, and I started to walk up to them, but Grace wasn't finished.

"Because you've been running for so long. I don't know if you're ever going to meet Mary. She's probably just as scared as you are."

I finally got the courage to walk up to them. I touched Grace on the arm. "Um, Grace?"

She whirled to look at me, and I almost dropped her arm and ran for it. Her eyes could have sent darts straight through me. "Yes?"

"We're all hungry, and um . . ." I pointed to Harrison's bag of food. "He's back. That's what matters. It's good for a person to go for a walk to clear their head. And he's back." I pointed both my hands at Harrison this time.

She slowly turned back to Harrison and said, "We are going to the gallery today."

"Yes," was all he needed to say.

Harrison spread out the breakfast food on the table, and for the next twenty minutes no one spoke. All we could hear were the sounds of our mouths chewing the most delicious food ever. Harrison had gotten a little of everything. There was lou buo gao, sao bing yu tao, soy milk, dang bing, lou buo si bing, sao bing with pork meat and eggs and lettuce, chive pockets, and xiao long bao. It was so good, and I made a note to get more of this delicious food tomorrow.

After we finished it was time to get ready to go to the art gallery. Harrison was very quiet the whole way there. When we arrived, he gawked at the line of people mingling outside the gallery.

"Are these people here for me?" he asked, his voice a touch awed.

"Maybe," I said.

"They don't know what you look like, so let's just walk in and find Bettie," Grace said firmly.

"Why don't we—?"

"No!" Grace and I both said.

We each hooked our arm through one of Harrison's and walked around the crowd and into the gallery. We went up the stairs and straight to Bettie's office—the same office I had first seen Harrison in all those months ago.

"You made it!" Bettie said upon seeing us. Her face was awed, and I saw her wipe a tear away from under her eye as she added in a whisper, "I can't believe you're here. You left so suddenly the last time I thought it was a dream."

I heard a small "humph" come from Harrison before Grace shoved him forward and said, "You have been so gracious working with us all these years, Bettie, and Anne and I weren't going to let Harrison miss another showing."

Bettie smiled and gestured to an adjacent table laden with food and refreshments. "Here, have something to drink. I had some snacks brought up too. We have not shown the new piece yet, as I was hoping you would come for the unveiling."

"You haven't?" Harrison looked startled. "Where has it been this whole time?"

"Safe. It's in a climate-controlled holding room, and my staff are currently getting it ready for display. I am so happy you are here." Bettie was beaming. I had never seen her so happy, and by Harrison's facial expression, he hadn't either.

"Maybe I should stay right—" Harrison began.

"No!" Grace and I said again.

"We should get down there, shouldn't we?" Grace added in a more persuasive voice.

I stood up to get us moving. "Yes, I think going down and seeing where we're supposed to be would be a good start." Anything to keep Harrison from running.

Thank goodness Bettie picked up on our cues. "Yes, yes, let's go down. I'll let the front desk know that we can let everyone come inside in fifteen minutes."

"Why are there so many people in line outside? I thought the museum opened at nine?" I asked.

"Oh, they're all here to see Harrison," Bettie said. "They love his work. People have been asking for years when he's going to come."

Bettie kept talking while walking down the hall, but the three of us had frozen in place. Harrison was rooted to the floor, whereas Grace and I had tightened our hold on him.

Harrison's voice was barely above a whisper. "You didn't say there would be this many people. It was supposed to be whoever happened to be in the museum at the time. It wasn't supposed to be a big event."

This time Grace humphed. "If we had told you it was a big event you would never have gotten on that airplane."

"So, you lied to me?" Harrison said, swinging his head to glare at Grace, who glared right back.

"No, I did not. I just didn't tell you everything, but that's nothing new."

Another glare from Harrison, but he knew he wasn't going to have his say.

And I knew right then we would be okay. Grace would never let Harrison back out of this now. We were in the building, and the only way out of here was down the stairs, which dropped us right into the foyer where all the people stood directly outside. I was certain at this point that Bettie wouldn't let him run out the front door, either.

Harrison started walking again, his footsteps heavy. Grace and I dragged him forward and down the stairs to where Bettie was waiting for us.

On the wall was what must be his painting covered in a white cloth. There were some chairs along the side of the wall, but otherwise, the space was empty. For some reason, I had thought there would be a table or a podium and rows of seats.

Bettie started speaking as if she had read my mind. "We decided to keep it informal. Harrison can either stand up front with both of you or by himself."

"With both of them." He said it with such finality that Bettie only paused for a second before moving on. We both looked at Harrison with a smile. I gave him a big hug, and he seemed to calm down a tad.

"There are so many people that we did not think chairs would fit in this space, so we only put some on the side for those who need a seat. Otherwise, everyone else will be standing. I'll do a short introduction, and then, Harrison, you can say what inspired you to create this painting. And then we'll reveal it."

"I have to speak." It was more of a statement than a question, and Harrison was gripping mine and Grace's hand pretty hard now.

"It can be a very short speech," Bettie said quickly. "Right after the reveal, we will have drinks and food brought in for everyone to enjoy. It would be great for you to meet with your fans, but I understand if you cannot stay."

At least she knew him well enough to know his limits. But to Harrison's credit, he didn't make a sound.

Bettie gave us all a huge smile. "I will let the guests in now. I'll be right back."

As we waited for Bettie to come back, the three of us turned to look at the covered painting.

"What are you going to say about this painting?" Grace asked.

"I don't know. It's very personal to me, and I didn't think I'd ever have to explain it to anyone."

Before we could respond, a bustle of people came swarming in, but Bettie was quick to stop them before they could approach Harrison. I was amazed at how well she managed the crowd. There were at least thirty here, and I could see more coming in. All of them were excited and taking pictures of the three of us standing up front. It was very disconcerting. I knew Harrison's work was famous, but it hadn't really sunk in as to what that meant. Noticing Harrison starting to shuffle back, it was obvious he wasn't used to this either. Knowing him, he probably had never shown his face anywhere before.

Bettie came up to us and asked Harrison, "Are you ready?"

Harrison just shrugged, and I couldn't blame him. I was overwhelmed looking at all the expectant faces, and I wasn't even the one in the spotlight.

In Mandarin, Bettie said, "Welcome to the Living Art Gallery. We are here today to celebrate Harrison Fei-Hong

Lin. This is our first time having him here in person, and I know you are all very excited to meet him, but we will save the questions till the end. Harrison has been with us for thirty years and continues to grow in his artistic abilities every year. What you see behind me is his newest piece. All his other works pale in comparison to this one. But I won't keep talking, as I know you want to hear from Harrison himself."

She motioned to Harrison, and with a light shove from Grace, he walked to the front. There was a few seconds of awkwardness, but when he started talking, you could tell people wanted to listen to his every word.

"These are my paintings. I'm not sure what to say except they came from inside me, but I couldn't tell you what inspired me or what they are about. My hands move across the canvas of their own free will, picking up color here and there and adding it where my muse thinks it'll fit best."

He walked to a small painting to the left. "I painted this one when I was sad and lonely. It was during one of the loneliest times in my life—a time when Grace was not there." He stopped to look at Grace and smiled. "And yet, you would never know because of the bright colors." The painting had splashes of purples and blues and dashes of red. It looked like a meadow of flowers rustling in the wind, paying tribute to the sole person sitting in the middle of the field.

Harrison continued on to the next one. "This one was when my first kid came. That was a joyous day." Again, he turned to look at Grace and gave her another smile. "It's why the focus is all on the child sitting in his mother's lap. I loved watching my wife and son interact."

The next one was dark, with shades of gray and black and flickers of white here and there. "This was during a happy time. It looks like happy times, doesn't it?" he asked, looking at the audience, who was hanging onto his every word. Some nodded in agreement with him. "I love playing with the darker colors, because it's what makes everything else pop off the canvas. The intricate work of shading draws attention to an area just by adding a little bit of darkness to the edges. You can see the butterfly here, even though all I used were grays and blacks."

He went around the room talking about the other six paintings hanging on the walls before he came back to the one that was still covered up. He stood in front of it, staring at it, and for a second, I thought he had forgotten about everyone else in the room.

"This piece, they say, is my coup de grâce—what I have been working toward my whole life. And if you had asked only a month ago, I would have agreed just to agree with you. I did not think it was special but just another painting. Now, I disagree because of this woman standing here with me."

He turned to look at me, and I could feel my face starting to redden. What was he doing? This was not about me.

"This is Anne. She is my niece," he said, gesturing at me. "We only met each other two months ago. She has opened my eyes to what I have missed—what my family has missed." He came over and put an arm around Grace. "I pushed my past down and pretended it never existed, but what you will see in this painting is that the past never really goes away. It's a part of you, no matter what you do, and you can choose to embrace it or let it eat away at you from the inside out." His eyes lingered on Grace for a bit. With a small nod from Grace, Harrison pulled the cord that brought the cloth down.

The gasp that reverberated around the room spoke volumes. It was his largest piece yet, showing the mountains from Taiwan and the house from Portland. Rose stood prominently in the front, looking down at a small Harrison as they splashed in the fountain before the mansion.

I heard Harrison start talking again, explaining to

everyone about his two halves—his family in Taiwan that he hadn't seen since he was thirteen, and his family in Portland, whom he had only met once and decided he didn't want anything more to do with them . . . until I came into the picture.

"Anne opened my eyes to what could have been," he continued. "And I am very happy she did. I can be a grouchy man." He sent me a quick smile before turning back to face the crowd. "I am probably not the person you thought you would meet today. I'm just an ordinary person who likes to paint, and my paintings happen to hang on the walls of this gallery."

He shrugged and turned to start walking away, but then someone started clapping. This was followed by a few more, and then everyone joined in. It was so great to see, and Harrison stood there dumbstruck. Grace and I stood on either side of him, beaming at this man who had never before opened up like this except in a journal. I could see tears running down Grace's cheeks; she was so proud of Harrison.

People started coming up to shake his hand and ask him questions. He seemed shell-shocked and didn't know what to say until Grace nudged him. Grace and I stayed next to him so the crowd wouldn't surround him, but my attention was elsewhere, searching for a certain someone and hoping that she had come. But the sea of people was too many, and I gave up.

Finally, after about ten minutes, Bettie came to our side and escorted us out of the crowd. More clapping followed us out, and I could tell Harrison was exhausted.

We ascended the stairs and headed toward Bettie's office, but on the way there Grace ran into the back of Harrison, who was now rooted to the spot. I peered around Harrison to see what had happened, and I felt a smile come over my face. Grace had recovered and was about to berate Harrison when

I grabbed her arm and pulled her around so she could see who was standing ahead of us. She gasped, and her hands flew to her face before she ran toward Mary and clung to her, crying. Mary wrapped her arms around Grace, tears also in her eyes.

I decided this was a good time for me to leave, so I started turning around to head back downstairs.

"Where do you think you're going?" Mary called out sharply.

I turned around with my hands in the air. "I'm just heading out. The three of you need time together."

"With you too," Grace pointed out.

I shook my head. "I'll just get in the way."

"You're the reason we're all here," Mary said. She gestured at Harrison. "If it was up to this man, we would never have seen each other ever again." The stare that Mary gave Harrison was as lethal as Grace's this morning. I wondered if I could perfect the eye stare.

Without letting go of Grace, Mary walked over and took my arm, marching us down the hall and then down the stairs. I looked back and saw Harrison was following along, and I breathed a sigh of relief.

"We are going to go to Ding Tai Fung," I heard her whisper to Grace. "If I remember right, Harrison has a hard time being mad or speechless when he has good food in front of him."

Grace smiled. "You remember right." They both shared a knowing laugh.

"What are you laughing at?" said a gruff voice behind us.

"Nothing you need to worry about, Harrison," Grace said.

"Humph," was the only sound we heard in response, which initiated more laughter.

While we were waiting to be seated, I noticed I had missed a call. I excused myself and moved off to the side to listen to the voicemail. The sound of Nick's voice floated through the phone, making my spine straighten like a pole. Had he found her? So soon?

Hi, Anne, this is Nick. I know you're off and about doing your thing. In the hope that we don't have to talk ever again, I am leaving you a message to say I found Sebastian's mom. I wrote down all the important information you'll need to find her and left it at your house. Bye.

That was it. I didn't even feel annoyed that he couldn't follow up with me in person. But he'd found her! I dialed Sebastian's number, hoping he would pick up, but it went straight to voicemail. At this point, Grace was waving at me to come back as we were being seated, and I headed over to join them.

We ordered enough food to feed ten and gobbled down all of it. I kept quiet as I listened to Mary and Grace catch up on the last fifty years. And there was a lot to catch up on. The babies, the adventures, the yearning from both to see each other again. I noticed them holding hands, and I wondered at the ability to touch those we loved. Just the simple task of holding hands was a miracle when they'd been separated for so long.

Harrison picked at his food and fidgeted in his seat, all alone in his own world and refusing to interact with anyone. Every once in a while, I'd see him steal a glance over at Mary. It was like he had reverted to his thirteen-year-old self.

I was fidgeting, too, and I realized halfway through lunch that I didn't need to be here. Grace was doing a good job talking with Mary, and they both seemed quite happy. And as

Harrison wasn't going to slip off without Grace, he was stuck here for the foreseeable future. He was also going to have to talk to Mary no matter what he thought or did, whereas I, on the other hand, felt like the fourth wheel.

"Harrison and Anne, are you going to say anything at all?" Mary asked.

A bit of grumbling came from Harrison amidst his chewing. He had eaten a whole tray of dumplings all by himself and was working on the second one while trying his hardest to ignore everyone there.

I said, "I'm so sorry, I just have a lot on my mind."

Mary smiled. "I can see that. You have a big wedding coming up."

"Yes! And I really hope you can come."

"That depends on Harrison." Mary turned to look at Harrison, who was doing everything he could to not look her in the eye.

"Anne," Grace said, drawing my attention away from Mary and Harrison. "You seem distracted. More so than normal."

"Oh, I know. I'm sorry about that. It's just Sebastian has been dealing with the aftermath of Geraldine, and now there's a problem with his uncle, who's trying to get some money or notoriety out of his connection with Sebastian. And through all of this, Sebastian has been nothing but supportive of me."

"He really is a nice young man," Grace said.

"I love him."

"Then what's wrong?"

"He found out his biological mother might still be around, and Nick just called saying he found her. I'm just antsy to talk to Sebastian about it."

Mary, who I noticed had scooted closer to Harrison, said, "Then it makes sense that you should go home. There's no need for you to stick around when you need to share this important news with Sebastian. Go home and be there for him. Grace and I can handle things here."

"Really?" I said, simultaneously feeling hope and guilt for wanting to leave at the same time.

"Of course," Grace said. "Harrison will be just fine. Right, Harrison?"

A grunt was what we got, but at least he was listening.

"Go," Mary said, waving me away. "I want some alone time with Harrison. You have done good, Anne. You have a life you need to carry on with and a wedding to prepare for."

"Okay, that's fantastic. Grace and Harrison, I'll see you back home."

"Yes, yes. Now go. Go to Sebastian."

"See you later." I was already standing, but I stopped to look at the three people who, only two months ago, I had no idea existed. Now, they were the closest family members I had besides Mom. "Thank you."

"Whatever for?" Mary asked.

"For welcoming me into your family."

"You mean *your* family," Grace said.

"Yes," I said, smiling. *My family.*

CHAPTER 24

I TOOK THE FIRST TAXI TO THE AIRPORT, AND AN hour and a half later, I had a ticket and was going through security. A smile crossed my face when I realized I had kept my word by only spending two days in Taiwan. I tried calling Sebastian again, but it went straight to voicemail. Trying two other times before my flight left didn't get me anywhere either. Where was Sebastian? I hoped he was at his office with Jack and just wasn't picking up his phone.

I hurried home, but Sebastian wasn't there, which meant he had to be at his office. I hurriedly dropped off my suitcases and collected the letter Nick had left. I was itching to open it but told myself this wasn't my mother.

I then hailed down my driver and jumped into the car, giving him directions to go to Sebastian's office in Downtown Portland. Even though it was only Jack and him using it, I knew Sebastian liked to spend time there. Having the office made him feel like he was going to work while also providing him with a suitable place to meet with clients. I think Jack also liked using the office.

When I got to the office, sure enough, Sebastian and Jack

were huddled around his table with piles of paper surrounding them. There was even paper on the floor, the extra chairs, and the sofa.

"I see you two are hard at work," I said as I walked in.

"Huh?" Sebastian said, looking up, and I could tell he hadn't slept again. I couldn't wait for our honeymoon so that he could start relaxing. Hopefully, the news of his mother would be good. "Hi, sweetheart," he said, coming over and giving me a kiss.

"It's good to be back," I said after I kissed him back.

"I know. Jack and I are almost finished. This is the last of the papers. We decided to bring it over here as there was sufficient room."

I looked pointedly around the office. "I see you two have used up every inch you could find."

Jack stood to give me a hug too. "It's good to see you again, Anne." He looked just as tired as Sebastian. "Would you like something to drink? We've got a new cup of coffee brewing right now." He pointed behind me to the kitchen on the other side of the hallway.

"That would be great. I didn't sleep a wink on the flight."

Jack went to see to the coffee while Sebastian and I caught up.

"I made it back in two days," I said, giving him a mock look of surprise.

"You sure did." Sebastian laughed. "I had totally forgotten you were planning to do that. Does that mean I have to walk Lady at night for the next month?"

"I won fair and square, and you know it."

He laughed, bringing me in for another hug. "When this is all over, I'm going to dote on you like you've never been doted on before. Actually, can we skip the wedding and go straight to our honeymoon?"

"No," I said, trying to wiggle out of his arms.

"I was just joking." His arms tightened around me. "But I can't wait for it to be just the two of us all alone in the middle of the ocean."

"Well, not completely alone."

"Close enough. There'll be no friends and family or work surrounding us. Speaking of family, did your trip go well?"

"It did. Mary, Grace, and Harrison are together now, and Harrison is going to make amends whether he likes it or not."

Sebastian smiled. "I don't doubt it for a second. I would never bet against Mary or Grace. The two of them together must be a storm unto itself."

I instantly sobered. "I have more news for you, though."

"Yeah?"

There was no other way to say it, so I spat it out. "Nick found your mother."

I had always read in romance books that a person's heart stopped for a split second when they heard sudden life changing news, but I had never thought it was real. I had been wrong. Sebastian's heart stopped so perceptibly that I looked up for a second to make sure he was okay. All the color in his face had drained away, and he was looking at me with big, startled eyes.

"My mother? He found her? This quickly?"

"What can I say? Nick has his ways. A bit scary if you ask me, but effective."

Sebastian's brow furrowed. "Should I find out if anything is amiss with his way of doing things?"

"No, let's just leave it be. He left a letter for us with the details of her whereabouts."

I stepped back and retrieved the letter from my purse. Handing it to Sebastian, whose hands had started to shake, I waited for him to read it first before he silently passed it to me.

. . .

Sebastian and Anne,

Here are my findings as pertaining to Cecilia Donaldson. It took A LOT of persuasion to agree to meet, but I can be quite persuasive. She is a lady of her own right and is open to a relationship, if you so choose. But she in no way wants you to intrude if your feelings are not mutual. Attached is a letter from her. Do with it as you wish. I found her quite charming, and as unhappy as I am to say this, she reminds me of you, Sebastian.

Nick

When Sebastian saw I'd finished reading the note, he took it out of my hands and stared at it for a moment longer before putting it to the side and pulling out the sheet underneath. He gestured at me to stand with him so we could read it together. It was written in neat, curly lettering, the type of cursive script that was used by someone who had gone through schooling where penmanship was important.

Sebastian,

I am surprised that you are looking for me. I didn't think you would want to ever see me again, much less have anything to do with this side of your family. With that said, did you look for your father too? I was sure your grandfather had covered my tracks very well, and sadly, I do not know what happened to your father. Benny found me once, but I had just settled into my new life, and I knew Mother would not be safe if Father knew she was in touch with me. I broke off all ties for her safety, believing I'd lost all connection to my family. However, since you've spent energy looking for me, I've written down some of my history so you can decide if you want to reach out or not. There is no pressure from me; you have a life, and I hope it's a good one.

After giving you up, my father arranged a marriage for me in Europe. He had a business acquaintance who was looking for a wife for his party-going son. I was repulsed, but Father was a force to be reckoned with. Mother was very much against the idea but had no real say in decisions of the household. We were both inanimate objects as far as Father was concerned. That was until I disgraced the family name by getting pregnant with the gardener—yes, it was the gardener as rumors claim—and who I was most definitely in love with.

Before I got shipped off to Europe, I visited you once with your new family. You were so precious, and I was tempted to run away with you. I know you probably won't believe me, but I very much wanted to keep you. I never wanted to give you up, and if I'd had a choice, I would have raised you. But I couldn't run off with you. Your adopted father was standing guard at the door the whole time, afraid I might do just that. I could see the fear in your adopted mother's eyes. So, I left a locket for you to keep to hopefully remember me by, although, I wasn't naïve enough to think that would bring you to me someday.

I went off to Europe chaperoned by two ladies who made sure I didn't run off. My future husband's father and my own had set up a meeting place for me and the boy to meet. I knew nothing about him except his reputation, which was not a good one. Lo and behold, he never showed up to the meeting, and my father was incensed. I hope you didn't inherit your grandfather's temper. It was an ugly trait, and I have tried very hard myself to control it.

My father had a knack for turning his back on people as soon as they displeased him. I have no idea how he hung onto the family fortune for as long as he did. But sure enough, Father broke the agreement about the betrothal because he claimed his business acquaintance had not held up his end of the bargain, even though it was clearly the son who was in the wrong. But that was fine by me, I wanted nothing to do with him. Thinking that Father would bring me home and think of a new solution to "my problem," I settled in for the night.

The next morning, I was greeted to an empty suite. The two women had left and taken everything in the suite, including a couple of the hotel kitchenette items. My father always had a fetish for kitchen appliances. Don't ask me why, and I hope you don't have that trait either. The only things left in the suite were my clothes and toiletries and an envelope containing cash, a birth certificate, and a passport. What startled me about these items is that the photo was of me, but my last name had been changed. My parents' names had been changed too. It took me a few minutes to realize Father had gone to a lot of trouble to give me a whole new identity. Essentially, I was no longer his daughter.

My first thought wasn't that I was abandoned or scared, it was relief that I was finally free. He'd left me behind to fend for myself, which I was more than happy to do. I missed you deeply, but I was only eighteen and so happy to finally be out from under my father's control. I never looked back as I ran toward my future.

I had been to Europe plenty of times before and had a few family friends through Mother. Europe was one place Father would let us vacation. Mother said he felt sophisticated here and could put on airs —makes me want to gag just thinking about it. One of Mother's friends was in London, and so, there I went. Thankfully, she took me in, no questions asked. I wouldn't have been surprised if Mother had called her in advance, knowing what Father was planning to do. I hope you're not like your grandmother either, letting people step all over you and controlling your every movement. But she always made sure I was able to go out and do things a child and teenager should. Though, now that I'm older, I wonder at the cost my rebellious nature had on her.

Mother's friend helped me find a job at a bookstore where I did very well. I now own my own bookstore and am married with two kids. One three years younger than you, and one five years younger than you.

So, now you know what happened to me. I would love to meet you and get to know you, but that will be up to you, Sebastian. I do not ever want to be like my father, who forced people to do his will. As you sent someone to find me, I extend my welcome in the hopes that we might meet again one day.

Love,
Cecilia Maphis

Sebastian and I stood there, not talking, just staring at the letter for who knew how long. Jack had come back and put down my coffee, which was cold by now, and gone back to sorting through the paperwork. His back was turned to us to give us some privacy, and I was glad for it. All sorts of feelings were churning through me that I couldn't even begin to imagine how Sebastian was feeling.

"Sebastian?" I rubbed my hand up and down his back. "Do you want me to get you anything?"

He turned to look at me, and I could see he had tears in his eyes as he tried to stay strong.

"It's okay to feel. You can let it out," I whispered.

He turned to look at Jack, who had just stood up. "I'm going to grab dinner. Do you want me to bring anything back for you two?"

Sebastian just shook his head, and I smiled at Jack as I shook mine too.

As soon as the door was closed, we sat on the sofa, and Sebastian put his head in his hands as the tears came. I held him while his body shook, as he let all the questions, fears, and unknowns out of his system so that he could think better about what to do next.

We sat like that for a long while until Sebastian was ready to talk.

"I'm hungry." Those were the first two words he said, and I had to laugh.

"The two of us really do run on our stomachs, don't we?"

"That's why I love you," he said, giving me a side grin and a kiss on my forehead.

"You want to talk about anything?" I asked him softly.

"Not really. It's a lot to process, and on top of all the paperwork that Jack and I are trying to finish up, I just can't think about it."

"Okay. Well, I just want you to know that I'm okay if you want to invite her to our wedding. She seems like a fully functional woman who isn't crazy."

"That's the first thing you think of? A fully functional woman who isn't crazy?" This brought out another laugh, which I was happy to hear.

"No," I replied, laughing in return. "I just wanted to see you smile."

"Thanks, Anne."

I leaned my shoulder into his. "But I really am okay if you want to invite her to our wedding, Sebastian."

"I'll think about it. It's all too new right now."

CHAPTER 25

THE NEXT MORNING I CALLED THE WEDDING planner back. She had left two messages while I was on my whirlwind trip to Taiwan, and I knew she must be stressing because I hadn't yet responded.

"Hi, Anne." Eda sounded cheerful. How was she so happy all the time?

"I'm sorry for my late response. I had to take an impromptu trip to Taiwan and just got back yesterday."

"That's not a problem. I just had some questions to run by you. I also wanted to check in and see if there's anything new you'd like me to know. Do you have time to meet today?"

"Yes, I do. I'll contact Lauren and Victoria too."

"That sounds great. How's two o'clock?"

"Two works. I'll see you then."

My next call was to Lauren, and I was surprised she hadn't picked up on the first ring.

"Hi, Anne." She sounded sad.

"Is everything okay?"

"Oh, not really, but the problem doesn't have anything to

do with me. It's Isabella. Something's happened, and she won't talk to me. I finally got her to open her door, and she shooed me away! I'm having to go through Nick to find out what's going on, but he's being pretty tight-lipped about it too. It's all very strange, and I'm very distraught and don't know what to do. Nick also mentioned something about Brian. He was your ex, no? I might have to ask you for help. I don't like seeing Isabella like this. She's usually the one picking up all the pieces and fixing all the problems, but right now she looks like she's ready to give up. I just don't get it. This isn't Isabella. What would you do? You seem so put together and know what to do all the time."

Her statement caught me off guard, and I had to pause a second before responding. "I think . . ." What could Lauren do that Nick wasn't already doing? Knowing Nick, he probably wanted to fix Isabella's problem all by himself, but Lauren knew her just as well, and two helpers would be better than one. "I think you should go visit her and not leave until she answers your questions, Lauren. If she's anything like how she was when I saw her, she could use all the friends she can get."

"You saw her?"

"Only for a little bit."

"And you didn't tell me she looked distraught?"

"She would not have wanted me to say anything, and neither did Nick," I replied. Besides, it wasn't any of my business how she was, and Isabella would never want me to tell anyone how she looked.

"But it's me—I'm her best friend! I feel so disconnected to her these days. It's like once I got married she decided to end our friendship."

"I'm sure it's nothing like that."

"You don't understand, Anne. We were supposed to get married at the same time and had this big wedding planned for the two of us. Of course, this was when we were still in elementary school, but still, we were like sisters. Inseparable. And now she's barely talking to me."

"Well, go and see her then. Make her talk to you. She needs more than just Nick."

"Yeah, I'll do that." Then, as if she'd just remembered I had called her, she said, "I'm sorry, you had called me about something?"

"It's nothing important. Eda wanted to meet, and I thought you'd like to come."

"Oh, I'd love to, but I should go see Isabella. You're in good hands with Eda. You don't need me there anymore."

"Sure thing. I'll update you on what's going on."

"Oh, no need. I'm sure everything will turn out well."

"Oh, okay. I'll talk to you later then."

"Talk to you later, Anne."

It was odd that Lauren was not gung ho on the wedding anymore. I had thought it overpowering when we had first started planning the big event, but I had gotten used to her being around and helping me out. At least there was Victoria. I phoned her next. "Hi, Victoria. Are you free this afternoon?"

"Hi, Anne. You sound so chipper!"

"I'm just excited because I have a good friend who wants to come with me to meet with Eda and help me finalize details."

"Oh, um, I'm not so free today. Paul asked me out for lunch. He said he has a surprise for me."

My excitement went down a notch, but I made sure that didn't show in my voice as I said to Victoria, "Oh, no problem. I'll let you know what's going on after I meet with Eda."

"That sounds great. I'm really glad you hired her, Anne. She called me yesterday to ask if there was anything I needed help with. How awesome is that when I'm not even the bride? But I told her I got your bridal shower all taken care of."

"Victoria, that's so nice of you! I totally forgot about the bridal shower." That made me feel heaps better, and my excitement returned ten-fold.

"Well, Leslie reminded me, and you're not supposed to have anything to do with the planning of it. She insisted, actually, but I would have done one anyways! You're my best friend, and you deserve the best. It's going to be so much fun, Anne! But, oh shoot, I have to go; Paul is here. I'll talk to you later, okay?"

"Okay. Talk to you later."

Leslie was supposed to fly in today, but now that I thought about it, she hadn't mentioned any flight informa-tion. I called her next, and she picked up on the first ring.

"Hi, Anne. Oh, I'm so glad you called!" Her voice was literally bouncing. I'd never heard her sound so excited. "I'm so busy," she continued. "I meant to call and tell you that I won't be able to come up this weekend. Jonathan surprised me with a night away, just him and me! I'm so excited! Mom and Dad are going to watch Madison and Ryan, and it's going to be like old times!"

"Oh . . . that's fantastic, Leslie!"

"I'm sorry, Anne. I know I said I'd come up this weekend, but now that you've hired the wedding planner, I figured you'd be okay. And now that I said that out loud, it sounds really callous of me. I'm sorry, I promise I'll make it up to you. We'll have a great girls' night out after you get back from your honeymoon, okay?"

"Leslie, it's not a problem. Honestly. And I'm so glad to hear you and Jonathan are going to spend some time together, just the two of you. Have a fantastic time."

"Thank you, Anne!"

I hung up the phone and stared at it for a second. Guess I was going to meet Eda all by myself then.

We met at Eda's office, and I was once again hit by the level of organization and crisp minimalism to the room.

"Anne, welcome. It's good to see you again. Do you want anything to drink or snack on?"

"No, thank you. I'm good, I just had a big lunch."

Eda smiled. "Then let's get down to your wedding. I've been working on your binder, and I believe I've got everything put together as you'd like it, but I wanted to go over it with you."

"That sounds fantastic."

"When we last talked, you mentioned you were wanting to combine a Taiwanese and Western theme together."

"Yes, it is what Sebastian and I had agreed on, but I'm learning that I need to include some tradition in it too. Is it possible to combine the two?"

"Of course, and I wanted to show you some of the flowers I had picked out. As you already decided on your bouquet, the wedding colors will be based on that. But I wanted to ask you if this is the right red color you had in mind?"

She pulled out a sample of silk that was definitely Chinese red. "Yes, that's the perfect color. How is it going to be used in the wedding?"

"I was thinking it could be used as an overlay for the tables, but do you have something in mind?"

"The tables?"

"Well, yes, we'd have—"

"Oh, I know there will be tables, but red silk tablecloths?" I raised my brows at the pure opulence of it.

"Too much?" Eda queried. "With the people you want to invite, I'm going big."

"Oh, um, why don't I leave that decision up to you? I think it's going to look fantastic whatever you choose to do."

"That's something I wanted to talk to you about." She sat back and gave me a long look, but it wasn't a prying or scolding expression; she looked worried. "Are you having the wedding you want?"

"What do you mean?"

"Is this big wedding—the red, the decorations—is it still what you and Sebastian want?"

"Yes . . ."

Eda gave me a small smile. "Honesty is what works the best."

"As you know, it wasn't what we initially wanted, but I think this is still the right thing to do. Plus, you said you already sent out five hundred invitations, so there's no turning back."

Eda frowned. "There's always a chance to dial back. Let me ask you this then: Are you looking forward to a big wedding?"

That one was easy, especially since I'd had some time to think on it. "I am, actually. It should be fun. Especially because I'm treating it more like a party—just like the gala I threw this past Christmas."

Eda nodded. "Yes, I heard about that one. I heard it was one of the best."

"It sure was, and I had a blast. That's why I'm sure I'll have a blast at my wedding too."

"Okay, that's what I needed to know. Thank you, Anne. Moving along, can you tell me in detail how you originally envisioned your wedding? There may still be elements we can add."

"Sure. I wanted it in my garden with Christmas lights

strewn overhead. Not the big weatherproof light-bulb-shaped ones but literal Christmas lights to offer a twinkle. There would be an open bar and a live band playing elevator music to invite people in. They would switch to dance music when the reception started, but the wedding and the reception would all be in the garden. There would only be about twenty people, so we'd only need three tables, and that's if they all could come. Servers would pass out champagne and hors d'oeuvres—and Cook has come up with some really delicious ones. Celebrating with food was what I was really looking forward to. Is that silly? I just love to eat." I gave a small laugh. "That's me being honest for you."

"That's not silly at all," Eda replied, giving me a warm smile and taking some more notes. "Anything else?"

I shook my head. "That's pretty much it. I planned on dancing through the night, and, at some point, turning off the Christmas lights to see if we could see the stars overhead."

"That sounds lovely."

"It does, doesn't it?"

Eda's head was cocked to one side, and she was looking at me like she was expecting me to say more.

"There's really nothing more," I assured her. "Were there other questions you wanted to ask?"

She didn't seem satisfied with my answer, but she didn't ask again. Instead, she looked at her notes and stated, "We have decided to have all five cakes, yes?"

"Oh, yes! They are all so delicious."

She nodded. "Cook and I decided to go the route of one cake per flavor. Would you like some during the cocktail hour or would you like to save them all for the cake cutting part of the ceremony?"

"Oh, that's a good question. I hadn't thought about that.

It'd be nice to have some during the cocktail hour, wouldn't it?"

"That's up to you, but we can cut the cake into tiny slices so they are part of the hors-d'oeuvres."

"That sounds like an excellent plan." I wished Lauren and Victoria were here to give their input. This would be right up their ally.

Eda then asked, "Do you have a preference on which cakes to use when?"

Was there a favorite? "Not really. Oh, wait—the carrot cake. Cook's carrot cake is the best ever, and I'd like that to be the one we do the cake cutting with."

"That's a fantastic decision." Eda beamed.

We talked about other details that needed refining before I left to go home. On the drive home, all I could think was that I should have hired a wedding planner a lot sooner.

CHAPTER 26

I watched Sebastian knotting his tie in the bathroom. "Can I help? You've attempted it a few times now."

He gave me a wry smile in the mirror. "That would be great. I usually get this on the first try."

"You're nervous?"

"Yeah . . . my hands are shaking."

I looked down and, sure enough, his hands were trembling. I'd never seen Sebastian so unnerved, even when he was about to go into a big case.

Today was the day. After all the late-night digging and filing of Geraldine's paperwork, Sebastian and Jack had gathered enough information to bring down Uncle Roger. On top of that, Jack and Sebastian's grandmother, Joan, had been pouring over paperwork she had found in Mr. Donaldson's things. Joan said they had given her the motivation she needed to start sorting through her late husband's papers, and she was glad they did because there were some interesting going-ons that she had never known about. Sebastian had joked that, at this rate, he might have a second client soon.

"Do you want me to come with you?" I asked.

"That would actually be great; I'd like that. You can meet my grandmother too."

I saw his shoulders drop a smidge, enough to see him relax, if only a little. "You think Uncle Roger knows what's coming to him?"

"Not at all. I called him yesterday to say you and I had come to an agreement on a payout fee, but that we wouldn't discuss it until we meet him at Schuster and Schuster at nine this morning."

"Probably good for all of us to be there, anyways. Don't want him saying we're doing anything behind other people's backs."

"I doubt my aunt even knows what he's up to," Sebastian murmured.

I gave him a hug. I don't know what I'd do if my family members blackmailed me. "All right, let's go and get this over with."

We showed up at Schuster and Schuster, and I was reminded of the first day I met Sebastian—right here in this building while he read a will that changed my life. I put my hand in his and gave it a squeeze. The wedding planning was going well now, and soon we'd have Sebastian's uncle off our backs. At least, I hoped so.

The building hadn't changed, and the people inside were just as monochromatic as last time—in stark contrast to whoever decided bright colors were great for the floor of a law firm. We took the elevator to the topmost floor and were ushered into a conference room. No one else was there, but coffee and a tray of cookies were readily available. I got a few for Sebastian and myself, and we sat down in the middle of the conference table.

"Anne!"

I turned to see Jack coming through the door. He was followed by a very dignified looking older woman around Jack's age.

I smiled at him warmly. "Jack, it's so good to see you again. Though, we did meet in the office not too long ago."

"You mean, where you made Sebastian a blubbering mess and he was completely useless to me for the rest of the day?"

"Hey now, I've been pulling my weight," Sebastian said, not taking his eyes off the stack of papers in front of him.

"Just joking, Sebastian," Jack said, giving him a slap on his back. He gestured at the woman beside him. "Anne, I don't believe you've met Ms. Donaldson?"

At this, Sebastian jerked his head up and stood so quickly, he almost knocked over his seat. "Ms. Donaldson, it's good to see you again."

"Sebastian, my dear. Joan, please. Is this your fiancée?"

Sebastian gestured at me. "Yes, this is Anne. Anne, this is my grandmother, Ms. Donaldson—ah, Joan, I mean."

"It's really nice to meet you," I said.

"Hopefully, we can get to know each other better once this whole farce is taken care of," the woman replied.

"Yes, of course. I'd love that."

"Sebastian, dear, can I sit next to you?" Joan asked, already pulling out the seat.

"Of course."

The four of us sat, with Jack on my other side, and waited for Uncle Roger and his entourage to appear. About twenty minutes later, Uncle Roger came strolling in, looking smug and round. The picture Sebastian had showed me was of a lean and mean gentleman with a fierce face, and it was clear the man in front of me had changed. He had gotten glutto-nous in his older age and appeared to hold his new physique in esteem. I didn't have time to study him more, though, because Sebastian gasped while staring at the door.

I turned to see who was coming in. It was an older version of a woman I'd seen in a photograph Sebastian had shown me —his Aunt Cassie. She hadn't changed one bit except for the fact that her hair was grayer and she seemed a bit stooped. A couple of men with folders followed her in, and I assumed they were people who worked for Uncle Roger.

"Well, it looks like we're all here," Jack said, kicking off the meeting. "Roger, I believe, wanted us to go first." He raised a brow at the older man in question.

Roger's face had turned into stone at the sight of us, and I knew then that he realized there was not going to be a payout. I watched as his cool features turned instantly into the lawyer I imagined he was—a man who never took no for an answer. His eyes were burning with hatred, and his mouth had become pinched.

Jack ignored the animosity in the room and continued, "We have been investigating Roger's interaction with my sister, Geraldine."

"She was a client and nothing else," Roger said sharply.

"Let's not interrupt, shall we? It's not polite and reflects badly on you, Roger," Joan said.

He sat down with a huff, and Cassie put a hand on his arm, which he brushed off.

"Hold on," Sebastian said. "Aunt Cassie, why are you here?"

"Why, to provide support for Roger. He told me to come in and be part of a family meeting."

"Cassie, be quiet!" Roger said.

"I'm just answering Sebastian's question," she returned.

Then she came forward, reaching her hands up to Sebastian's neck. "You need to straighten your tie, it's a bit crooked. There you go. Much better."

"Cassie, go wait in my office," Roger snapped.

She raised a brow, but her features were as mild as her voice when she asked, "You don't want me here?"

"Not anymore," Roger said.

"Oh, okay." Aunt Cassie shrugged and turned away from him to glance at us. "Sebastian, dear, I'll see you later, okay? You haven't come by to visit in so long that I was hoping we could all go to dinner tonight."

"Cassie," Roger seethed.

She held up a hand. "Okay, okay. I'm going."

We all silently watched as Cassie left the room.

"Why did you bring her?" Joan asked, breaking the silence. "This meeting isn't going to look good for you."

"He thought he could make Sebastian buckle," I said.

"It clearly didn't work. You must not love your aunt as much as you say you do," Roger spat, staring at Sebastian like a hawk.

"I love her as much as my own mother."

"You mean her daughter?" Roger said, pointing at Joan.

"No, the one who raised me."

"Ah, the one who left the family fortune and married a good-for-nothing."

"Roger!" Jack, Joan, and I said at the same time.

Roger sat back looking smug. Did he not know what information we had on him?

Jack continued, "As I was saying, we've found some important information. It seems that Geraldine kept a fair amount of detail on the projects she and Roger worked on."

"She wouldn't have. Those were all classified," he growled.

Jack continued as if Roger hadn't interrupted, "Geraldine even recorded all of their conversations."

"What?" Roger shouted, standing up and pounding his fist onto the table.

A booming voice was heard on the other side of the door. "Cheryl! Hold that call for me. I have a meeting to attend, and I don't want anyone to interrupt me." In the next moment, a man, towering close to what looked like seven feet, came storming through the door.

"Mr. Schuster," Roger said, instantly coming to his feet and rushing to his boss's aid.

"Sit down, Roger," the man said, sitting himself at the head of the table. "I want to hear what Jack has to say." He waved at Jack to continue, and I watched as Uncle Roger sat with a decidedly green look on his face while I tried hard to wipe the smug one off mine.

"Thank you, Mr. Schuster. As I was saying, we have found evidence that Geraldine and Roger were running schemes on their clients, one of them being the Donaldson family."

Roger didn't interrupt, although I saw his eyes swivel to Mr. Schuster. I was glad the head boss had joined us, since this was the quietest Roger had been up till this point.

"Geraldine didn't work for us," Mr. Schuster said.

"Roger paid her on the side," Sebastian explained.

"That's a dirty allegation and a bunch of lies!" Roger said, pounding the table again. "You can't prove it!"

"But we can. It's contained within this document here, and there's more where that came from." Jack passed a sheet over to Roger, who accepted it while shooting daggers at Jack.

We waited until Roger had read it.

Mr. Schuster stood up then and beckoned to Jack and Roger. "Come to my office."

The two men stood up and followed him out while the rest of us waited, not knowing where to look. Roger's two workers were still standing in the room, looking quite uncomfortable.

I turned to Sebastian. "You going to be okay? Just remember you have a lot of detailed evidence against Roger that nothing could go wrong," I reminded him as I ran a hand up and down his back.

His shoulders tensed. "Roger can talk himself out of anything. I've seen him in meetings before, he has the tongue of a snake. And Aunt Cassie comes from old money; her family would never allow her downfall if Roger was to be let go. I honestly don't know what Mr. Schuster can do."

"We can only wait and see," Joan said, giving Sebastian's hand a pat.

I felt Sebastian flinch, but he didn't pull back, only raised his eyes to look at his grandmother. "Would you like to come to our wedding?" he suddenly asked.

Wow! He asked her! I looked at Ms. Donaldson, wondering if she was aware of the significance of his request, and in one glance, I could see she had been hoping he'd ask, because a slight breath came out of her mouth before she smiled and said, "Of course, I will. My only grandson? I wouldn't miss it for the world."

Sebastian reached over and gave Ms. Donaldson's hand a squeeze. "I'm not quite ready to call you grandmother yet, but I'm so glad you'd like to attend."

Joan gave him a small smile. "That's okay. You can spend the rest of my life calling me whatever you want, and I'll still be as happy as can be."

A commotion sounded in the hallway, and we all turned to see Roger being escorted by a security guard with his hands in cuffs. Aunt Cassie was close behind, her face streaked with tears as she asked Roger what was going on.

Sebastian got out of his seat and rushed to the door. "Aunt Cassie!"

"Sebastian!" Cassie came running toward him. "What is going on? Why is Roger in cuffs? Did something happen?" Then she put a hand to her chest. "Oh, what am I going to tell the kids? They look up to their father so much. What am I going to do?"

Sebastian grasped her shoulders. "Aunt Cassie, do not worry. I'm going to take care of you, okay? As for your kids, they will understand. I talked to all three of them earlier this week."

She blinked up at him. "You did?"

"Yes, just to prepare them. I tried to get ahold of you earlier, but clearly no one gave you the message that I called."

"Oh." She sniffed and ran a hand over her cheeks. "I'm not going to leave him."

"No one said you needed to, but I'll make sure you're safe and taken care of, okay?"

Cassie reached up and patted his cheek. "You were always a nice boy."

"It's the least I can do after you've taken care of me and my family for so long."

"Nonsense, it's what family's for. Your mother was the one person I could count on. And I thought, well, I thought I could count on Roger too."

Sebastian squeezed her shoulders. "Well, now you have me."

"And me," I said, stepping up to put my arm around Aunt Cassie.

She looked at me and smiled. "I'd like to get to know you better."

"I'd like that too," I said.

"Good." She dabbed at her eyes again. "Well, I better go to your uncle." And with that, she pulled away and ran after Uncle Roger.

"Do you think she's going to be okay?" I asked Sebastian.

"Yes, I'll make sure of it. She's the only family besides Father who I have left from when I was growing up."

"And your cousins," I added.

"Who I never kept in touch with," he said with regret. "I called them earlier this week, and they were indifferent to what we'd found about their father."

"Well, you have a new family to get to know now."

"Yeah." Sebastian turned to see Joan talking with Jack, their heads together as if conspiring something.

"Do you know what you're going to do about your mother?" I now asked him.

"No. No, I don't. But I am going to start getting to know my grandmother. That's the first step."

CHAPTER 27

WE GOT BACK TO THE HOUSE IN A SUBDUED MOOD. Even though Roger got what he deserved, he was still Sebastian's uncle, and his wife was still someone Sebastian loved very much. How was I going to remedy this and help put him in a better mood?

"Anne, you want to have ice cream for dinner?" Sebastian asked as we alighted from the vehicle.

"Yes! Very much yes."

"Good. That's about all I can stomach right now."

I put a hand on his arm as we walked up to the front door. "We'll take care of your Aunt Cassie, Sebastian. Maybe she could move in with us? We have the room."

Sebastian laughed. "I love that you're open to helping her, but I wouldn't go that far. She likes her space, and I don't know that I'd want her around all the time."

"Miss?" came another voice.

I turned and saw Ben standing at the front door, holding it open for us.

Sebastian stepped inside first. "Thank you, Ben. Anne and I are just going to head to the kitchen for some ice cream."

Ben cleared his throat. "You two are needed in your bedroom, actually."

"Our bedroom?" Sebastian and I both asked.

"Yes. Something's come up, and Victoria is waiting there for you both."

We glanced at each other, then hurried through the foyer and up the stairs. What could be happening that Victoria would request us to all meet in our bedroom? I told myself that if it was important, we'd meet in the library or sitting room.

I opened the door to our room and found not just Victoria, but a man with what looked like a hair salon set up.

"What in the world is going on?" Sebastian asked, hooking an arm around me.

"I'd like to know the same thing," I added. "We're really not in the mood for surprises right now. It's been a hard morning."

Victoria walked up to me and put both of her hands on my shoulders. She had a big smile on her face. "You're going to love this surprise! We have everything planned. Sebastian, you too. Both of you have been running in circles since you met, and it's time you sat back and relaxed."

"What are we doing?" Sebastian asked, now holding onto me even tighter.

Victoria only smiled. "You'll see." Then she ushered Sebastian into the adjoining room, where I saw a man waiting with scissors in one hand and a drape you would see in a salon in the other.

"Victoria, are we getting some sort of spa treatment?" I asked her.

Her smile got wider. "Yes, you are. Now, sit right here and let Thomas do your hair and makeup."

For the next hour, Thomas primped and primed me for I didn't know what, but I allowed myself to sink into the moment and enjoy it. Victoria even brought me some dinner that Cook had made with a side of ice cream. By the end, my hair had so much hairspray and pins in it I knew it wouldn't be going anywhere. My makeup was flawless too. Every blemish was covered up, I had nice rosy lips, and my eyes looked much bigger and brighter than normal.

Victoria pulled out a red floor-length gown. It was a gorgeous satin ballgown that poofed out from the fitted waist. There was a slight train in the back, the sleeves were banded around the arms, and it had a sweetheart neckline at the front and a V at the back.

"Is that for me?" I gasped.

"Yes," Victoria said, smiling. But there was a look on her face that told me she was hiding something.

"What aren't you telling me?"

"Just put this on and you'll see."

"Victoria . . ."

"No questions. You and Sebastian both deserve this. Just let it happen."

She had unzipped the dress and was waiting for me to step into it. I did as I was told, wondering if this was what I was thinking it was—but it couldn't be! I had just talked to Eda, and everything was on schedule for the big wedding in a week's time.

Victoria zipped me up and then gave me a once-over.

"I feel like a princess," I whispered when I saw my reflection in the mirror.

"You should. Okay, I think you're all done. Would you like to go see what we've been up to?"

"We've?"

Victoria walked to the door and beckoned me forward. "Just come down and see."

I looked toward the door that led to the adjoining room. "What about Sebastian?"

"He's been down there for a while now."

"Really?" *What was going on?*

I followed Victoria down, careful not to step on my dress. The heels Victoria had given me were a beautiful red and matched the dress well; however, they were impossible to walk in due to their three-inch height. She led me to the back doors, but when I was ten feet away, I stopped. Were those voices outside? And what were those sparkling lights beyond the doors? I could hear soft music as well.

"Victoria . . ." I faltered. I could feel the threat of tears about to spill and roll down my cheeks.

She came and gave me a hug. "You deserve this. And it's the perfect way to start off your life together—with just family and friends."

"Family and friends?" All those voices floating through the door . . . was it who I hoped it was?

"Come on, we're almost to the door." Victoria took my hand and led me the rest of the way.

When I stepped out onto the balcony, I gasped.

"Don't start crying!" Victoria whispered under her breath. "I asked them to use waterproof mascara, but you never know."

"Anne," came a gasped voice behind me.

I turned to see Mom and almost ran into her arms. "What are you doing here?"

"To see you get married, of course. You didn't think I'd miss my own daughter's wedding?"

"But the wedding isn't till next week."

Mom smiled at me. "We thought you'd like to have the wedding of your dreams before doing the big wedding that you felt obligated to do."

Eda came up behind Mom, and I went and gave her a hug. "I don't know what I'd do without you," I whispered into her hair before pulling away.

"Don't thank me. It was Victoria and Sebastian's idea, and your bridesmaids did most of the work. I just helped with some last-minute coordination."

"What?" I whirled to look at Victoria, but she was nowhere in sight. "Sebastian was in on this too?"

"He didn't know the details, but he gave us his blessing to put something together," Mom said. "And I think we did a pretty good job."

"I agree. I love the Christmas lights." They twinkled in the evening air like fireflies on their nightly adventures.

Mom came forward. "I've been saving this to give you when the time was right. I think this is that time." She handed me a wooden lacquered box not much bigger than my hand. On the lid was painted a plum blossom. I opened it to find a hair pin that was about five inches long. The brown wood ended in a point, and the other side held three pink plum blossoms of varying sizes. Two pink beads hung off them, dangling delicately. "It belonged to your grandmother, Rose," Mom said softly.

I looked up in shock. "This belonged to Rose?"

"It's the only thing I have left of hers that I can pass on to you. It's your 'something old' for today."

"Thank you, Mom." I gave her a hug so tight I didn't want to let go. We had both gone through so much over the last few months.

"And I have something new for you," another voice said.

I turned to see Leslie, and I also gave her a big hug. "You made it here today too? Wait! Did Jonathan even have a night out planned?" Then a thought occurred to me. "You didn't cancel your night out without kids for me, did you?"

Leslie laughed. "Anne, don't worry. We didn't cancel anything. Jonathan did plan a night out for us, but it's for another night. We wouldn't have missed your wedding for the world," she said, smiling. "I do have something to say before I give you this gift, though." She looked solemn all of a sudden.

"Okay . . ."

She took my hands. "I wanted to apologize for pushing you so hard to include Taiwanese traditions in your wedding. Ever since the kids were born, I've felt guilty for not teaching them more Taiwanese traditions and for not having them speak Mandarin. I've been wound up so tight about it that it kind of flooded over into your wedding. I'm sorry."

"Oh, Leslie." I enveloped her into my arms again and held her there for quite a while. I didn't care if there were people waiting for us. It was my wedding, and my cousin was feeling guilty for something that I probably would have done, too, if I was in her position. I let go and pulled back to look into her eyes. "I'm glad you had all this knowledge about Taiwanese traditions, because I sure didn't. Neither did Mom. Yes, it was a bit overwhelming at times, but at the end of the day, I'm really happy to include them."

"Thanks, Anne." She gave me another hug, then broke away to show me a small, wrapped present. "Here, I thought it only appropriate after hounding you about tradition that I get you this. It's your something new and blue."

I opened the box to see a blue garter belt and burst out laughing. "This is fantastic! Sebastian will have a fun time getting this off."

We all laughed, and I looked around feeling more loved than I had ever felt before. Old and new family were together.

Leslie pulled up a chair and had me sit down. "Let's get these on you."

Between Mom and Leslie, they got the pin in my hair and the garter belt up my leg. When I stood up, I was surprised to see Harrison standing at the top of the stairs, waiting for me.

"Harrison!"

"You didn't think I would miss your wedding?"

"Well, no, but you flew all the way here for this surprise one? What about Mary and Taiwan?"

"Who else was going to walk you down the aisle? Ah . . . if that's okay with you?"

Now tears were really starting to fall down my cheeks. Leslie was there within seconds, dabbing at my face and reminding me to hold it in.

"I don't know what to say," I choked out.

"Don't say anything," Mom said, giving me a kiss before walking down the stairs with Leslie to take their seats.

Before I could wrap my head fully around what was happening, I heard the wedding march start.

"You ready?" Harrison asked, holding out his arm to me.

"Yes," I said, smiling. I was.

We walked down the stairs and behind the last row of people to the center aisle. One glance showed me that everyone was here, at least all the ones in the States. Victoria, Leslie, and even Lauren were standing up at the front, and I could see Sebastian—who had the biggest smile on his face and one that I hadn't seen in a long time—standing next to two of his close friends. Mom, Jack, all my cousins and their kids, Lucia, Cook, Ben, and even Ms. Donaldson was here. A man I didn't recognize stood in the first row, but before I could figure out who he was, my hand was getting passed into Sebastian's, and I was being pulled to stand next to him.

Sebastian leaned over and whispered, "You look absolutely gorgeous."

"Thank you. You look quite handsome yourself. I can't believe you knew about this!"

"Trust me, it was hard to keep it from you, but from the look on your face, I think it was well worth it."

My heart burst inside my chest with such incredible warmth. "I love you so much."

"I love you too, Anne."

The ceremony went by in the blink of an eye. At some point, I remembered handing Victoria my bouquet of red roses and turning to hold both of Sebastian's hands as we said our vows to each other. I hadn't quite written mine yet, but I just spoke from the heart. He was everything to me and he'd been right by my side through all the adventures we'd had over these last many months that had irrevocably changed my life. There was no one else I wanted to spend the rest of my life with. We had so many more adventures to embark on, and I couldn't wait to make those memories.

Next thing I knew we were putting rings on each other, and Sebastian bent me over and gave me the longest kiss. I wished the world would melt away and let me stay in this bliss, but our private time together would have to wait.

We resurfaced to a thunder of applause and cheers. My face must have turned a deep shade of red, but I didn't care, I was so happy. This was the wedding we wanted, and we were so loved that our family and friends had made it happen.

Someone yelled, "Let there be food!" And everyone burst out laughing as they filed out behind us to go into what I could only imagine was a feast, as Cook would do nothing less.

While we had been outside, someone had decorated the whole first floor. They had done such an amazing job. There were red cloths over every flat surface in the hallway, complimented by red flower arrangements in beautiful red and gold vases. There were also red rose petals strewn over the floor, leading to the ballroom where a faux wall had been set up to make the room more intimate.

Inside the room, each table had a bright red tablecloth and matching red chairs. Lanterns hung from the ceiling at differing heights, each one surrounded by a plethora of plum blossoms.

Sebastian and I were ushered to a table for two that was located at the front of the room, facing everyone else. Small strands of Christmas lights had been sewed together with white satin ribbons and were cleverly situated in the middle of the table. Opulent candles finished the delicate setting. I immediately noted that on the candles and walls was the word 囍—which meant double happiness for the bride and groom. And in the corner was the live band, who were setting back up after moving in from outside. I also saw an open bar in the other corner of the room and noted there was already a line.

"I'm completely amazed," I said as Sebastian rubbed my hand, his finger running over my wedding ring.

"We have great family and friends."

I smiled at him. "We really do. Do you think there is any need to even do the big wedding anymore?"

"Yes, because I think it'd be fun to finally let loose and just enjoy a nice big party."

"Yeah, that does sound like fun."

We took out seats, and the food came out almost immediately. Cook had outdone herself, of course. There was a thirteen-course meal with the obligatory roasted whole pig that held an apple in his mouth, lobster and chicken, crab over sticky rice, roast duck, abalone and sea cucumber, whole fish, noodles, hot red bean soup, sliced oranges, three different types of vegetables, and sweet buns. Everything was served on red platters and bowls, and even the band started playing some famous Taiwanese songs intermixed with western dance music. It was amazing.

Near the middle of the meal, Eda collected us both and took us around each table.

We approached my mom's table first. It held Mom, Harrison, Grace, the man I didn't know, Lucia, Jack, and Ms. Donaldson, who I noticed was sitting pretty close to Jack. Everyone seemed to be getting along fine.

After speaking with my mom and the others, Sebastian brought me to stand in front of the man I didn't know. "Anne, I'd like to introduce you to my father, Frank."

"Oh! It's so nice to finally meet you."

"The pleasure is mine. Sebastian speaks highly of you."

"I'm flattered," I said, looking at Sebastian, who was staring back at me with the most adoring eyes.

The next two tables accommodated my cousins, the bridesmaids and groomsmen, and the last one held all the kids. They were lively to say the least, and I couldn't blame them. This was the best surprise ever, and I was so glad to have everyone here.

I heard clinking behind me and turned to see Victoria getting everyone's attention.

"We have one more surprise for Anne and Sebastian tonight," she announced. "I know Sebastian already had his bachelor party, but Anne is not one to really get into that kind of thing, so the girls and I decided that we'd do a bachelorette/bridal shower tonight. So, Anne and Sebastian, if you could take a seat."

"Did you know about this?" I said to Sebastian as we walked back to our table.

"Nope. I'm curious what everyone got you," he said, nudging my elbow.

"Me too!"

"Okay," Victoria said. "For someone who already has all the money she'll ever need and therefore can buy whatever she wants, it was a bit hard for us to come up with what to get you, Anne. But"—she looked at everyone else, who all had expectant looks on their faces—"we finally came up with something that we knew you would never get for yourself."

"Uh oh," was all I could say. This was going to be embarrassing.

"I believe your mom would like to go first."

Mom stood up with Harrison and Grace. "We wanted to get you something special, and we thought both of you like to travel, so a trip around the world might be of interest."

"Really?!" I cried.

"Really," Mom said. "We want both of you to get away from here for a bit. Get to know each other more away from all this history."

"Thank you, Mom!" I stood up and ran to her as best I could and gave her, Harrison, and Grace a hug.

"We're not done yet," Veronica piped in.

"I'm next," Leslie said, standing up. "This is not Taiwanese tradition. This is just me getting you something that I know you would never get yourself." She handed over a silver-wrapped box with a big bow on the top.

"Thank you, Leslie."

"Open it," someone shouted from behind.

"Right now?"

"That's the whole point," another person shouted.

"Okay then." I took off the ribbon and unwrapped the box. Lifting the top off, I heard chairs moving as people tried to see over others at what was inside. I opened the tissue paper and quickly put it back down, bringing the box under the table. Howls of laughter burst out from the cousins' table and some clapping came from the parents' table. I was so embarrassed.

Sebastian leaned over to me when I sat down. "I want to see you in that."

"Stop it. I'm not going to show it to everyone right now, and you'll only see it in private."

"I'm okay with that," Sebastian said, laughing along with everyone else.

Sebastian's father stood up and gave us an envelope, where inside were sheets of hotels that he had booked matching the dates of the flights Mom had given me. Ms. Donaldson had added on events in each city we were at, and not to be outdone, Lucia had booked dinners for us at a Michelin star restaurant in every city we were to visit.

Last, but not least, Victoria stood up and walked over with a device that was wrapped in red leather. "In keeping with today's theme, I thought red was appropriate. Open it."

I opened the cover and smiled. She knew me so well. Victoria announced for everyone else's benefit, "It's the latest Kindle, and I downloaded thousands of romance, sci-fi, cozy mystery, and fantasy books on there. I also subscribed Anne to some travel magazines as well to help her get back on that blogging she used to do."

"This is the best gift ever!" I stood up to give Victoria a hug. We held on for as long as we could. I whispered into her ear, "You're the best friend a girl could ever have. This was all a wonderful surprise, and I can't believe you pulled it all together."

"Thank goodness you hired that wedding planner. But I know, I'm that good." She laughed.

At the end of dinner, the band was playing. The lights dimmed low, and we were then dancing the night away. This was the wedding we wanted, and it had turned out perfectly. Thanks to my family and friends, we could look forward to the big wedding without trepidation now. At least, I hoped it would go off without a hitch.

Memories of Isabella's cousins and Geraldine's husband had been flooding my brain these last few days. Sebastian and Victoria had both said I didn't have to invite them, but I didn't want to exclude anyone. That was the whole point, right? To invite everyone who had come to the ball? To make them feel welcome and show them I wasn't a threat?

CHAPTER 28

THE WEEK FLEW BY. WE TRIED TO TAKE THE FAMILY to as many tourist attractions as we could, but we ended up just lounging at home and watching movies, which I loved. There was no need to impress or manage anyone. The kids were happy running around the garden and in the house playing hide and seek. Leslie and Jonathan were even lucky enough to go out on a couple of dinners by themselves, which was a huge thing, and it was the first time I'd seen the two of them smile at each other in a long time.

Erik was still being followed around by his daughters, who still held phones in their hands, and it melted my heart to see Paul and Victoria together. Victoria had caught the bouquet last night, and I hoped Paul would propose to her soon.

Mom had surprised me this morning with a photo, framed in a simple gold trim. It was of me at one years old, sitting on Rose's lap. It was the only photo she could find from that period, and I couldn't stop looking at it. That was Rose, my Ah Po—the lady who had begun this whole journey to find our family. As I stared at her picture, I fervently hoped that, after all the tragedies she'd experienced, the rest of her life really had been good. Rose deserved no less.

"That photo needs a prominent spot in this house," Sebastian said, coming to sit next to me.

"It sure does—as soon as I'm willing to let go of it."

"You've been holding it all morning."

"I can't stop staring at it. This is Rose, and that's me. We were together once. I mean, I knew that we had met before, but this picture makes it real."

Sebastian wrapped his arm around my shoulders. "You know, I was thinking—I know you want to give any money donated in the red envelopes to a charity, and I also know you've had a hard time figuring out whom to gift it to, but what if we used it to start an endowment in Rose's name? That way we can ensure there will always be money for any causes we deem fit to fund."

I jumped up to face Sebastian. "Oh, I love that idea!"

He beamed. "Thought you would."

"Anne!" Madison cried as she came running into the library, her eyes bright with excitement. She gestured out the door. "Look who's come!"

Sebastian and I walked toward the foyer, and when I saw who was standing there, I ran the rest of the way into Mary's arms. "You made it," I said, holding her tight.

She patted my back. "I didn't have a choice. Once Harrison got talking, he wouldn't stop, and then he and Grace both insisted I come. They booked my ticket without telling me! Of course, Ming-Yue is also here to help me, but I'm here to rest before your wedding. Where is my room?"

I turned around to see if Ben was nearby.

"Already taken care of, Anne," he said, coming down the stairs. "Can I escort you to your room, ma'am?" he asked Mary, who was more than happy to oblige. She looked so tired from the trip that I hoped the journey hadn't weakened her too much.

"Are you my great grandmother?" I heard Madison asking as she followed Mary up the stairs. "I heard you're my great grandmother. Not my real great grandmother is what Mom said, but close enough. Is that true? Can you tell me stories? I know lots of stories. I think we're going to be best friends."

I couldn't help laughing. Only Madison would be this comfortable with Mary at first sight. I imagined the two of them had lots to talk about.

"Nice to have all your family here?" Victoria said, walking in with a bowl of ice cream.

"Sure is. Let me have some." I took a bite before she could swing it away from me.

"Tomorrow's the big day. You excited?"

"I am, actually. We're already married, so I don't feel that pressure that everything has to go just right."

"But you're still nervous," she stated.

"That obvious?"

"You forget I've known you forever," she pointed out.

"True." I laughed. "I keep thinking about those Wilkens cousins, the ones who were mean."

Victoria lifted a shoulder. "It's your party. You didn't have to invite them."

She made it sound so easy. If only she knew. "I didn't want to exclude anyone if the whole point was to bring everyone together."

"It will all be fine. You'll just need to stick with Sebastian or me, or one of your own cousins for the night and forget about them. They'll be too busy stuffing their face with the delicious food Cook is making."

"Yeah, how did you get that ice cream? Cook kicked me out of the kitchen earlier today, saying I wasn't allowed to set foot in there until after the wedding."

Victoria slid me a smile. "She kicked me out, too, but I'm a bit more stubborn, so she enticed me with ice cream. It was a win-win for both of us, because she kicked me out and I left with yummy treats." She lifted her bowl to show me the contents.

Mom entered the room then, sweeping through with that look of organization on her face. "All right, girls, I think it's time to watch a movie and then call it a night. We have a big day tomorrow."

"That sounds like a grand plan, Mom." And just what I needed.

We woke up to morning fog on the day of the wedding, but the atmosphere in the air was unmatched. There was a peaceful stillness that instantly made me calm. Even though I had told Victoria I was excited for the wedding and didn't feel pressure, I still did a little bit. It was still my wedding day, and Sebastian and I would be the center of attention in front of hundreds of people.

I had seen the wedding venue only once—a big open field on Sauvie Island. I had agreed to a large marquee and the many decorations it would require, as well as several chartered jets that would pick up and deliver our guests from all over the world. I was sure the venue would look beautiful. Anything in Eda's capable hands would. I just wished that I could feel as confident about the guests themselves.

The only thing I had wanted to add to the occasion was the provision of a polaroid camera for every single guest. Eda had suggested we also provide photo albums so our guests could pop their pictures immediately inside them as tributes and memories for Sebastian and I. Of course, these photos wouldn't replace the professional photographer and videographer we had also hired, but I thought the polaroid cameras would make a fun addition to the event.

Thomas was back to do my hair and makeup. It was an evening wedding, so the morning had been quite serene. I'd treated the bridesmaids to a spa morning before we were required to head back for hair and makeup.

After everyone was ready, we got into our SUV limousines and drove to Sauvie Island. I remembered how Mom would bring us to the island for day adventures to pick fruit. It was surreal to think I'd be getting married here.

As we got closer, I started wondering where the field was. There was no way we could have taken a wrong turn. On each side of the road were trees covered in Christmas lights, all twinkling in the setting sun. As we started to slow, I rolled down the window to stare at what appeared to be a land for fairies.

There was a parking area to the left and a huge white marquee in the middle—as huge as one I'd seen at a Cirque du Soleil show. The doors were open, and there was a canopy overhanging the entrance. A red carpet had been rolled out to greet guests. My jaw dropped.

We swerved to the right and went behind the big tent, where we were dropped off outside one of two smaller tents. I was directed to the one to the left. It had a feminine aspect to it, which meant the other tent was for Sebastian.

A soft inviting light poured from the doorway. Intrigued, I walked up to my tent to find that flowers seemed to be growing around the entrance, and I entered to find there was a shaggy rug, numerous fluffy pillows, and a soft, luxurious couch inside that I immediately sank into. Like the outside entrance, flowers also decorated the edges of the tent. There was a big wardrobe with its doors open off to the side, and I could see it held my wedding dress with my blue heels peeking out from the bottom. I looked up to find that, just like the walls, the ceiling was also draped with white silk. The final touch included an array of electric candles, cleverly placed along the walls to create a warm ambiance. I had no idea that any of this could be put together in a simple place like a tent! It felt like a different world.

"Time to put on your dress," Mom said, after we'd oohed and aahed at the room. She had taken the dress down and was holding it out for me to step into. Even though Sebastian and I had gotten married only a week earlier, this felt different. It felt like we were doing it for real this time; that last time was just practice. I couldn't help but smile—we were lucky to be able to get married twice.

I stepped into the dress, Mom pulling it up at the back and Victoria holding the front.

"Did you eat one too many ice creams?" Victoria asked as Mom struggled to zip the dress up.

"I did not! This dress will fit."

They kept pulling and pushing, and I was starting to get a little concerned. Did we bring my red dress to wear in case this one didn't fit?

"Oh, wait!" Mom let go of the dress suddenly, and I went toppling into Victoria's arms. "I just remembered where the actual hook is. Stand up straight, Anne."

I straightened, and soon after I felt Mom snap the dress in place with no effort at all. "Really? All it took was that?" I asked her.

"Sorry, there's just too many buttons and snaps on this dress. I forgot which was which."

"The good thing is your dress is on, and you look absolutely gorgeous," Victoria said.

The three bridesmaids put on their dresses next, and we all made final touches to our hair and makeup. Eda came in then, and we went over the schedule.

"I cannot believe all the things you did! This is magical," I gushed.

She smiled. "I had a lot of fun doing it. You gave me free reign, which most brides would never do, so I did everything I wanted, and, well, this was it."

"Well, it's beautiful," I said sincerely.

"Wait till you see the big tent."

Eda then escorted us out of our tent, and I immediately saw that a red carpet had been installed from mine and Sebastian's tent all the way to the rear of the main tent. It must have been done while we were getting changed! And it was so thoughtful because no one was getting their shoes soiled tonight. A string of lights lit the way, hanging high above our heads on either side of the red carpet, and garlands of flowers were wound around the poles holding up the lights. The smell of them was intoxicating, and I floated down the walkway in a dream.

"Are you ready?" Eda asked when we stopped in front of the back entrance.

"Ready as I will ever be."

"Remember, there's a lot of people who came, most you don't know. It might be a shock, so I'm just preparing you."

"Thank you."

Eda turned to the others. "The rest of you girls ready? Great. Okay, Victoria, you first."

I watched as my friends walked into the tent with Sebastian's groomsmen. The music was beautiful, and my mind started drifting with the music.

"Anne," Harrison whispered.

Startled, I whirled and almost lost my balance, but Harrison caught me.

"I didn't hear you come back here," I gasped.

"I could tell. You were in your own world." He smiled. "Are you ready?"

"Yes." And I was.

I had been standing off to the side so hadn't gotten a good look inside the tent. All I'd had a chance to see was the glow of more Christmas lights and the sound of rustling dresses.

When Harrison escorted me to the entrance, I was stunned. Eda wasn't kidding. There were a lot of people here, at least a few hundred. And not one face did I recognize. But even more astounding were the flowers. They were everywhere. And just like my tent, white silk also draped the ceiling and walls, covering up any sign of the tent's original material. The red carpet extended all the way to the aisle, and I saw Sebastian at the end of it.

My mind cleared at the sight of my husband, and I focused on him until I felt Harrison transfer my hand to Sebastian's. I then turned to give Harrison a kiss on the cheek. "Thank you."

"Thank *you*." He squeezed my hand before letting go and taking his seat.

"Just focus on me," Sebastian whispered.

"Can you tell I'm overwhelmed?"

"Absolutely. You look like a deer in headlights."

I laughed and quickly caught myself before I got too loud, but that was all I needed to relax. I held Sebastian's hand as we faced the pastor. The rest of the ceremony went off without a hitch, and we shared a secret smile when we put our rings back on—so none of the guests were any wiser, we had taken off our wedding rings in order to reuse them for this ceremony.

Everyone cheered when the pastor announced us husband and wife. At that point, I forgot all about the audience, I was so happy to be married to Sebastian! We exited the tent to thunderous applause. Eda was at the entrance to greet us, and she escorted us to yet another tent directly behind the two small ones we had prepared in. We entered, and then both of us stopped, staring in amazement. The inside was a complete garden, even accommodating a walking path and a bench under a tree.

"How . . .?" I started.

Eda just smiled. "Only the best. You got married at sunset, so photos outside weren't feasible, even though I do have you booked to take photos at Multnomah Falls after your honeymoon. What do you think?"

Sebastian spoke first, as I was still tongue-tied. "Eda, you've outdone yourself. This is amazing. I am very glad Anne hired you."

"Thank you." Eda beamed.

"Is that a plum blossom tree?" I whispered.

"Yes, Victoria said that was meaningful to you two."

We looked at each other and my tongue-tiedness seeped away. "I can't believe you did all this. I would never have thought of any of this."

"That's why I'm here," was her simple reply.

"Eda," I said, holding her back for a moment. "How did you pull all this off in such a short time? I mean, this is really amazing."

Eda smiled as she looked around the room, landing on the staff that were waiting for us. "It helps to have vendors and staff who are a well-oiled machine at my disposal. They know exactly what to do at a moment's notice with only the slightest of instructions. It also helps that we all have years of experience. Now, let me introduce you to your photographer."

We did no less than forty-five minutes of photos. I felt like a model as I posed sitting or draping while staring into Sebastian's eyes, and we had to redo a number of shots because I kept giggling.

Halfway through, Eda and Lauren showed up with my qipao. Ms. Lu had flown up with the dress this past week to make sure it fit. I had to say I loved the dress, especially how simple it looked.

"I got you some new flats, too, to match your qipao," Leslie said, pulling out a pair of bright red flats from the bag she had brought in.

I couldn't take my heels off fast enough. The flats were slipped on, and my feet gave a sigh. "You are a life saver, Leslie! I hadn't even thought about shoes. I figured I'd be stuck in heels for the whole night. Wow, I think I can start feeling my toes again."

"I remembered the tip from my wedding. I'm glad you like them," Leslie said, beaming.

The rest of our close family and friends joined us near the end, and we were having so much fun we almost forgot we had hundreds of guests waiting for us. But when it was time, Eda ushered us to the back of yet another big tent where we were going to be presented as Mr. and Mrs. Gole.

When the music started playing, I turned to Sebastian. "That's our song."

"I know," he said, smiling at me.

It dawned on me. "You requested it!" He'd remembered the song we had heard when we went to dinner for the first time!

"Of course, I did. It's our special night."

Again, as soon as I looked inside, I was stunned at the amount of people that had come and on such short notice. It was unbelievable that this many people were interested in our wedding. They didn't even know us! But I had been replaying what Isabella had said over and over again. She was right. This was our time to show these people who we were, and that we weren't scared of them or of having them around. We were going to live our lives and enjoy it.

Right then, Eda came up to us again. "You two are next," she announced, gently ushering us forward.

We walked in to a sea of people all clapping and smiling. That was a good start seeing how we didn't know most of them. Eda directed us to the front of the tent where the band was located. They seemed like they were waiting for something.

As we sat, we heard the masses sit down behind us and then the lights dimmed low. A spotlight came on, and a solid silence permeated the room. On the stage was Lauren. She waved at us and swayed to the music that had suddenly started up. I could hear some whispering behind me—people were wondering what she was going to do.

The song sounded familiar, but I really was not good with names of songs. Then Lauren started singing, and the whispering around us was replaced with little gasps that seemed to roll through the crowd. My mouth dropped open. I had no idea she could sing so well, and, apparently, neither did anyone else.

Lauren's voice flowed through the air, sending a calmness through the crowd. It was mesmerizing, and I felt like time had slowed. I couldn't sing worth anything and was always amazed when someone I knew could. When she finished, I felt like my heart had taken a stroll on a cloud of music and was now trying to catch up to the present. I started clapping and stood up to give her a standing ovation. Sebastian whistled next to me, and more and more people joined us. I could see Lauren's face start to redden, but she was smiling as she gave a low curtsy before straightening and tapping on the microphone to get everyone's attention.

"Anne and Sebastian, we haven't known each other for long but I feel like we're the best of friends. I know others in this room don't feel the same and might never will, but I've got your back, and I know others who do too. We love you so much, and I'll be the first to say welcome to the Wilkens family. We're made up of all types, but you couldn't have found a better family to join. I love you, Anne and Sebastian!"

The room didn't give as big an ovation as they did after her song, but Lauren was beaming, and I knew I was too. Fate did strange things sometimes, but I was grateful she had come into my life.

Lauren stepped down from the stage and made her way toward us while the first course was being brought out. I disliked salads so had insisted on something else, anything else really. The waiter sat a soup of minestrone in front of me. It was only then I realized I had barely eaten all day, and I took up my spoon and was halfway through it before Lauren reached our table.

"Congratulations, you two," Lauren said, standing next to me.

We stood up to exchange hugs, and Lauren and I hung on for a few seconds more.

"That was the most beautiful song I have ever heard," I told her, pulling back to squeeze her arms. "I had no idea you could sing like that."

"Not many people do. I do it for fun, and it makes me happy, so only close family and friends know. I wanted it to be a surprise for you. And I wanted a chance to let my family know not to mess up your night tonight." She gave a little laugh. "I think I got my point across."

"I noticed and thank you. I have been nervous about tonight."

A man walked up then and put an arm around Lauren. "Lauren would never let any harm come to you. I'm almost jealous how much she loves you. I'm Stephen, by the way. I don't think we've formally met."

"Stephen! It's great to finally meet you." I really was happy to finally put a face to Lauren's other half.

"I know you two only met recently, but once Lauren

latches onto someone she rarely lets go, and she defends them with all her might," Stephen said.

"I do, you know," Lauren added. "So if anyone gives you trouble, just let me know." She winked as Stephen whisked her off to their table.

"I can second Stephen's sentiment," Sebastian said. "Lauren is a feisty one and will defend her loved ones and chosen friends with her life. She's proven that with Isabella, and I'm pretty sure you're under her wing now too."

"I have no idea how I deserved her friendship in the first place. We didn't even know each other two months ago."

"Sometimes friends come and go, but every once in a while you meet someone and you just know." There was a twinkle in his eyes, and I couldn't help but smile. This was exactly how Sebastian and I had met. Sudden and quick, and here we were, married and surrounded by family and friends and so many people we didn't know. At the realization that there were hundreds of people behind us, I turned to take a good look around for the first time.

Most were eating and chatting, but every so often I saw a pair of eyes studying me. It made me uncomfortable, but I wasn't going to let that get to me today. Instead, I focused on the room for the first time and really took in what the place looked like.

Flowers, five feet tall, adorned every table, and I had never seen so many combinations of plates, bowls, silverware, and glasses. The tablecloth was a light shade of pink. It pooled around our feet and was soft to the touch. The same silk drapes covered the ceiling and walls, and a faux floor covered every square inch of the ground. Eda had also hung red lanterns from the ceiling, nestled amongst a sea of flowers and lights. Lights that you couldn't actually see, as they were disguised among the vines and flowers—they looked like twinkling stars in a forest. But the main centerpiece was the big tree in the middle, covered in plum blossoms.

I was awed. This was amazing. It felt like we were in a field of flowers and the sun had just come out after it had rained. Dew drops glistened in between the flowers, and soft music was drifting out from somewhere among the branches. And to think I didn't want a large wedding? This was beyond anything I could have imagined, and from the look on Sebastian's face, he felt the same.

"I never thought I'd have a wedding like this," he said, echoing my thoughts.

"Me either." We smiled at each other and finished our soup.

Before the main course started, Eda had our table merged with the wedding party. With Victoria and Lauren on either side, we ate the delicious food being placed on the table. Halfway through, we saw the band setting up and, just like in rehearsal, we knew it was time for our first dance.

We danced our way onto the dance floor and went straight into our first dance. I had to laugh. Sebastian had been in charge of picking the music, because I never remembered the songs I liked. He had chosen an upbeat tune for our dance, and he twirled me around the dance floor with a smile as big as the Cheshire Cat.

I didn't even notice when people started joining us until Madison was giving me a hug, and I looked down to see all my cousins' kids behind her.

"We want to dance with you too," Madison said.

"She's my bride today," Sebastian teased.

"But she was our aunt first." She stomped her feet at this, and the others looked on with wide eyes, no doubt wondering if Madison was going to get her way.

"All right, you can have the next dance." Sebastian bowed and started walking away.

"We want to dance with both of you, though," Ellen piped in, so quiet that we almost missed what she said.

"Well, that can be arranged," I said.

We had two kids on either side of us and formed a circle as we started dancing to the next song. A few other people joined in, too, and before we knew it, it seemed like everyone in the whole room was circled around us.

I saw a hand tap Sebastian's arm, and a man who looked familiar stepped into the circle.

"Excuse me, but may I have this dance with the new Mrs. Gole?"

I could tell Sebastian wanted to say no, and then I remembered who he was—Geraldine's husband, Walter. He was the first person I met at the Christmas Gala, the same man who set the snowball of ill intent for the rest of the night.

I might as well get this over with. It was time to put this dread aside. "I'd be happy to."

"Anne . . ." Sebastian looked at me with a questioning look.

"I'll be fine. He just wants to dance."

"I have no ill will toward you, Anne," Walter said, taking my hands and whisking me off into the crowd.

"I hope you don't."

"It's my wife you should be worried about, but I heard you got her locked up, so congratulations. You're the first to have tamed the great Geraldine."

"I didn't lock her up," I said, offended.

"Of course, you did. If you hadn't inherited the fortune, she would not have gone off her rockers." Walter held up his hand before I could object. "I have nothing against you, Anne. I'm actually in full control of my faculties tonight. I thought I'd take advantage and come and tell you 'well done.'"

"Well done?"

"You outsmarted and stood up to the queen of bullies."

"Your own wife . . .?"

"Only on paper." He winked at me.

"Okay . . ."

"I've rendered you speechless, I see. I think my time here is done. Oh, here's Jack. A much better companion for you. Hi, Jack!"

"Walter."

The two men shook hands, and then Walter was off. I watched him head to the bar.

"Congratulations, Anne. You look very happy today," Jack said. "May I have this next dance?"

I gave him a smile and a nod, and we started dancing. I breathed a sigh of relief that I was no longer in Walter's arms. "Thank you, Jack. I'm glad you asked for a dance. I wanted to tell you that I wouldn't be here if not for you. You've been such a support since I inherited Anthony's estate."

Jack shook his head. "No need to thank me. You were brave, Anne. You were willing to take on the negativity and turn it into something good. You found your family, and I hear you're making a foundation for Rose."

"Yes! Oh, I meant to tell Eda to make a sign for the red envelopes."

"Already done."

"What do you mean?"

"I'm assuming Eda is your wedding planner? The lady who has an earpiece and has orchestrated the most elaborate wedding I've ever attended?"

"Yes, she's the one." I flushed. Now that I looked at the tent through Jack's eyes, it did appear outrageous. Did I overdo it?

"I see you haven't stopped overthinking." Jack laughed.

"I'm still Anne," I said.

"And I hope you stay that way. In answer to your earlier question, there is a beautiful sign at the entrance where we were to drop our red envelopes and sign our name in a book. There's a photo of Rose with you on her lap and a story for anyone interested to learn more about who she was."

"Oh!"

"I think your family and friends did a good job working with Eda on this wedding." Jack gave me a knowing look.

"They did, and they've all been supportive the whole way through."

He smiled. "Remember the advice I gave you when we first met?"

"Yes—don't let the others get to me."

"That's right. Never let anyone in my family bring you down."

I returned his smile. "Thanks, Jack. Can I ask you something?"

"Of course."

I said quietly, "What's going to happen to Geraldine?"

"I don't know. She's responding to treatment, but then she's also very good at acting, so I don't know if it's genuine. But she's my little sister, and I feel obliged to take care of her."

"I see . . . ."

Jack made a show of looking around. "I noticed Isabella is not here," he said, directly changing the subject.

"I did invite her," I was quick to respond.

"Out of obligation?"

I ducked my head. "Yes."

"Even though you two are like oil and water, you still see something in her that draws you to her?"

"Not really. It was more because I had invited everyone in the Wilkens family."

"It's not you, though, Anne. You only wrap yourself with

people who are close to you. This wedding has more strangers than I think you've ever let yourself be around, and this is an intimate occasion."

I tilted my head. "What are you getting at, Jack?"

"Lauren told me how she and Isabella had talked to you about holding a big wedding that included all the guests we had at the Christmas Gala. That this was a way to introduce yourself to this new world you have been thrust into."

"Well, yes."

"You listened to Isabella."

Jack paused to let that sink in. I had listened, hadn't I? I looked around the room and saw all the happy faces dancing, chatting, and just hanging out with each other. Yes, they had all come to my wedding. "So I did," I mused.

"Did you ever think why she shared that with you? Why she even bothered to?"

"I asked her. She said it was because the sooner I settled in, the sooner she'd hear less of my name."

This brought a loud laugh from Jack, and I flinched.

"Isabella is an enigma to those who don't know her," he replied. "She only shows one side of herself and lets very few into her private life. And yet she does care. Sebastian would never have dated her for all those years if she wasn't a caring person. You know that much about your husband, don't you?"

Yes, I did know my husband.

"I wouldn't give up on Isabella too soon," Jack continued. "Lauren seems to have taken to you, and Isabella is never far away if Lauren is around. It might behoove you to find a way to bridge a truce with Isabella. And, if you haven't noticed, the other cousins follow Isabella's lead. If you really want to win over the family, Isabella would be the first you'd need to convince." He held up a hand to prevent my response. "You know as well as I do that Isabella won't be the one to reach out. Though, in her own way, she already has. You're a lot more open-minded, Anne, and Isabella . . . well, I worry about her. Her family life hasn't always been the best. The finery that surrounds her does a very good job of covering the hurt she holds inside."

"Why are you telling me this?"

"I'm old and won't be here for much longer. I want to see my family members all happy and getting along in the time I have left. Seeing Geraldine fall apart almost broke me. This is not what my parents would have wanted. In a way, I'm thankful the fortune has now passed on to your family. Maybe your children and grandchildren will handle it a lot better than we did."

I smiled. "Yes. And that goes for you too, Jack—being happy."

He smiled. "Ah, but I am."

"You always see the good side of others, don't you?"

"Not always, but when it comes to family, I don't give up on them."

I beamed at those words, and I knew he knew that he had hit home with his point.

We danced to the edge of the dance floor, and I saw Ms. Donaldson coming toward us. Jack saw her too.

"This is my queue to leave," he said quickly, letting go of me and sliding right into Ms. Donaldson's arms. But before he disappeared into the crowd, he looked at me and gave me a wink, and I couldn't help but notice how his arms encircled Ms. Donaldson a little tighter.

Jack's words bounced around in my head, but I put them aside for later. This was not the night to ponder his advice about Isabella.

I took advantage of being without a dance partner to wander about the room for a bit, saying hi and introducing myself to people here and there.

"If you always throw a party like this, we will be there," a voice said from behind me.

I turned to see Isabella's cousins, the same ones who had made me cry at my Christmas Gala. Tingles started racing up my arm, and my first instinct was to bolt, but then their words seeped into my brain. "Oh, thank you . . . I think."

"It's actually tastefully done, and the idea of having it in a tent in the middle of a field—very niche," Jessica said. The other cousin behind her was nodding and smiling. "I'm going to have to tell Monique about this. She should totally do this instead of at that church she wants it at. Anyways, you've passed for now."

Jessica walked off with me gaping after her.

The girl who had nodded slid to my side. "Don't take what she says to heart. She tries to emulate Isabella but with less class."

"I hadn't noticed," I said, raising one of my eyebrows.

She laughed. "Isabella isn't the only one in our family who thinks she's all that. You just haven't met the nice ones. I'm Emily."

"And I'm Anne."

"And we want to say on behalf of our cousins how sorry we are at the comments they made at the Christmas Gala. We have nothing against you."

"Thanks."

All this niceness was getting to be a bit odd. Where was Isabella? I needed some of her snark, but I doubt she'd show up tonight. I felt a sense of sadness roll over me, and Jack's words came back to mind.

Unaware of where my emotions had led, Emily said, "I'm going to get some more shaved ice. See you later."

That got my attention. "Wait! Shaved ice?"

"Yeah, you have some in the corner by the bar. The

bartender will even use some of his drinks on the shaved ice. It's soooo good."

I felt my smile return. This party just kept getting better and better. I kept waiting for the other shoe to drop, but after talking to Emily for a little bit longer while we waited for shaved ice, I decided to let go for tonight and just enjoy myself.

I found Sebastian outside playing bocce, but the closer I looked, the more the balls didn't look like balls. I laughed when I realized what they were. Someone had brought golf balls, and they had been painted different colors.

I walked up to Sebastian and put my arm around him. "Hi, sweetheart."

He turned and enveloped me in his arms. "There you are. After I left you on the dance floor, I couldn't seem to find you again. Then these boys challenged me to a game of bocce."

"And you couldn't say no." I laughed.

"Of course not. Someone was willing to stuff their pockets with golf balls just so we could have some fun."

"Sebastian, it's your turn!" a man on the other side called out.

"Randy here is going to take over for me," he called back. "I have my bride now, and I'm not letting her go."

He pulled me away from the group, and we started walking into the darkness. We laughed as a bunch of whistles followed us.

"I'm so happy right now," I said.

"I am too. Did anyone bother you inside?"

"No, actually. Everyone has been weirdly nice. Makes me wonder if Lauren did anything."

"She doesn't have a mean bone in her body, but she does

a good job standing up for others, and her family respects her. You've got a good ally there."

"She comes with Isabella."

"Anne—"

"Before you say anything, Jack was telling me to give Isabella another chance."

"Ah, I was wondering when he would try that."

"You knew?"

"He's been trying to talk to me about it, but I kept telling him he had to talk to you directly. I am not getting in between you and Isabella. It's up to you if you want to attempt a friendship with her, just know I'm always on your side."

"That's very sweet of you."

We fell into each other's arms and danced in the middle of the field under the night sky to the music that was seeping out of the tent. Stars galore hung over us, and I was the happiest person in the world.

My thoughts wandered to what Jessica had said. I didn't think I'd be throwing anything like this for a long while, if ever again, but it was really nice to hear our guests were enjoying themselves. Well, maybe the Christmas Gala could be spruced up a bit. Eda could do wonders to a party like that, especially with Christmas decorations at her disposal.

CHAPTER 29

The next morning, we were all a bit groggy. Mom, Mary, Harrison, Grace, and their family had all spent the night at the mansion. Victoria had joined us too. Cook had put out a mouthwatering breakfast spread on the balcony, and we all ate without talking for quite some time.

Victoria was the first to break the silence. "The wedding was *so* nice, Anne. Eda outdid herself. I'm so happy you hired her."

I gave her a look. "I know you and Lauren conspired on things with her, so not all the credit goes to her."

"Only a little," Victoria admitted, but she was smiling, and I knew she was congratulating herself for contributing to all the little details that really counted—the plum blossoms and Rose's Foundation most of all.

"Did anyone notice how Jack and Ms. Donaldson hung out with each other all night long?" she then said while spearing a piece of bacon.

"I did!" Leslie said. "They were so cute. Did you see that young woman Ms. Donaldson was talking to? They looked so much alike. It's like they were mother and daughter."

This time Sebastian almost choked on his eggs. I gave him a glass of water, and with a couple of startled glances at Leslie, who was looking really worried, he was finally able to say, "You saw someone who looked like Ms. Donaldson's daughter?"

"Yeah . . . she looked similar, but I might have been mistaken." She paused. "Did I miss something?"

Everyone was silent, waiting for Sebastian to speak. He looked at me with pleading eyes, and I bent over to give him a hug. I whispered to him, "What if it was her? Wouldn't you want to know?"

He nodded and turned to look at the others. "There's the possibility that the lady you saw is my mother."

Jonathan spoke up, confusion written all over his features. "Your mother?"

I cut in before anyone else could ask any further questions, "Sebastian was adopted, and we only recently found out that his biological mother is alive. We sent her a wedding invitation but heard nothing back, so we assumed she wasn't coming. But now it seems that she did come." I turned to look at Sebastian. "I wonder if she's still here. She wouldn't have flown all the way here, talked to her own mother, and then not stayed to talk to you."

"You never know. She might have taken one look at me and decided to run for the hills."

A gasp sounded from Grace, but otherwise, everyone had stopped what they were doing and were staring at Sebastian. Grace was the first one to move. She stood up and walked over to him, turned him around in his seat, and put her hands on his shoulders. "Sebastian, as someone who knows the loss of family, I would go find her. Take every opportunity you can get to see and hold your family before they are no longer with us. If this woman really is your mother, and she's come to your wedding to see you after all these years, she must want to speak to you. But I'll bet she's scared too. Don't let years go by until it's too late."

Harrison spoke next, looking strangely resigned yet relaxed at the same time. "She speaks from experience, Sebastian. You're now family, so I can be blunt with you. What Grace is telling you is don't be like me. Go call this Ms. Donaldson and see if this mysterious woman really is your mother. She might just be a look-alike."

"Baba!" Leslie said. "Don't be so callous!"

"I'm not being callous. Look at what we could have had if I hadn't been so stubborn."

Mary walked in right then. "You didn't wait for me for breakfast."

"We waited, but we all got hungry," Harrison said.

"Well, I don't know what this conversation is about, but I heard what Harrison just said and I agree. He was stubborn. I was stubborn. And look at us now. I've missed my own grandkids growing up and almost missed my great-grandkids growing up."

"Yeah, we never knew a grandparent from Baba's side," Paul said.

"Yes, you really should go find her," Leslie added.

"Okay! Okay, I'm going." Sebastian pushed back his seat and rushed inside before any more of my family could hound him.

"You guys didn't need to gang up on him," I said, giving everyone a look.

"Oh yes, we did," Grace said. "He would never have gone to make the call otherwise. There would have been excuse after excuse. I know—I'm married to someone who did that for fifty years."

"Humph," Harrison said.

We all laughed.

I decided it was time to change the subject. "Mary, when do you head back to Taiwan?"

"Tomorrow. And you and Sebastian and everyone here are coming with me."

"What?" more than one person said, all heads turning to look at Mary.

"You've had your American wedding here, and now you need to go to Taiwan to have a wedding there. I've missed out on too many weddings, and I insist. Anne has enough money to cover all of us, and we're doing a big feast. I'll invite all the family to get together, and all of you can meet your cousins, aunts, uncles, and other relatives. I've already decided. Anne, you need to look for flights for all of us. We should all fly together. After being separated for so long I'm not letting any of you out of my sight."

Leslie and I looked at each other and just shook our heads. We both knew how the older generation liked bossing us young ones around. It was kinda nice to have our own grandmother figure with us now. Little did she realize I wasn't going to let her out of my sight either, not until we got to know each other a bit better.

"That sounds good, Mary. I'll get right on that. But keep in mind we have a lot of people, and Sebastian and I are going on our honeymoon first. It might be a while before we can leave, especially if we all want to fly together on one flight."

"Yes, yes. You can figure it out. I have nowhere to go, and Harrison's store is being fixed, so he can't go work there right now. Grace is retired. Erik, Leslie, and Paul, you are bringing your families too. You have time to tell your work you're going on vacation with your family. It's a very important matter. We all just found each other. It's time to celebrate."

Jonathan looked like he was about to protest, but I saw

Leslie give him a look, and she must have kicked him hard, because he doubled over and began muttering under his breath. Mary gave him a disapproving look, and all I could think was I was so happy everyone was here.

Mary wasn't finished though. "It's going to be a joint banquet because I missed Harrison and Grace's wedding too. Yes. Yes. Yes." She seemed to lose herself in her thoughts after that, and some of us went back to eating.

I thought it was time to change the subject before Jonathan could find a chance to object to the trip again and before Mary could come up with another plan. "Harrison, I'm glad to hear your shop is finally getting fixed."

"Yes, I got a generous check in the mail for the purposes of bringing the shop back to pristine order." Harrison looked intently at me. "You wouldn't know where this check came from, would you?"

"I do, but I'm not going to tell you. I'm just glad to hear that he came through."

"Ah, so it was a he."

"You could see that it was a he in the video," I pointed out.

"Very true, but you've confirmed it."

Grace piped in. "Harrison, we've talked about this, and there's no need to find out who that person is. Anne's already taken care of it."

"Humph. I want to know. He destroyed my store."

"Maybe one day I'll bring him by to meet you, Harrison. How's that?"

Another "humph" was his response. I was about to ask Victoria something when Harrison started talking again. "Don't you want to know what I'm changing the store to?"

"You're changing the store?" everyone echoed.

"Yes." Harrison looked satisfied that he now had everyone's attention. He looked at Mom. "In honor of my little sister, who I am glad is now part of my life, I am no longer going to have a postcard store. There will be a studio in the back where my office was so I can still paint—and room enough for someone to join me." Again, he looked at Mom, who had now turned a deep shade of pink. "And the front of the store will now be a gallery where I will be showcasing Josephine's artwork."

A gasp came from Mom, and she stood up and ran to Harrison, whom she engulfed in a hug. We all laughed at the surprised look on Harrison's face.

"Thank you, Harrison! That is such a fantastic surprise. I don't know what to say," Mom gushed.

He patted her arm. "Don't say anything. Come visit and see the space and bring some of your artwork with you. We can hang some up as soon as the walls are done."

"It's—"

"Super generous, I know. But you're my sister, and your art is fantastic. It's crazy you're being overlooked by others. So, I will provide the space for you to exhibit your wonderful art. Now, please stop hugging me."

We all laughed. Mom gave Harrison one more hug before returning to her seat. I looked around the table and felt my heart swell. The only one missing at the table was Sebastian. I excused myself to go and search for him.

I looked through all the rooms downstairs but saw no sign of Sebastian. Did he go to our bedroom to have some privacy? But one look into our bedroom only showed me our open suitcases that contained the initial items we would be taking on our honeymoon. We were leaving tonight for Bora Bora; a place I had always wanted to visit but could never afford. We were both super excited for the two-week trip, but right now, I could feel my heart starting to race. Was Sebastian okay?

I decided to check outside and went to the barn where the

sled was kept, the same one we had used on our first date. I had found him here in the past when he wanted to hide. Sure enough, there, sitting in the sled with his head in his hands, was Sebastian. I climbed in next to him and put my arms around him. "Was it her?"

He nodded as he leaned into me.

"Are you going to meet her?"

Again, he nodded, but this time he sat back and looked me in the eyes. "I'm terrified. What if we don't get along? What if she takes one look at me close-up and runs for it?"

"I don't think she'll do that."

"How do you know?"

"She flew here to see you, Sebastian. She talked to you on the phone and is willing to meet with you. She wouldn't do all that if she was going to make a run for it. She's had plenty of opportunities to do that since yesterday."

"That's true." He released a deep sigh and leaned his head on the wall behind us.

"Where and when are you going to meet her?"

"My grandmother—which is still weird to say—is going to bring her to the airport before we leave so we can meet. My mother is going to be staying with her until I return. It'll give them a chance to get to know each other again. I could feel my grandmother smiling through the phone. I could tell she really loves her, and I can't believe they were separated all these years." He shook his head and ran his hands through his hair.

"Well, we better get packing if we're going to make it to the airport."

"Right. What would I do without you?"

"You wouldn't know which end was up," I teased. Then I ran as fast as I could before Sebastian could catch me, laughing all the way to our room.

CHAPTER 30

WE GOT TO THE AIRPORT A BIT TIGHT ON TIME. Sebastian was a wound-up ball of tension and was driving me crazy as he would sit down for five seconds before standing and pacing, only to sit and start the process all over again. Even the people around us had started staring at him.

"Sebastian, why don't you sit down with me and look at the trips we've been gifted," I suggested.

"Not now. I'm so nervous."

Thank goodness that at that moment I saw Ms. Donaldson, who was walking beside a woman who really did look like a younger version of her. "They're here, sweetheart." I put a hand on Sebastian's shoulder to steady him, but maybe I was really steadying myself. I was nervous like Sebastian was, because I didn't want him to get hurt. But both women were smiling, and I thought I could see tears in his mother's eyes.

They walked over, and his mother immediately enveloped him into a hug. Sebastian was still for a few seconds. I think he was shocked at the sudden physical contact, but he recovered fast and wrapped his arms around her.

His mother pulled back and looked directly into his eyes. "Sebastian, I know you might not forgive me, but I really have loved you all these years. It broke my heart that I couldn't take you with me to my new life."

"I know," was all he said.

"I wanted to meet you before you left so I could tell you that I'm not going anywhere. If you want to see me after you get back, then I'll be here. There's no catch. We're finally able to see each other again, and I will be here for you however you need. It'll be on your terms."

"Thanks . . ."

They stared at each other for what seemed like forever. Ms. Donaldson broke the silence by enfolding them both in a big hug. "I am never letting the two of you go again, no matter what you say. Sebastian will return home from his honeymoon, and we will start from there. I have no idea what will happen, but nothing can be worse than us being separated for this long again."

Sebastian and his mother both wiped their eyes and let each other go.

His mother looked at me, as if realizing I had been there the whole time. "You better go, Sebastian. Your bride is waiting."

I walked up to stand by my husband's side. "I hope to get to know you, too, when we come back," I said to her.

"Of course," his mother said, taking my hands into hers. "We are family now. But as I said, I'll take the cues from Sebastian."

We got on our plane and the stewardess had some champagne flutes ready for us. As we waited for the pilot to give the okay for takeoff, Sebastian asked, "What did you bring with you to do on the plane?" He was taking out his sci-fi book that looked more like a tomb.

"I brought this." I pulled out the little red journal Sebastian had given me.

"You still have it?"

"Of course, I do!"

"I was just teasing. I never saw you writing in it, so I thought it got stuffed in a drawer again."

"No, I would never do that. I just couldn't figure out what I wanted to use it for."

"And now?" he asked, a brow raised.

"We're on a new adventure, and I think I'd like to start our new life in this journal. Maybe one day our kids will want to read it."

His lips curved. "Already thinking of kids, huh?"

"One day—I didn't say now. We have a lot of travels to do before having kids."

"I can agree on that."

I squeezed his hand and then asked, "You feeling okay about your mother?"

Sebastian was silent for a moment, deep in thought. "Yeah, I think I'm okay. Her hug shocked me for a second, and I thought I'd have more of a wall up. But seeing you find your family and being open to accepting them, even with all the drama, showed me that I can at least give my mother a chance. We should talk and get to know each other a bit before I make any big decisions. No one said we have to become good friends."

I nodded. "You never know what will happen."

He shot me a look. "Yes, well, I might get sucked into a whole family drama. Is that what you're saying?"

I laughed. "She does have a whole family that you haven't met yet. Who knows what secrets they might be hiding?"

"I doubt my family will be as dramatic as yours. I still find it mindboggling that what was a very straightforward inheritance turned into you finding your extended family, and not just in one country, but in two."

"Family is a funny thing, isn't it?" And I couldn't wait to get to know mine better.

EPILOGUE

FIVE YEARS LATER

"Oh my goodness, will she ever stop crying?"

"Maybe she needs a diaper changed?" I suggested.

Sebastian was holding our daughter and bouncing her around the living room, hoping she'd calm down and go to sleep seeing how it was two in the morning. But Joy didn't seem to have any intention of stopping.

"What about if I sleep with her tonight?" I said. "It's worked before."

"You were the one who said you didn't want her getting used to us sleeping with her, that she needed to get used to staying in her crib."

"Be quiet," I hissed. "I already have a headache. And I know what I said, but I'm desperate!"

"Why don't you read her your journal? That's bound to put her to sleep."

"You think my journal is boring?" I shot him a look.

"I don't know, I haven't read it. Why don't you enlighten us? We've tried everything else; let's just read to her and maybe she'll calm down."

I had found my little red journal tucked in the back of my

drawer just the other day. Sebastian had been teasing me that he was going to peek in it one night and read about all my secrets. I had told him to go ahead, as everything in there detailed our first six months of marriage; nothing he didn't already know. That seemed to deflate his excitement and probably why he thought what I'd written was going to be boring and a good reason for our daughter to go to sleep, or at the very least, stop crying.

"Fine, I'll give it a try."

I grabbed the red journal off my nightstand and turned to the first page.

Saturday, June 25, 2011
Sebastian is snoring next to me as we fly to Bora Bora.

"Hey! Is that really what you wrote in your journal? As in the very first sentence?"

"Sure was," I said, turning the book around to show him. "Shall I continue?"

"Yes, please. She's still crying."

We just got married—twice! Two gorgeous, extravagant weddings.

"They were nice, weren't they?"

"Are you going to let me keep reading, or are you going to interrupt me after every sentence?"

"Yes. I mean, no. Keep reading," he said, waving me on while still rocking a crying Joy.

. . .

All our family were there, both Sebastian and my newfound extended family.

"And it's grown bigger since," I heard Sebastian whisper to Joy, whose crying had just turned into simpers.

I closed my journal, given I wasn't getting very far. "You know what? Why don't we just talk about our new family members who we've gotten to know over the last five years?"

"Who do you want to talk about first?" Sebastian asked.

"How about your family?"

"My family? Well, there's my grandmother, Joan Donaldson, and my mother, Cecilia Donaldson—or Cecilia Maphis as she's known now. I have two half-brothers, both boys, who have families of their own. You'll get to meet them one day, Joy. You're the first grandkid, so Mother and Grandmother are very excited to spend time with you. And I wish they would come now, but they are currently on their annual mother-daughter trip. I've also met some of my relatives on the east coast from the original Donaldson line, and they were pleasant. Maybe one day we'll do a family reunion with the ones who are interested. But all in all, Joy, I definitely didn't have drama like your mother did."

"That's not true," I protested.

"Okay, there was my Uncle Roger, but he is now behind bars, so let's not talk about him. We bought Aunt Cassie's house so she could stay in it." He looked at Joy with a sad expression. "One day, I'll tell you about my parents who raised me and how I might dislike Geraldine and her daughter, but them buying my childhood home so I had a place to live when I most needed it saved my life."

"It all turned out well," I said, giving Sebastian's arm a squeeze.

He looked at me with somber eyes. "Why don't you tell

her about your family?"

"Well, there's my mom, my aunt and uncle, and their kids and grandkids, and then there's Victoria. She's my best friend in the whole wide world, and she married my cousin, Paul, and they are expecting their little one soon, too, so you'll have a playmate soon. Victoria has already claimed the favorite aunt title, so there's no taksie-backsies as she says—which your other aunt, Leslie, is not too happy about, but I'm sure she'll have her moments with you too. Then there's Lauren, who has become family. She has a two-year-old that will be like a big sister to you. A very sweet girl and talkative, just like her mother. Who else?"

"What about the Wilkens clan?"

"Oh yes. Joy, you'll soon realize that our family isn't all blood relatives. We've accumulated quite a bit of outside families too. I've gotten to know the Wilkens family more, and some of Lauren's cousins are actually really nice. They're helping with Rose's Foundation, who I'll tell you all about when you get older."

"Or now, because while she doesn't understand it right now, it will calm her down and hopefully put her to sleep," Sebastian said under his breath.

I gave Sebastian a look, but he waved at me to keep talking, and I continued, "Even Isabella, who you might meet at some point, is finally giving Nick a chance, especially after what he did for her with my ex, Brian, who I hope we never hear from again. But that's another story. Isabella still hates my guts, and the feeling is mutual, but somehow . . . somehow, we've come to a truce. And Lauren never lets us forget it."

"She's asleep!" Sebastian turned Joy around so that she was sitting on his arms with her back against his chest. Her eyes were closed, and she was slumped against him.

"You think it's because we're not yelling at each other

anymore?" I asked him.

"That's a good guess. We're quite calm right now."

Sebastian put her back in her crib, and we tiptoed out of her room.

As we walked back to our adjoining room, Sebastian said, "Maybe she'll be like her mother and learn about her family through journals."

"The only difference is we are still here, and I don't plan on going anywhere until she's old enough to be on her own."

"Doesn't mean we can't take her places as she's growing up," he pointed out.

"Of course, but in the meantime, let's give her the gift we never had—let's let her grow up knowing all her family."

We were now at the top of the stairs, looking down at the foyer where I had set foot for the very first time five years ago. Sebastian encircled me within his arms, and we danced to a silent tune only we could hear.

"To family!" Sebastian suddenly said out loud.

"You're going to wake Joy!" I said. But I couldn't help smiling—I loved the sound of those words echoing off the walls of this house.

Want to read more stories in the Skyline Mansion world? Explore the Companion Stories that deep dive into Isabella, the Wilkens siblings, Josephine, Charlie, and Gillian's younger selves and how they meet the love of their lives.

Join Nola's newsletter to be the first to learn about new releases and receive a FREE copy of *Something Gained*. https://www.subscribepage.com/nolalibarrnewsletter

MORE FROM NOLA LI BARR

Skyline Mansion Series

Forbidden Blossom
Hidden Blossom
Secret Blossom
Family Blossom

Companion Stories to the Skyline Mansion Series

Summer of New Love
Summer of Second Chances

ABOUT THE AUTHOR

Nola Li Barr is the bestselling author of the Skyline Mansion series. She writes family sagas in women's fiction and young adult with a touch of sweet romance. When she's not writing she can be found reading, making photo books, and navigating the path of motherhood.

Receive a FREE copy of *Something Gained* when you join Nola's newsletter. Be the first to know about new releases and giveaways.
https://www.subscribepage.com/nolalibarrnewsletter

OR

nolalibarr.com to find her on social media.

If you enjoyed reading this book, please consider leaving a review on Amazon, Bookbub, or Goodreads. Reviews go a long way in helping independent authors get the word out. Your review is one of a kind, and I can't thank you enough for your support.

9 781956 919097